DEATHLESS DUNGEONEERS

BOOK 1

J. D. ASTRA

Deathless Dungeoneers Book 1 is a work of fiction. Names, characters, places, and incidents either are the product of the author's imagination or are used fictitiously. Any resemblance to actual persons living or dead, events, or locales is entirely coincidental.

Copyright © 2022 by J. D. Astra and Shadow Alley Press, Inc.

All rights reserved.

No part of this publication may be reproduced, distributed, or transmitted in any form or by any means, including photocopying, recording, or other electronic or mechanical methods, without the prior written permission of the publisher, except in the case of brief quotations embodied in critical reviews and certain other noncommercial uses permitted by copyright law. For permission requests, email the publisher, subject line "Attention: Permissions Coordinator," at the email address below.
JStrode@ShadowAlleyPress.com

1
THE DUNGEONEER

Rhen was about to die a horrible, gruesome death. The eight-foot tall, slavering moth monster grabbed Rhen's feet and began wrapping them in acidic silk string. The moth monsters liked to eat their prey alive, like most spiders, and wrapped them in silk in a similar fashion for meal preservation.

The young dungeoneer carefully played at being unconscious, waiting until the monster's tender underside was closer to his blade-hand. He only had one good chance at saving his life and, boy, did he not want to die. For one, Rhen hadn't saved his essence in the dungeon's Resurrection node recently; he couldn't afford it. So, if he died now, he'd get set all the way back to syntial level Prima I—and a different realm—losing about five months of progress.

More importantly, getting spit out of the gelatinous *between realm* after weeks of incubation, naked as the day he was born and missing all his gear, powers, and memories since his last check-in was just about the most unpleasant experience of his life, aside from the dying he didn't remember much of. Was Rhen even himself if he was reborn from the between realm?

A philosophical question that would have to wait.

The moth's tubular tongue slapped against Rhen's neck, tasting him. The slippery tongue slid across his cheek and lips with a wet *schlick* that made Rhen's stomach tight with fear. He remained deathly still, for if he didn't, he'd be dead for sure. The moth's silk burned on his shins, and Rhen knew the acid was eating away his simple leather boots.

The monster's mandala tattoo on its lower abdomen flared with purple light, and the silk grew stickier, and thicker. The moth picked Rhen up at the waist as it began wrapping his thighs in the anima-enhanced silk, trying to ensure its prey couldn't escape. But that lift gave Rhen just the edge he needed to close the distance with his blades before the monster's razor-sharp wings could slice him in half.

It supported Rhen's back as the cocooning process moved up to his waist, and Rhen tensed his grip on his crescent moon blade. He triggered Swift Twitch with a thought, significantly increasing the speed at which his muscles could contract. A surge of hot anima poured from the syntial; a mandala-like spirit tattoo that directed the flow of his energy. The anima coursed down his arms in a burst of blue light and the moth screeched in fear, but too late.

Criss. Cross. Slash.

In three swift movements, he diced the moth's thorax, spilling its guts all over him. The monster didn't even know it was dead, its body frozen in the wrapping pose before it collapsed to the ground. Rhen breathed a deep sigh of relief.

That.

Was.

Close.

He ran his blade down the sticky, acid-covered silk, then stepped out of the half-completed cocoon. The monster's entrails slopped off him to the ground and a shiver ran down Rhen's spine. He could've been *in* those guts.

There among the gory mess was the small, glimmering purple gem. It was the anima crystal—the storage apparatus for all beings' power, which allowed them to cast spells, even nasty ones like acid-infused cocooning silk, or awesome ones like Rhen's Swift Twitch. Rhen thanked his luck for that ability, which had saved his bacon more than a few times now.

"Are you okay down there?" the concerned voice of Rhen's delve leader called from above.

Rhen slipped the anima crystal into a secret pocket on the inside of his leather jerkin. He looked up at the hole created by careless anima drilling and gave a thumbs up. "Just another horromoth, higher level though, and big. It had an ancilla level syntial on its abdomen that infused the silk with acid that, I assume, was to start pre-digesting me."

"Gross," the delve leader said with a shiver. She was a squat woman from the Dwarvish realm of Fjagrasill, competent and kind. She'd led the delve without incident—up to now.

But, so long as none of them reported the incident of collapsing rock because the knucklehead drill operator wouldn't listen to Rhen, they'd all be fine. Incidents meant a docked pay, and no one wanted that. If Rhen had died, that would've been another story.

Deaths got reported directly to the Dungeon Delver's Guild by the dungeon's Resurrection node. The reports were all reviewed scrupulously to ensure it was a dungeon death, not some back-alley robbery, or fighting ring games. Rhen wasn't certain *how* they derived that information, but it wasn't his business, or his problem.

"See any good veins?" the knucklehead with the anima drill asked as he popped into the opening he'd created with his careless extraction methods.

Rhen inhaled deeply through his nose and activated the small [Primordial Breath] syntial on his diaphragm.

"Light," Rhen whispered.

The anima heat mounted in his lungs until he could hold it no longer. He blew all the air out with force, blanketing the room in a brilliant shimmering fog. It poured from his mouth like a steaming kettle and filled up the space. The sparkles faded to a dim, silvery glow, and the walls of the cavern winked back at him.

"Veins-a-plenty!" Rhen called back.

This was going to be an excellent payday.

The careless driller whooped. "All right, you make sure there aren't any more of them horromoths down there and I'll get some equipment loaded."

"No backup, Delve Leader? I almost died by cocooning just now."

"Other team's workin' a dungeon node boss right now. Can't spare any more fighters."

The dwarf woman disappeared from the hole above, leaving Rhen with the careless man whose name he hadn't bothered remembering. They were on a temporary dive together, not a long-standing team. That was fine. Rhen preferred not to make too many connections or stay in one place for long. He followed the flow of the dungeons, like many other dungeoneers, and with it came the wealth he needed to one day be a dungeon owner himself.

Rhen walked the perimeter of the circular cavern. The black rock was rich in silver and turquoise veins of ore. Lafite and Auramine. Not rare materials, but mid-tier. They'd fill his pockets with coin all the same.

A small fissure in the wall caught his attention and Rhen stopped. He squatted down, peering through the gap. It was too dark to see, so Rhen took another deep breath to fill the space with light. His breath clung to the walls, lighting up the narrow passage, before spilling into the cavern beyond.

It was enormous, and the angle of the fissure put his position at the top of a slight incline. There was a screech, and another horromoth flap-ran past the opening. This one was a beast of a thing, with even more spindly legs and a longer, thicker tongue for sucking up liquified guts. Maybe that was a node boss! If there was a dungeon node in that room, that'd be the real prize. Ore veins paid out well, but the dungeon nodes were the true objective for any dungeon owner.

Each node could be activated with different levels of anima to transform them for four distinct purposes. Resurrection nodes allowed anyone to save a copy of their essence and be revived on death. Well, reborn on death. Rhen still didn't want to think about that.

Then there were Mastery nodes, which gave holders of anima crystals the ability to integrate that crystal's power into themselves, unlocking new spells, traits, and abilities. Third was the Control nodes. They could be used to map a dungeon and rearrange areas that were cleared of all large living creatures. These nodes were essential to set up bases of operation and delve deeper.

Last was the most important: Nexus nodes. This was what Rhen so craved to find in his own dungeon one day. Nexus nodes connected dungeons by way of portal, sometimes even to different realms. Seventeen realms had been discovered and connected over the several hundreds of years that Rhen's people, the Shin'Baran, had been dungeon diving.

A wide grin spread over Rhen's face. "We might have hit the motherlode."

"A node?" drill-man asked, excitement in his voice.

The delve leader was back at the opening with uncanny speed. "Stake it and get out. We can't delve deeper here tonight if there's a node boss. We don't want to risk *another* collapse." She glared at the drill-holder.

The glowing breath in the cavern faded, and with it, his enthusiasm. Going against the delve leader would get him kicked from the raid, and he couldn't afford the dings on his record with the Dungeon Delver's Guild; he had two already.

With a sigh, Rhen put his hand against the fissure and channeled his anima through the identification syntial on his side, then down his arm to the wall. A glowing white circle appeared in the rock with Rhen's name and a three, his team number. Now the other greedy delvers couldn't drill this spot without the tools registering Rhen's mark. There was a *lengthy* legal process for anyone who stole another delver's location that could have them removed from the Dungeon Delver's Guild, but it typically wasn't worth risking.

The drill-man dropped a rope through the opening. He pressed his hand against it and green anima flowed down it, popping the rope out into a runged ladder. Rhen was grateful to not have to climb his way out. Despite wanting to press on, he had been delving for a good nine hours already.

When he reached the top, the drill-man patted him on the back. "It was worth it, right?"

Rhen glared at him. "You owe me new boots."

He looked to Rhen's feet to see his big toes were popping out of the dissolved leather. "Every man's responsible for his own losses." The drill-man retreated down the well-lit cavern to the sounds of buzzing tools and cracking rock.

"Fluffer..." Rhen muttered, wiggling his toes.

It was an arduous hike back up to the dungeon base, with several different biomes to traverse. Rocky caves that had once been populated by the horromoths, slimy tubes used by thick slugs called grubbers, big, open swampy caverns full of glowing mushrooms, and even a few spaces with open lava pits.

This was Desedra I, the largest dungeon in Resplendare, owned by Adelus Desedra—the wealthiest man for many realms. Rhen had worked Desedra I a few years back, but the pay rates were scandalous. Rhen, having a small scandal of his own at his last dungeon, didn't have much else left to turn to. He was a good fighter, an intuitive diver, and those things mattered for something despite his record.

Finally, Rhen made it to the exit checkpoint where he was stopped by Reclaimers.

"Deposit here," the Cadrian woman said, pointing to a bucket with her sharp nails. Her skin was black as night but glimmered with gold as if she'd been dusted in it. Her eyes were a sharp garnet, and two sawed-off horns protruded from either side of her forehead.

Rhen patted himself down, then removed the crystals from his many pockets—save for one. When twelve crystals, all mostly the purple of horromoth and decently sized, had been dropped in the bucket, Rhen grinned. "That's it."

In his periphery, Rhen noticed the floating orbeye, the monster turned monitor through anima control. The orbeye was a head-sized, all black eyeball encased in crystal that walked on twelve, noodly legs. The crystal glowed a soft blue, a syntial lighting up on one of its facets. It must've been sending a visual feed back to the headquarters right outside the dungeon, because the glow of the crystal was strong. Rhen put his attention back on the pat-down agent.

An ancilla level syntial on the Cadrian's stubby horn glowed a brilliant orange. That glow filled up her eyes, and she combed over Rhen with scrupulous care. He hadn't expected to get such a thorough inspection on departure but knew that even a tiny anima crystal couldn't escape the piercing gaze of Detect Anima.

"Oh, wait!"

He pulled the secreted crystal from his jerkin interior pocket and plopped it in the bucket.

"Missed this little one." He grinned brighter, and the Cadrian scowled.

She finished her inspection, but held him another moment. Everyone tried to sneak out little treasures; it was normal. But with Rhen's record, he supposed it was only fair he got the strip-down treatment.

The Orbeye approached, glowing a soft blue, and then the syntial on the Cadrian's horn flared to life again. The blue anima flowed to her temple and her oversized ears twitched. She cocked her head, listening intently, then nodded.

"Sen Thun-Desedra would like to see you."

Sen wanted to see him, huh? That couldn't be good.

The Desedras were an enormous family. Everyone who wed into it took Desedra for their familial name for obvious reasons. Power came with it, even in small measures for someone as low down as Sen Thun—a man who married into the family through a cousin of the main familial line.

So no, an invitation to see Sen was not good, but it was far better than a visit to Zeichen IV, named for her late father. She wore the real crown in the family. She was a first-born in a long line of first-borns. A trip to her would take Rhen most of the evening, and there probably wouldn't be a trip home. But Sen and the other extended family members scrambling for power stayed close to the dungeons and didn't have the brazen guts of Zeichen.

Rhen beamed, hiding his apprehension. "Great, so... I can go?"

She waved him off without a word.

It wouldn't have been that tiny anima crystal he'd "forgotten," would it? That was too small an infraction to get an instantaneous notice to appear. It had to have been something else.

Rhen hadn't misbehaved in any way—well when there'd been witnesses. Maybe there had been witnesses...

Rhen walked with a swagger out into the wide dungeon opening, a wide-mouthed cavern of blackened rock and stacked pallets of goods. It was buzzing with activity. Anima-powered train carts flowed up the left side from the exit checkpoint he'd just come from. Those carts were dumped into a sorting station. People of all races sorted the crystals and ores, lifting them with a magical flick of their wrists and tossing them to the next appropriate station for size and power assessments. After their assessment, the minerals and gems were stacked into the pallets that were lifted by powerful machines and dropped onto vehicles bound for distribution centers. Desedra ran a profitable business of selling off their power to others; they had more than enough for themselves... Zeichen was practically a god, or so he'd heard.

The fast-paced chaos to the left was offset by the extreme, sluggish order on the right. A single-file flow of bodies on either side of a blocky checkout station moved in and out of the dungeon, all waiting to be verified. Travelers with packed bags were headed to Nexus nodes, delvers headed in for work, and businesspeople of all kinds headed in for their various reasons.

It was *maddeningly* slow.

Rhen finally made it through the procession line and jogged to the sturdy stone building just outside the entrance. It was six stories tall and looked like some patchwork quilt of rocks. With every new level to the dungeon discovered and every Nexus node providing access to yet another dungeon, they had added another wing or level to the building to host all the managers who would observe those operations.

This dungeon was a shitshow, as made apparent by the dilapidated, mixed-media building that housed its operations.

Rhen moved through the overcrowded building lobby and

went for the stairs. Knowing a Desedra, Sen would've posted himself up somewhere near the top. Rhen found a guard easily and asked for directions once he reached the top level.

He patted himself off when he reached the closed office door, covering the carpet with dungeon dust. There was laughing on the other side of the door. Rhen waited for it to die down, then knocked.

"Come in," came Sen's muffled voice on the other side.

He opened the door. Sen and six others were gathered around the table at the far end, ogling the projection of the Cadrian coming out of the orbeye crystal.

Sen, who had married into the Desedra house, was a Shin'Baran like Rhen. He had the kind of stature that required six goons for him to feel safe. At five foot nothing and a mere hundred and twenty pounds, he relied heavily on his magic and his guards to protect him. Sen had bought his way into Tertia Level III, a master level of magic use.

Prima was the base tattoo, large and multifunctional, but usually not very powerful. Next was Ancilla, which was an add-on to the Prima. It provided specializations and additional power on top of the Prima ability. Tertia was yet another extension on top of the Ancilla, which increased the power and specialization of the ability significantly. Rhen doubted Sen had ever used his tertia ability in a dungeon... or any other worthwhile pursuit for that matter.

Rhen stepped into the room and straightened up. "You wanted to see me, boss?"

"Yeah, c'mere." Sen ran one boney hand through his brown hair and put his other over the Orbeye crystal. He twisted his wrist, sending blue anima into the crystal. The projection shivered, then the bodies in it moved in reverse until Rhen appeared in the projection.

Projection Rhen patted down his body, then reached into his

hidden interior pocket with a grin. He dropped the crystal in the bucket and the Cadrian scowled. Sen made a fist and the anima stream cut, leaving Rhen looking at the man square in the face.

"I don't want trouble in my dungeon."

Rhen shook his head and shrank. "Same."

"You've got a little record. You didn't think anyone would notice at a place so big, huh?"

"That's not it—"

"I'm not stupid."

"I don't think you are."

"Then don't lie to me. What's this about?"

Rhen patted down his gear, which was form fitting to his body. "I don't have a lot of pockets, you see. I have to stuff the crystals anywhere I can. I just forgot that little guy."

"I'd hate to add more to your record. Could make you ineligible for the Dungeon Owner's Guild."

Rhen kept up the innocent play. "I wouldn't want that either. I will sew up the pocket. No more mistakes."

"See that you do."

Sen waved him off just as the Cadrian had.

"Thank you."

Rhen turned to leave and let out a slow, quiet fart as he did. Just a little something for them to enjoy. With a smile, he watched the first goon gag, then closed the doors behind him.

2

NEXUS NODE

Rhen picked up his backpack and his week's earnings on the way out; a measly ninety Dra, which was the Desedra's own currency. That one anima crystal he'd pulled from the horromoth would've been worth at least sixty on its own. It was heinous robbery to snub the delvers so bad.

Rhen preferred to work in imperial marks, good in all seventeen realms, but in Desedra City, there was a discount for anyone using Dra coins. The city that had sprung up around the dungeon towered overhead as Rhen made his way onto the streets. The tallest buildings were at least three hundred feet, and even the smaller ones were a good five stories. They were of various construction, the shorter ones being mostly stone, but the taller buildings were crafted of strong metals, like Lafite, from within Desedra dungeon.

The city spanned several miles, with different districts for different types of business—delver's areas, crafter areas, markets, living quarters, and ancillary businesses to dungeon delving, like shipping, storage, and mineral processing. Of course, there was food *everywhere*. Not that Rhen could afford good food. Street vendors leaned their carts up against the sides of buildings just beyond the opening of Desedra dungeon. The smells were divine, even if it was all monster meat. His stomach groaned, but it would have to wait. He had business to attend.

It was only midday and already so crowded. Carts on thick tracks hurried by, powered with silvery anima that flowed through the metal wire just above it. Monster-drawn carriages, bicycles, and speedy pedestrians filled up the wide, paved roads leading away from the dungeon.

Rhen activated Swift Twitch and grabbed onto the back of a cart as it sped by. He crouched low to be out of the view of the driver's mirrors. The cart slowed and Rhen hopped off, walking casually. He pushed on through the thinning crowd until he reached a twenty-story building that looked all orderly and neat with its metal beams and clear glass windows. A meticulous welcome banner hung over the entrance reading "Dungeon Owner's Guild."

In stark contrast to the Desedra operation, the Dungeon Owner's Guild ran a smooth, efficient, tight business. They had figured out how to coordinate dungeon plots and active delve spots across seventeen realms without batting an eye it seemed. Meanwhile, Desedra's massive family could hardly keep their operation legal with all the missing resources and dead delvers.

Rhen entered the building like he had a dozen times and walked over to one of the many "Beginners Plot" desks, which had a magical mirror attached to it. Rhen took a moment to observe his reflection.

He looked worse for wear with the dark bags under his green eyes, and his brown, curly hair was a bit greasier than he should've let it get. His face was narrow, in part from his genes he assumed, but mostly due to the strict diet his budget put him on. He had tanned skin, which was certainly due to his genes and not his lifestyle. He spent most of his time in the dark reaches of the dungeons, away from the suns of the realms. The black leather jerkin he wore had been repaired more times than Rhen cared to count, and the gray undershirt sported a few holes of its own.

So what if he looked like a crazy hobo? What mattered was his money.

Rhen pressed the glowing button on the side of the mirror and in a burst of sparks, green anima flowed across the glass. A teller appeared in the depths of the mirror, disappearing Rhen's reflection.

Rhen smiled at the man behind the shimmering anima portal. "I'd like to see if plot SB9102 is still available, please."

The teller made several sweeping hand gestures, and the plot information appeared in the mirror.

[Unclaimed Dungeon Plot – SB9102]

Anima Type: Kinse, Cebrum
Depth: ~Four levels
Nodes: 1= 99% | 2-3 = 55% | +4 < 10%
Monsters: Prima Syntial = 99% | Ancilla Syntial = 82% | Tertia Syntial or Higher < 1%
Price: 7,105 Dra | 3,200 imperial marks
**Notice, all statistics are based on the D.O.G.'s certified inspection process. All statistics are subject to change and cannot be guaranteed by the D.O.G.

=====

"Is this the one you want?" the teller asked in a bored tone.

SB9102 was nothing to write home about—not that he had a home to write back to... The Kinse anima was all body related, much like his Swift Twitch, so the monsters would have advanced physical abilities. Cebrum was all mental, things like inducing fear, hypnosis, suggestion, and the like. Rhen wasn't exactly immune to Cebrum abilities, but years of practice in the delver school had made him more resistant.

With less than one percent of the creatures having tertia level syntials, the third power level that put combatants on a completely different level from prima or ancilla, he wasn't worried about running into anything too tough for him. And at only four levels, it was a good starter dungeon, exactly what Rhen wanted. He needed to get out of the system that was crushing him. Even if he had to work around the clock to exhaustion, he would be far better off than staying at Desedra.

"Check my balance, please?" Rhen asked.

The teller swished his hands through the air and Rhen's account appeared at the bottom. Six thousand nine hundred and twenty-one Dra. It had taken him three years to save up that much, moving from dungeon to dungeon like a ghost. He was getting so close now, he could suffer just a little more.

"I'd like to deposit eighty-five."

Five would hold him over for the week at the Down-N-Out, a guild of delver's shelters he'd frequented over the past few years.

"Place your hand on the Control node."

A dark crystal whirred into view overhead, suspended in a beam of blue light. It dropped down to the desk and with a few clicks, connected into the system. It hummed to life with a soft yellow glow, flashing to indicate it was ready.

Rhen placed his hand on the device and felt the id syntial on his side flare to life. His heart pounded, fear pricking the back of his mind. *What if it doesn't work this time?*, he wondered with horror, but kept his face still and relaxed.

Warm anima flowed from his hand to the identification syntial on his side, then back to his hand and into the Control node. The teller received the information on the other end and nodded. More anima flowed back through Rhen's arm and to his side.

"I've updated your account and withdrawn the money from your id syntial. Anything else?"

"Nothing else."

"You know, you could get a loan if you wanted it now," the teller said, a bit of life entering his voice.

He knew the guy was just doing his job, but Rhen couldn't keep the contempt from his voice. "And let the Guild drain the wealth out from under me in interest? I think not."

Rhen was certain that the teller would get some kind of a bonus for selling a loan, and while he wanted to help out the little guy stuck behind a desk, Rhen was little guy number one that he had to look out for.

The teller shrugged, then deactivated the view. The Control node lifted on the blue beam of light and moved back into the ceiling. Their system was *mighty* efficient. Rhen practically bounced out of the Guild office, his smile bright.

Just one more week and he'd be a dungeon owner.

Rhen caught another trolly cart down toward Desedra I dungeon and hopped on a third that would take him west. The sun was still too high, around four in the afternoon, so Rhen made a stop at the open market first. He couldn't get into Down-N-Out until nearly sundown anyway.

He spent his time perusing various wares, like Enon syntial reinforced boots that would passively suck anima out of the ground to power its Kinse ability, Super Jump. Rhen's boots did something similar, but instead of having an ability, the anima flowed directly into him to power his abilities. It wasn't fancy, but it worked.

Among the wares were Mana syntial swords that could channel fire down the blade, or cause a gust of wind that would slice enemies open from a distance, and even Enon syntial capes that could teleport a wearer with a flourish. Yes, syntials were a wonder. Rhen wished he had more gear with powerful abilities, but with the possibility of dying and never getting it back, maybe it was better to wait until he had his own dungeon, where gear retrieval wasn't so spotty.

When the sun was low, and Rhen's toes were raw from scraping against the stone pathways, he made his way to the delver's shelter. The building was utilitarian, simple, and depressing. Gray slab exterior with windows just large enough to stick one arm through. The front door was thrown open in welcome, and Jakira stood beside it.

The cute Cadrian smiled when she spotted Rhen. The golden flecks in her black skin shimmered brilliantly in the setting sun. She still had her dark horns, which curled up and back over her head. One had a wide crack running along the side that she tried to keep together with straps of leather. Rhen wondered if it was painful. Some of her long, red hair was braided in a crown around her head with little flowers, while the rest flowed down her back to her thin, spade-shaped tail.

"Here for another night?" she asked, hardly able to contain her glee.

"If there's room, I'll take a week."

She held out a small Control node. Two syntials under each of her hands glowed brightly when Rhen placed his palm on the smooth, worn crystal. The light traveled up her arms and into her eyes as she read his information.

"Cutting it a bit close, aren't you?" she asked, concern wrinkling her brow.

"Don't worry about me, Jak."

She pouted. "How can you do this to me? Show up broke as a joke and tell me not to worry? What are you going to eat in the dungeon, huh?"

"Plenty of horromoths in the new wing."

The glow faded from Jakira's eyes and receded back to the crystal. "I left you with two dra. That should be enough for something a little better than monster meat."

"Wait, but isn't that what you serve here?"

Jakira scowled. "You take that back!"

"The stew needs work, Jak. I'm just saying." Rhen stepped past her into the inn.

"You don't have to have any, then!"

He turned to her. "Why so mad? It's not like you cook it—wait, do you?"

"Just go to your room already!" Jakira turned back to the procession of delvers coming in for the night.

"You're the best, Jak. Never change."

Rhen took the concrete stairs two at a time up to the second level. He was grateful for Jak's sympathy; it kept his stomach full. He knew she gave the help willingly, but he wanted to pay her back somehow once he had his own dungeon. Maybe an anima crystal, or some ore to help fill the crack on her horn.

The second level was already full, and hotter than the lava chamber in Desedra dungeon, so Rhen made his way up to the third. It was ten to a room, BYOB—bring your own bedroll. He unclipped the blanket secured on the top of his backpack and rolled it out, then dug through his bag. There was still a good half-bar of soap, and his toothbrush was in decent condition too.

He took off his boots and inspected the anima syntial on the sole. It was still intact. The anima syntial was simple, but so, *so* necessary. It allowed him to passively absorb the anima from anything he walked on. In a dungeon loaded with monsters, ore, and powerful crystals, he was absorbing little bits of their power just by standing there. It was crucial for long sustained battles.

When his hygiene was handled, he went down with his worn bowl for a stew serving. There was no way it wasn't monster meat. But Rhen was so close to being a dungeon owner, he could only taste success—okay and the bitter undertones of horromoth wing powder. Who thought that was seasoning?

The evening's entertainment was a homely bard. Kinse syntials came alight along his arms while he played a fat lyre that was missing a few too many strings to make a decent noise. But the Kinse syntials made up for it. A ghostly purple mist drizzled out of each string as he plucked his three-chord melody. The mist smelled of lavender and made Rhen's eyelids droop.

When he couldn't take another note, Rhen bid the other delvers a prosperous tomorrow, and staggered up the stairs to his bedroll.

Before long, there was a heavy pounding on the door to wake the sleepy dungeoneers.

"Sunrise! Up and out with ya!" the morning crew member called.

Rhen much preferred the sweet Jakira's rousing, which came with hot honey bread and a smile. He rubbed his eyes and pulled his worn clothes from the hanging line next to the narrow window. There were still acid marks on his pants, but the blood and guts had all washed out with the soap, thankfully.

Rhen rolled up his bed and pinned it under the flap of his backpack, then secured the bag to his shoulders. Another six days of grinding and he'd be free.

There were stale rolls from the night before piled high on a table near the door and Rhen took two on his way out. He made his way across town to the dungeon entrance, stuffing his mouth full of dry roll as he went.

Desedra dungeon was just as disorganized as the days, weeks, and months before. Rhen argued with the dungeon level manager about the claim he had staked, and the crew that would work with him on it. He was assigned Captain Careless once more, and only one other fighter he hadn't worked with.

Rhen made a complaint about just a single point of backup, but it was ignored.

When they reached the collapsed floor Rhen had fallen through the other day, he brought the party to a halt. Rhen tiptoed to the edge, listening intently. Sure enough, the flapping of razor wings and chittering of a hungry horromoth met his ears. Damn thing had resurrected already. The node on the other side must've been powerful to pump out another full-grown monster in less than twenty-four hours.

Rhen sucked down a deep breath, activating the Primordial Breath syntial on his chest.

Fire.

The syntial responded to his mental command, and heat mounted in his lungs, threatening to burn him up too. Rhen blew the air out with all his might, releasing the fiery spell into the hole in the ground. The unsuspecting horromoth caught a face full of flames and shrieked, flapping for the back of the cavern while its wings curled and crisped.

Rhen jumped in after it and pulled his crescent blades from the holster on each hip. The horromoth was easy pickings, and it went down with a few swipes. Rhen dug through the chest and removed the anima crystal, carefully handing it off to the party pack-mule, Captain Careless. He could deal with Sen this time.

When the little cavern was clear, Careless brought the anima drill down and got to work on widening the crevasse. The monsters on the other side were all going berserk, thirsty for the blood of whoever would damage their home. Rhen had to hold the creatures at bay with several bouts of fiery breath until his esophagus ached.

Finally, the drill punched a hole wide enough for Rhen and the other fighter, who looked like a "Pat" to Rhen. Pat threw his hands out, fingers splayed wide, and the cavern walls glowed from the anima flowing through them, providing just enough light for a romantic battle.

The floor where they were deposited sloped down toward the node at the center of the wide-open cavern. There were thick crystals poking out of the walls that maintained their glow far brighter than the stone. A little stream trickled through the lowest part of the cavern, and Rhen grinned greedily. Water meant another passage down, and perhaps even another chamber type.

Four horromoths flapped in from the edges of the walls and surrounded the dungeon node. Rhen wasn't sure if the monsters knew their resurrections depended on that node, but there had to be some basic understanding of its purpose, lest they wouldn't have crowded it like that. One of the monsters was a good two feet taller than the others, and perhaps a minor boss.

The big one stepped forward, flapping its wings hard. A purple syntial glowed to life on its back and the wind took on a deadly glow of anima. Rhen activated Swift Twitch and leapt out of the way. Pat screamed as he caught a wind-blade to the hand, losing two of his fingers.

"Get it together!" Careless yelled from the gap in the wall.

"I don't see you coming in," Pat screamed. He clamped down on the bleeding and growled.

Rhen dashed right, circling around the back of the cavern. He sucked in a deep breath, though his throat still ached. He reached the little stream and kicked a swath of water up against the closest moth.

"Freeze."

The Prima II Primordial Breath syntial on his diaphragm twisted for the altered command, sucking the anima from his core in response. His lungs contracted as the cold air mounted inside him. He blew all the icy air out in a huff, crystalizing the water on the moth and freezing its thick tongue. Rhen dashed in, crescent moon blade tight in his grip, and slashed at the tubular appendage. The moth dodged but Rhen's second slash came in faster than the bulky creature could move.

Its tongue shattered at Rhen's attack, and the moth gurgled a shriek. Rhen followed with a quick set of slashes to the moth's wings and arms. It staggered back and Rhen pressed his advantage, but the glowing purple in his periphery alerted him just in time. Rhen dropped to the ground as a wave of razor-sharp air blades passed overhead, dicing the moth monster in a bout of friendly fire.

Rhen rolled to his feet, ready to pounce on the next creature when Pat's scream caught his attention. He glanced back to the entrance to see the fighter kicking at the moth trying to cocoon his lower half, while he tried to rip his bleeding arm free from the second moth that was eating him alive.

"Hold that thought," Rhen said to the moth that'd just killed its friend.

He dashed toward the downed Pat, stuffing his left crescent blade back into its holster as he did. With a thought, he gathered anima in his left hand and triggered Tremor Blast at a high frequency. The vibrations rocked through his fingertips and exploded into the air in front of him in a burst of pink waves. The spell smashed against both moths, and the wall behind them.

The moths screamed, dropping their prey and retreating in a heavy flap of their dusty wings. The cavern wall trembled, groaning. Large cracks appeared in the slabs of stone around the opening, threatening to crush the bloody fighter. Rhen grabbed Pat by the leg and dragged him away from the entrance as huge chunks of rock broke away. The stones smashed against the cavern floor, sending shards exploding through the air.

"You stupid or something?" Pat cried out, shielding his face.

"You're welcome!"

Rhen turned back to see the two horromoths were still flying about in chaos, rubbing at their heads, but the third he'd been tussling with was retreating through a tall and narrow passage near the back.

"Oh no you don't."

Rhen activated Swift Twitch and sent the infused anima to his legs. He dashed for the exit, right crescent blade ready. Just before the tip of the monster's wings disappeared into the darkness, Rhen slammed his blade down into it, pinning it to the wall.

His anima reserves were getting low, but he had enough for one more breath. He inhaled deep, and despite his raw throat, activated the anima for fire. The concentrated gout of flame blasted over the moth, lighting the hairs on its abdomen and thorax. The creature flailed and cried, trying desperately to escape, but the knife in its wings held it in place.

The horromoth slouched to the ground, the smell of burnt hair and flesh making Rhen's eyes water. He gagged and staggered back and turned away from the smoking hole in the wall. Blurry purple light appeared above him. He rubbed the tears from his eyes just in time to see that light was attached to the syntials on the moth, ready to cut him to ribbons.

Rhen dove forward. The wing blades slapped against the wall he'd been resting on, peppering Rhen with shards of ore and stone. The moth's hooked forelimb grabbed him by the collar of his jerkin, then a sticky, slimy tube slid across his cheek.

Not again.

Rhen flipped over and pressed his feet against the monster, willing his boots' Anima Drain ability to work fast enough to save his life. The horromoth snaked its nasty tongue around Rhen's throat, compressing his esophagus. He sputtered, inhaling only a tiny breath to keep him going.

Damn things *were* smart.

But not smart enough.

Rhen pulled the left blade from its holster and slashed through the creature's tongue. The horromoth retreated with a scream, splashing blood over Rhen's face. He rolled to the side and climbed to his feet, using the back of his sleeve to wipe his messy face.

Pat, despite his missing fingers, was back in the fight. He summoned a green anima lance with a trailing chain that attached at his shoulder. He hurled the spirit weapon at the last flying moth, nailing it through the thorax. Pat did a quick jump and spin, wrapping the anima chain around his body and jerking the moth to the ground.

Rhen pulled his second blade from the wall and gave chase to the screaming, tongueless moth. He put it down with a few quick swipes, then slumped to the floor. The Tremor Blast had taken a lot out of him, and his throat ached from the constant use of his breath syntial. He'd have to get that reinforced with some kind of shield or soothing agent when he had all the anima crystals he could want from his own dungeon.

Careless crawled out of the cavern opening and stumbled his way down to the dungeon node. He placed his hand on the fat, round crystal protruding from the stony pedestal and grinned. "We. Are. *So*. Rich."

"How rich?" Rhen asked, his voice raspy.

"It's a Nexus node."

3

DUNGEON OWNER

Rhen and the delve crew reported the Nexus node to pats on the back from the delve leader. She'd get a little cut of it, too, but it would be an extra five hundred dra coin added to Rhen's, Pat's, and Careless' weekly earnings. It was a gross underpayment for such a find, but Rhen wouldn't turn it down. He just had to survive the rest of the week now. No more wild risks. He'd play it safe and hang back.

In an effort to not die and set himself back considerably, Rhen made a stop at the Mastery node. He'd battled hard, and used his spells a fair amount all week, so it was likely he had expanded his anima and syntial capacity. There was a long line to get to the east wing Mastery node, the one with good fighter abilities, but Rhen had some time to spare before he needed to get to the Down-N-Out.

When it was finally his turn, Rhen shooed off the other fighters, not letting them watch his selections. Rhen felt he was one of the better fighters in the realm for his versatility, and the other fighters knew it. He didn't want anyone else copying his designs and giving him too much competition, though that wouldn't matter so much when he owned his dungeon at the end of the week.

Rhen laid his hand upon the Mastery node and felt the dungeon anima flow into him, assessing him. Light swirled into view in the long, glassy mirror on the wall that reflected his anima state.

[Rhen Zephitz – Full Assessment]
[Spell Assessment]

Number of Syntials: 4 | Highest Syntial Level: Prima, II
{Prima II: Swift Twitch}
{Prima II: Primordial Breath}
{Prima I: Tremor Blast}
{Prima I: Identity}
Syntial Build Analysis – Fighter Type, High Damage

[Anima Assessment]

Anima Capacity: 100% *Ready to apply a new syntial or upgrade an existing!
{2x Kinse – Light & Chaos Alignment}
{1x Mana – Chaos Alignment}

=====

The more he used his syntial spells, and pulled in anima, the greater his body's capacity became. But the greater his capacity became, the more likelihood of his body exploding, which is where the syntials came into play. Because Rhen's body couldn't grow any bigger to support the additional anima swell, the magical syntials created a barrier around him, keeping his anima and his body intact under all the pressure of the power.

Prima syntials were basic, the lowest level but some of the most versatile spells. Ancilla became more specific and powerful, and once two or three ancilla were acquired, the delver was registered as an advanced combatant. Tertia, the third level, was where the more "godlike" powers came into play. By the time tertia syntials were applied, the body's capacity would far exceed any creature naturally created in the realms.

There were levels after tertia that few had achieved, but they were legends, and Rhen had never encountered such a being himself. But even Prima II delvers were powerful, having more advanced powers than any creatures without syntials.

Bonding with monster cores expedited the process of anima growth, though Rhen couldn't afford it, much like most of the poor fluffers working Desedra. They had to slowly, passively restore anima—or suck it out of the dungeon floor through their boots—and so their progression was like that of a snail.

Since he was at full capacity, Rhen would be able to apply a new syntial to help strengthen the anima barrier of his body. The syntials, magical mandala-like tattoos Rhen could adorn himself with, would strengthen his anima channels and allow the body to hold even more anima in it. Though difficult to accomplish, it was possible to overstuff the body with anima. Rhen had heard rumors of spontaneous combustion, gory explosions, and worse from anima overload, and had zero desire to experience it himself. He'd stick to applying new syntials and leveling up his skills.

The mirror flickered to life with additional options.

[Syntial Additions and Expansion]

Available Options: 22 {Expand? Y | N}
Recommended Options: 2
{Vibrational Dampening}

Prima I | Passive | Kinse | Chaos | No Anima Cost
Absorb vibration and convert into functional anima. Current vibrational force absorption potential at Level I; 50 pounds per hour.

{Swift Healing}
Ancilla I | Passive | Kinse | Life | Cost: 10% Anima/Hour
Append this syntial to Swift Twitch to increase passive healing. Passive healing increased by 25% at Level I. If anima well is emptied, passive healing will deactivate. Passive healing will reactivate as soon as the anima well reaches 20% capacity.

=====

There was no contest. If Rhen wanted to survive longer, Swift Healing was the right choice. Vibration absorption was useful indeed, but could wait. Rhen idly wondered what skills were in the hidden twenty options, but he was running out of time with the Mastery node and needed to hurry along. Desedra didn't charge for the use of the Mastery node, a blessed fact indeed, but workers only got five minutes alone with it per week, so choices had to be quick.

Rhen selected Swift Healing and cringed as the power flowed from the Mastery node up into his arm. The Prima II syntial on his pec flared to life, and a new teardrop shaped blossom appeared poking out from the left side. A symbol inscribed in it that Rhen could not read, but knew that was the source of the power channeling. Words, especially in script, had power in his world.

With that complete, Rhen headed out, which took another good hour. It was late in the day when he made it to the market, so he only managed to peruse a few vendors before the sun began to set. He turned up back at the Down-N-Out for the evening, toes protruding from his boots, face covered in gore.

Jakira's nose wrinkled in revulsion at the sight of him. "You need a bath."

"Can't afford a bath."

"Your stench is going to drive away the other customers."

"But I already paid for the week."

Jakira growled. "Fine. Free bath. You'll go after Mr. Aki. He's on the third floor."

Rhen grinned and headed toward the stairs. "You're the best, never change."

"I wish you would!" Jakira yelled after him.

Rhen turned back, a hurting pout on his face. "Say you don't mean it."

She rolled her eyes, then smiled. "Get out of here with your filth."

The third floor was crowded with familiar faces from the night before, except "Mr." Aki, whom he found waiting outside the bathing chamber. Rhen had never seen a Prelusk himself, but had heard wild stories of the cuttlefish-like creatures entrancing anyone who crossed their path. They used magic in mysterious ways, with and without syntials, controlling raw anima in logic defying feats of psionics and hypnosis. Stranger than all the other species, Prelusk refused to join the modern culture. They had a special accord with the Imperial Kingdoms to keep anyone out, except on express invitation, and they rarely left their realm.

This Prelusk was a bit different than Rhen had imagined. He stood six feet tall in a man-shaped body made entirely of muddy water. At the top was his actual body, protruding up like a long, cone-shaped head. His skin glowed a gentle blue, but under the muddy water it was hard to tell if that was all. He had fins on the side of his head shaped sort of like ears that fluttered gently, and long tentacles trailing down the water body's chest like a slimy beard.

"So, I'm bathing after you?" Rhen asked the Prelusk.

"You are?" Aki's resonant voice vibrated through Rhen's chest and then surged up to his head. The feeling was disconcerting, but Rhen tried to shake it off.

"That's what the Cadrian downstairs said."

"No. Who are you?" The voice moved through him smoother this time, as if he were adapting to its vibration, or maybe Aki was adapting it to him.

"I'm just a filthy delver who's been ordered to bathe."

Aki's fins fluttered and his color shifted between blue and green. "Your name?"

Rhen's stomach turned, willing him to spit out his name.

Maddox.

Maddox!

He mashed his lips together and shook his head, trying to dislodge whatever magics had willed that word to the surface. It was wrong. That wasn't him.

Rhen pinned Aki with a stern gaze. "That was rude."

"Not telling your name to someone who has asked is rude."

He wasn't wrong, but fluffer didn't have to use hypnotic magics against him to find out.

"It's Rhen."

"Good to meet. I am Aki."

Rhen was getting the sense that this Prelusk was new to the common language. Maybe he was new to being not a fluffer, too.

"What's brought you to Desedra?" Rhen tried for small talk as they waited, listening to the water run into the tub beyond the door.

"Pilgrimage."

Rhen nodded. "I've heard about that. You tour the dungeons, fighting and gaining powers before you can return home. It's some rite of passage, yeah?"

"Indeed."

Dude was chatting his ear right off.

"Why do you do it?"

Aki turned to Rhen, his skin glowing brighter blue. His yellow eyes opened wider, and the black, star-shaped pupils dilated.

"Do you not know, or did I just ask a really dumb question?" Rhen was feeling a bit queasy under the Prelusk's intense gaze.

"It is tradition for the last hatched. We must prove our worth."

Touchy subject. Rhen thought of his own upbringing. Whether it was the Prelusk's hypnotic ways, or just the feeling Rhen got from how he'd said *worth*, he wanted to share some insight.

"My parents gave me up to a delver's guild before I was even weaned. I get the whole *prove yourself* thing, but trust me, it's way more important to live up to your own expectations than any of theirs."

Aki looked him up and down. "And are you?"

Rhen smirked. "That's the trick. Have low expectations."

The water was still running on the other side, and Rhen felt uneasy in the quiet as the Prelusk watched him.

"So, why do you look like that?"

"This is my physiology."

"No, I mean why do you have a body shaped like mine made of water, and your... body at the top like a head?"

He dropped down into the center of the watery mannequin and the water changed shape to be more like a Cadrian. He even grew watery horns and a little spade tail. "This is realm norming. I can pass in the population better if I look more like you."

Rhen nodded thoughtfully. Prejudice was definitely a thing, especially in the war-realms. While the wars had ended long ago, the old hatred still burned between Shin'Bara and Resplendare, the Desedra's home realm. Resplendites looked very similar to Shin'Barans, with just a few subtle differences in the eyes, hair colors, and height. It was thought they were one race many millennia ago, having traversed the dungeon Nexus nodes and populated the new realm. But something happened to disconnect them, leaving the populations separate and stranded until a few hundred years ago when they connected once more.

The door to the bath opened and a young Cadrian boy emerged, his skin glossy with steam. "It's ready for you."

Aki's watery body moved just as Rhen's own legs would and he stepped into the closet-sized bathing room. He turned back to Rhen, hand resting on the door. "I will consider your words."

He closed the door, but not a minute later, opened it again. His watery body was clear and clean... and the water left in the tub looked like warm diarrhea. At least it didn't reek as bad as Rhen did.

"My apologies," Aki said as he passed Rhen through the door.

"Free bath is a free bath."

Rhen discovered the brown tint was just dirt, which settled to the bottom of the tub after a minute of being still. He reserved a bucket of the cleaner stuff off the top, then washed his face and hair first. When the water was really starting to smell, he submerged the rest of himself, using a sliver of his precious soap.

He drained the water away, then slowly poured the bucket of mostly clean water over himself to rinse the soap when he was done.

Ah, a delver's life.

That night they were entertained by the same old bard and Aki, who used his psionic abilities to create dancing lights over the crowd. Pinks, purples, and reds streamed overhead like a river. Little blue and green bursts popped here and there, like a fish jumping out of water. They caused ripples through the streams of color that bounced along to the bard's rhythm.

Rhen could watch it for hours, but his drooping lids said otherwise. He stayed as long as he could, until the crowd had thinned to just a few delvers and the performers. Rhen finally stood, bade the others a prosperous tomorrow, and made his way to the stairs.

"I must sleep." Rhen felt Aki's words dimly, like they were being spoken at a whisper. He wondered how the Prelusk did it, communicated that way. So strange.

Aki crossed the floor and followed Rhen up the stairs. "You work in Desedra dungeon?"

"Doesn't everyone here?"

"I would like to work with you tomorrow."

"That'll be up to the delve leader... Are you even registered? I thought you were on a pilgrimage?"

"All travelers must be registered so we may collect power on our journey. I am still in need of a tertia syntial before I move on from this realm."

"Tertia?" Rhen stopped at the top of the stairs.

"Yes, I must acquire a tertia syntial before I depart each realm."

"That'll take you fifty years of delving Desedra. You're better off finding a smaller dungeon group you can work with. Try the Dungeon Delver's Guild tomorrow, they'll point you to the right place—especially with skills like yours."

Aki blinked, his fins fluttering. "I understand. Thank you for the advice."

"You're welcome. G'night."

Rhen waved at the Prelusk and headed to his room. He plopped down with a heavy thud on his thin bedroll to vapid snores all around him. Soon enough, the droning sounds became a symphony that helped him off to sleep.

The following five days flew by for Rhen, following the same pattern as every day that had preceded it. Wake, stuff face, work —saving Careless' skin more than once—check on his dungeon, walk the market, stuff face, sleep.

Rhen was practically bouncing out of his skin the morning of payday. He took special care in making sure he didn't get himself killed and set back two thousand dra. The exit line from the dungeon took far longer than Rhen thought was possible, and for a moment, the idea that he might never get out of that line crossed his thoughts.

Preposterous, as it was...

Rhen leaned around to look at the procession, which was still plugging along slowly, when he noticed Aki's dirty mud-body not too far ahead. So, he had decided to work for Desedra. Poor fool.

He made it out of the dungeon and a feeling of weightlessness took over. He was just a few steps away from being his own boss, a dungeon owner. Rhen floated over to the payments office and stood in yet another line, the euphoria battling with the anxiety.

What if the dungeon was taken?

It'd been listed for months, and no one had wanted it. It was fine.

What if Sen gave him trouble for quitting the delve after a score?

Sen could piss up a rope once Rhen was a dungeon owner. Nothing could touch him, not even a Desedra, once he had that shiny "D.O.G." badge on his id syntial.

His pay was just over four hundred dra, to which he argued that the node find should've put him well over five hundred. The desk jockey sighed, referencing some old Desedra rule stating any injury sustained on the delve would come out of the delvers' pay to cover repairs... damn that fluffer Pat and his missing fingers.

Either way, his pay was more than enough to free him, and give him some tools to get started. Rhen couldn't help but run from the payment office all the way down to the Dungeon Owner's Guild that moment. He skidded through the lobby with his toeless boots and came to a stop at the teller's station. The same bored teller as the days before appeared. "Let me guess, SB9102?"

"Yes please," Rhen said, unable to contain his grin.

The information pulled into view. It was still available.

Rhen's heart pounded as he made the deposit that would get him the rest of the way there.

"You understand that by purchasing this dungeon outright that the D.O.G. is not responsible for any losses of life, limb, personal belongings, nor do we ensure—"

"I agree!" Rhen interrupted.

The teller shook his head, a tiny smile playing on his bored lips. He made a few sweeping gestures and the control in front of Rhen came to life. "Place your hand on the crystal to receive your mark of ownership."

Rhen slapped his palm down on the node. Warm anima trickled up his arm to his id syntial on his side. There was a tingling ache as a new petal blossomed out from the mark, the light of it visible under his clothes. After a few short seconds, the pain stopped and the anima receded.

"Congratulations Rhen Zephitz, you're a dungeon owner now."

Rhen jumped from his seat, fists pumped in the air. "I'm a dungeon owner!"

"Shh," the front desk attendant hushed him.

"I'm a dungeon owner," he whispered with glee.

"Anything else I can do for you?"

Rhen caught his breath. "This has just been... I mean wow. Finally. I did it."

"Best of luck out there."

The magical glow faded, taking the teller with it. Only Rhen's reflection remained. He looked at himself. No longer a boy fighting for his place in the world, but a man who'd seized it. He'd scrapped the bottom of the scummiest dungeons, bathed in filth, slept in a room with thirty other dudes, ate stale bread and monster meat... and it was all worth it.

He was a dungeon owner.

4

DUNGEON DISCOVERY

The cross-country train plugged along at a good speed, rattling now and then. Rhen's eyes were fixed on the petal sticking out of his id syntial that read, "D.O.G." in flashing letters at the center. There was a single hashmark on the top of the petal to show he owned one dungeon, and within that tiny hash was the dungeon identification number.

His finger traced the mark, lingering on the faded scar that ran around the id syntial. Rhen battled to keep his thoughts from going to the dark, caved-in dungeon of his childhood. Eleven years wasn't long enough for him to forget the pain, nor his mentor's face.

"You'd be proud," Rhen whispered, assuring himself he'd made all the right choices from back then to now, at least to the best of his ability.

The door to his train car rattled open and Rhen pushed his jerkin down, smoothing out the material.

The woman who'd opened it was a busty fifties-something with a fat cart full of delver's goods. "Need anythin' for your dive?"

Rhen patted his overstuffed backpack. "Got it all right here, thank you."

"You sure you aren't in need of... this!?" She pulled a small mooring piston from the side of her cart. It was intended for pumping fresh air through a tube run underwater, for dungeon levels that were separated by lakes or rivers. Rhen was most certainly not in need of it.

"No, thank you."

"What about one'ah these?" She removed a multi-purpose pressure gauge and anima sensor that was missing one of its needles.

Rhen scowled. "That one looks broken."

She stuffed it back in the cart. "You just ain't seen it clearly. Who's dungeon you divin', anyway?"

Rhen beamed proudly. "Mine."

She laughed, her whole bosom bouncing. "Hope ya have enough to save a resurrection profile in town."

She slammed the door shut, leaving Rhen to scowl alone in his little alcove.

"Hope ya die on ya first run," he mocked in her voice, then turned to the tiny window.

The wild landscape flew by in blurs of blue and green. He'd seen his fair share of forest dungeons, but somehow seeing it outside with a wide-open blue sky made it more enchanting. SB9102 was the perfect plot, situated close to a decent-sized dungeon town, but well enough into the wilderness that he wouldn't have random people wandering by.

The trees thinned and little pockmarks of building clusters appeared. The train slowed gradually, letting Rhen take in the setting of Yu City. It was a *far* cry from Desedra City, with its towering skyscrapers, packed streets, full markets, and multitudes of temptations.

The buildings of Yu were constructed with wood and brick

and didn't make it past three levels in most cases. The roofs were thatched with straw from the agricultural fields on the east of the city, and there were a good number of fruit trees as well as livestock shelters. It was a mom-and-pop type town. Everyone probably knew everyone else.

The streets weren't paved, or really maintained at all. Thick wagonloads of ore bumped along, losing chunks of material out the back with every divot in the road. A child picked up the dropped pieces, throwing them back into the wagon that was pulled by a simple horse. Horses were strong, but not like dungeon monsters. Anyone who could afford a monster drawn wagon was much better off than one with a horse. It spoke to the state of the city, and what Rhen could expect.

He spotted an inn not too far from where the train came to a rest. The sun was setting, and his body ached from a full day of work on top of two and a half hours of train travel. He knew he might not get another chance for a soft bed and a hot meal for many weeks, so he decided to splurge a little.

The city smelled of dirt, raw ore, and horses.

Blech.

Rhen covered his face with his sleeve to prevent powdered horse poop from flying up his nostrils and pressed on for the inn. A cute little sign hanging over the door read Bustling Brood and colorful roses bloomed on either side of the stained-glass windows. It was a nice place—maybe too nice for Rhen to afford.

He stepped into the scents of fresh bread and roasting gamey meat. His mouth instantly salivated at the thought of having meat that hadn't come off a horromoth or some other slimy dungeon monster. The music hit him next, a jaunty little tune being performed by a Sephine, lizard-like humanoids with two extra arms.

This orange and yellow Sephine played a tall bass in two

arms and a lyre in the other, creating a sweet harmony. She started in on her chorus, singing something about high wages and better times. A fuzzy Taalite—a monstrously big and well covered creature from the ice realm of Ptahl—clapped along nearby, and two twin males with dirty blonde hair, Resplendites if Rhen had to guess, held out donation buckets on either side of the stage.

Rhen liked this place.

He approached the bar where a man with a thick moustache waited. "Hello, sir. Room and board for one night?"

"It's Perry. One private room left at ten imperial marks, or you can sleep in the entertainment hall for one."

Rhen cringed. Ten marks was a quarter of what he had left, and quite steep for a private room. Yu must've been in dire need. Rhen couldn't afford it at that price. Ah, what was one more night in a room full of thirty dudes? He'd have eternity alone with his dungeon soon.

"Group situation please." Rhen placed the shiny imperial mark on the counter. He didn't like carrying a lot of coin with him, preferred storing his money on his id syntial, but he knew going into a small town like this, he'd need cash on hand.

Perry ferried the coin away with a wink and a gap-toothed smile. "Welcome to the Bustling Brood."

Rhen kept his pack securely about his shoulders and looked around. Several tables were already packed full of scrappy looking dungeoneers, but there was one near the bard's stage that was empty save for one man. His hair was graying on the sides, and what was left on top had been slicked back. He wore a tattered green-gray jacket tied off at the left elbow where he was missing the rest of his arm. He had dark, stained pants, and his boots were in about as good shape as Rhen's.

Rhen made his way over to the older man. "Are you saving this spot?"

His furrowed, bushy brow of salt and peppery hair nearly obscured his purple-hued eyes. The old man looked down at Rhen's feet, then scanned him all the way up to the top of his head. After a long beat, his eyes went wide with delight.

"Is that you, Gerald?"

"I'm afraid not, sir. My name is Rhen."

The old man's eyes lost their sparkle, and his face sagged. He kicked out the chair across from him. "Sit yourself down, Rhen."

Rhen set his pack on the other seat, then plopped down in the offered chair. He opened his bag and took inventory of the tools he'd bought before he left Desedra City. He'd been able to get a small hand operated drill, not the industrial-sized stuff Desedra rented out, but it would do fine alongside his Tremor Blast ability.

Next was a good length of rope, some carabiners, and a simple harness. He didn't know how deep his dungeon would be after he got in it, but the assessment said at least two levels, and up to four, so he'd need to climb. He preferred not dying alone at the bottom of a dungeon because he was too stupid to strap in, so he'd spent the three marks on the basic climbing gear.

Lastly, he inspected the small canvas tent. It was used and a little holey, but it would serve him fine for the time being. He didn't plan on living in a tent for long. Rhen wasn't too bad at carpentry and planned on building himself a little cabin just as soon as the funds allowed. A tent would do for now.

"New dungeon owner, huh?" The geezer's voice was gruff, but friendly.

"I am."

"Thought you could do it better than Desedra, saved up everything you could, bought yourself a little plot?"

Rhen nodded.

"You know how to mine, or just delve?"

"What's the difference?"

"For six marks, I'll tell ya, and my secrets. All my secrets..." he whispered conspiratorially, like he knew something no one else did.

Rhen had a good forty marks left, but he needed to save those for when things inevitably got tough. Not to mention he'd need healing salves. His natural regeneration was passively increased because of Swift Twitch, but not enough to save him from ruin if he broke a leg—or lost an arm. How hard it must be to get by as an old, one-armed man.

"How about two marks and you can have my ale?" Rhen offered.

The old man laughed in a kooky way. "I know my worth, kid. It'll be six marks."

The barkeep dropped a bowl of stew and a mug of beer in front of Rhen. He slid the mug across the table to the old man.

"My apologies, but I'll have to decline your expertise for now, mister...?"

He accepted the drink. "It's just Wyland, no mister about me. What about you?"

Rhen faltered. Had he not introduced himself? "I'm Rhen, no mister here either."

Wyland took a long pull of the hoppy beer, then muttered to himself. "Looks like Gerald."

Rhen dug into his meal and turned his attention to the performance on the stage. The Sephine had moved on to a slower song, something to help the dungeoneers towards sleep. It seemed too early for that, but then again it was a smaller city. He probably wouldn't find all-night parties here like in Desedra.

When all the delvers had finished their meals, and yawns proliferated around the room, the barkeep ordered everyone to start preparing for sleep. They dragged the tables to the edges of the room and sat them up on their ends to help make space. Everyone claimed a spot for their own and rolled out their beds.

Rhen was exhausted from travel, and was asleep in a matter of minutes.

By sunup, the inn was bustling again—hence the first part of the name, Rhen realized—but where the "brood" part came in, he didn't know. Perhaps some inside joke. He tucked his bed back into the flap of his pack and gratefully accepted a steaming roll from the barkeep. These smelled like nothing he'd ever had before, and he'd had a lot of breakfast rolls.

This roll was coated in a syrupy sugar on the outside, with flecks of cinnamon and sugar inside. The bread was hot, fluffy, and sweet on the inside, with little chunks of fruit and meat, left over from last night he assumed. While strange, it was also quite divine.

The door to the inn opened and a well-dressed beefslab of a man with orange hair strode in. He looked like a Shin'Baran, but Rhen couldn't tell without a closer look at his eyes. He moved around the lounging delvers with mild disgust and stopped at Rhen's feet.

"You're Rhen Zephitz?" he asked, an unimpressed scowl on his face.

Rhen stood and turned to face the wide man with arms so thick they could no doubt crush every bone in Rhen's body if the man so wished. There was no way he could've offended someone so soon, right?

"Who is it that's asking?"

He hooked a thumb at his chest. "Peter Welsh, owner of the Welsh Dungeon Cluster."

"It's good to meet you, Mr. Welsh." Rhen held out his hand for a shake, but Peter didn't return the gesture.

"The delvers in here work for *me*. You got that?"

How was it possible that he was outed the *night* he arrived in town? Welsh must've been watching that plot... Why hadn't he bought that plot if he didn't want the competition? Rhen wasn't here to give him competition, yet he couldn't help but stoke the man's anger.

Rhen smirked. "And what if they want to change dungeonship?"

"You think sleepin' on the floor makes them like you, like you're one of 'em? They're *my* delvers because I've got the profitable dungeons."

How dare he storm in here just after dawn to accost him over an offense he hadn't committed and then claim to know *what he was*?

"I'm not here to pilfer *your* delvers, Mr. Welsh, though my dungeon will no doubt be profitable," Rhen said a little louder than he needed.

Peter leaned in closer. "I'll hold you personally responsible for any of my losses. Now, do you got that?"

"I'm sure the D.O.G. would have something to say about your claiming ownership over the delvers in your dungeon, Mr. Welsh."

Peter bared his teeth in an attempt to smile. "You're makin' a mistake."

"That's to be seen."

Peter turned and stormed off, smashing his way through the inn door with a growl.

The other delvers looked between each other with glazed-eye confusion. Rhen was confused, too.

What an idiot.

He bade Wyland goodbye, who offered his secrets once again at six marks. Rhen strapped on his pack and took one last look at the city behind him. In a few days' time, he'd be back to trade. Maybe then he could afford some of Wyland's secrets, or boot repairs. There were a lot of things high on Rhen's list of to-buys once he had the marks for it.

The trail out of town shrank in width until he was at the

precipice of the forest, walking on a narrow strip of dirt overgrown with blue-green grasses. The tall blades danced in the breeze, looking like waves on an ocean. Birds chirped, squirrels chittered, small predators rustled bushes, and the whole forest sang with life.

Rhen pulled a deep breath all the way down to the pit of his stomach. Now, to find his dungeon.

Rhen followed the softly trodden trails through the forest for about thirty minutes when he came to a large, white-barked tree with pale green leaves. He opened his bag and pulled out the map he'd been gifted from the Dungeon Owner's Guild. It was magically infused and linked to the id syntial on his side, making it valuable, but only to Rhen... or whomever had that three-by-three patch of skin over their ribs.

Rhen placed his index finger on the seal of the map and it unfurled with a magical flourish of purple sparks. It laid itself out flat between his hands, black ink seeping onto the page from seemingly nowhere. Eventually the ink revealed the tall white tree to his side as the Waiting Willow, a common meeting point for the cluster of dungeons in the area.

Rhen's marker appeared on the map beside the tree, a purple pulsing orb, and then his dungeon came into view, scrawled out in elegant script: Zephitz Dungeon. It was still a good three hours away, but excitement swelled in him from the pit of his stomach. He felt like a jittery lizard, itching to take off in every direction at once.

Several paths snaked off from the Waiting Willow, but none in the direction of his dungeon. He'd have to build that path himself, starting now.

With his crescent moon blades in hand, he slashed his way through the tall underbrush toward his prize. The passive syntial in his boots allowed him to absorb anima from the severed plants and even the ground itself, which was enough to give him an extra two hours of energy. He paused at a stream, panting like mad and dripping sweat.

The water looked clean enough, so he splashed himself with some and reviewed the map again. His previous trek time hadn't been indicative of carving his way through the forest without a trail. But *now* he seemed about two hours out.

The anticipation was making him hungry.

But there was no time to stop for a meal. He filled up his water skin, strapped his bag on his shoulders, and headed on his way. The stream cut through the forest quite nicely in the same direction of his dungeon, so he made better time by following close to the bank.

Energy, like a buzzing swarm of bees, tickled his skin.

Rhen stopped. He'd felt that every time he delved close to a strong monster. The raw anima pouring off it would cause a disturbance in the air, detectable by anyone attuned to using anima.

Rhen crouched, becoming still and quiet as he looked for a threat. A distant snap pulled his attention. It wasn't a twig breaking, but a whole branch. He opened his map and found that his dungeon was right in the path of that noise. It wasn't uncommon for monsters to roam out of their dungeons in the nearby areas, but if the volume of that sound was any indication, the monsters in Rhen's dungeon were going to be *huge*. Huge monsters were a double-edged sword. Usually harder to kill, higher level, with more syntials, but also bigger cores, more anima, and greater powers to impart.

Rhen crouched lower, hiding himself amongst the waving grasses, then crept toward the noise. A shadow moved between the branches ahead and Rhen slowed, focusing his gaze on the movement. Horror dredged through his guts when Rhen realized it wasn't a wandering monster from within his dungeon...

It was a defiler.

5

DUNGEON DEFILER

The dungeon defiler, a twelve-foot-tall monstrosity of hulking muscles and a long maw of thick teeth, marched in a circle, likely right over Rhen's dungeon opening. Its canine nose sniffed at the air, pulling a deep inhale. It must've smelled Rhen's unoccupied dungeon and thought it'd scored big.

Defilers rarely rolled up on dungeons that were actively being mined, unless they were desperate. They survived off a diet of anima and meat, the latter which could easily be found in the forest, but the former was hard to come by in large quantities—except in a dungeon.

Rhen took a deep breath and calmed his nerves. He'd never fought a defiler before, but he imagined it was just like killing any other dungeon monster. If he defeated it, he'd get the thing's massive crystal core, loaded down with anima from however many dungeons it'd suckled from... but that also meant it'd have a wide variety of syntials from different dungeons, and abilities that did not mesh in cohesive ways. It would be a wildcard battle.

And if he didn't win, well he'd cross that rainbow bridge

when he came to it. Rhen hadn't saved at a Resurrection node recently. A death now would mean losing months of progress and a trip back to Shin'Bara.

He couldn't distract himself with those thoughts right now. He needed to focus.

The defiler turned toward Rhen, sniffing again. Could it smell *him?* Rhen had been sweating profusely.

The dungeon hunting monster growled low in its throat, like a warning. "This is mine," its guttural snarl said.

Rhen sucked down a deep breath and activated Primordial Breath, thinking, *Darkness,* when he exhaled. A black cloud billowed out from his lips and filled the air between him and the defiler. The monster roared in anger. Rhen moved, circling around left behind the cloud and into a cluster of bushes.

He knew he'd be able to use his breath another five or six times before his lungs couldn't take anymore, but he'd rather use his other abilities with the anima he had left. If he ran his skills to the limit, the lack of anima in his body would make him weak, and could cause him to collapse... it had happened before, and now would be the worst time for it.

The defiler pushed through the trees, snapping roots with simple shoves. The trees bent under the monster's immense strength, allowing it passage to the dark cloud Rhen had left behind.

Rhen wanted to pounce when the monster's back was turned but waited. He wanted to see just what kind of spells this thing had up its metaphorical sleeve.

The defiler was still a good ten feet from the spot Rhen had been when a green syntial glowed to life on its muscled back. It dropped to all fours, arcing its spine as a rumble grew in its chest. With a loud bark, it spat about a gallon of acidic green mucous into the black cloud.

What was it with monsters wanting to melt his skin recently?

The black mist dispersed, revealing not acid burned plants, but colorful glowing mushrooms sprouting at a much too advanced rate. The caps bloomed, and when the defiler stomped, they released spores.

Nope, that wasn't good at all.

Rhen pulled in another breath and imagined a raging fire. He activated Swift Twitch and leapt forward ten feet in a single bound. The fire spell belched from his lips, eating up the mushrooms, their spores, and lighting the defiler's sparse fur.

The defiler howled and swung around with a beefy arm. Rhen ducked, then slish-slashed with his crescent moon blades along the monster's unguarded side. The defiler kicked hard, catching Rhen in the chest, and sent him pinwheeling into the air.

Rhen activated Swift Twitch again, twisting midair and landing in a somewhat graceful roll. His sternum hurt, and he couldn't breathe as deep as he wanted. The defiler pursued him, its crispy skin oozing and its side bleeding.

Despite his limited lung capacity, Rhen activated his fire breath again. The defiler shied away from the flames, giving Rhen just enough time to turn tail and run for the rushing river. A thick branch sailed past him with near-deadly accuracy and Rhen looked back. The defiler pulled a sapling from the ground, lining up to spear Rhen through.

Rhen grabbed a fist-sized rock and ducked behind a thicker tree for shelter. The sapling crashed against the trunk behind him with a sickening crack. Rhen imagined his bones crumpling against the tree when the defiler got hold of him.

No, Rhen had a plan. A stupid plan but whatever.

He pulled the rope from his pack and tied one end to the rock. The ground trembled at the defiler's coming. Rhen dashed for the next tree, getting to its shelter just before another something smashed against it. Sounded like a rock this time.

The retching sound of mushroom spore splat came again. Rhen made one last mad dash around the nearest tree, spinning the rock-ended rope in a tight circle. The defiler spat out his mushroom goop over the tree Rhen had been taking shelter behind.

The passive healing had done its work on Rhen's chest, and he was able to take a deep breath again. He thought *light* this time and charged toward the beast.

The defiler flexed, activating a deep blue syntial on its chest. Rhen didn't want to discover what that was, so he unleashed the light spell early, a few feet out. The defiler growled in pain. Rhen squinted through the bright mist, finding the creature had reared back, trying to avoid the spell it thought was fire.

Rhen activated Swift Twitch and fired his makeshift grappling rope at the closest tree trunk big enough to hold the defiler. The rope swung around the trunk, smacking the defiler in the face, and disorienting it. Rhen ran around the tree, pulling the rope tight and slamming the defiler against the trunk.

The monster pulled and the rope whined. It wouldn't hold long, but hopefully long enough. Rhen ran around the tree again. The defiler reached for him, and Rhen dodged wide, managing to wrap a loop around its wrist. He ran around the tree and pulled hard again, pinning the defiler's arm across its body. He wrapped one last time, then tied an awkward, shaky-handed knot.

The defiler pulled and strained, red syntials lighting up along its arms. The rope began to slip into the defiler's arm, like he was phasing through it. Rhen couldn't give it a chance to finish whatever it was doing, and crescent blades wouldn't do their job fast enough. Rhen summoned all his anima and channeled it into his arms. He placed his hand on the beast's stomach and activated Tremor Blast, imagining the strongest vibrations he could.

His hands shot backwards at the force of the spell that ripped the defiler's guts open. Thick, yellowed blood exploded out of the defiler's back and splashed against the tree. It gave a weak groan, legs kicking into the bloody dirt, and then its syntials went dark. The defiler slumped forward, held against the tree by the rope running through its body.

Rhen sat back and sighed. "Shoulda just let me have my dungeon."

He allowed himself a quick rest to regain some anima, then cut through the nasty, goopy guts to find the thing's core. It wasn't as large as he'd hoped, but still considerable. As soon as he found a Mastery node in his dungeon, he'd be leveling up again, and getting whatever cool powers his new dungeon had to offer.

The river was near enough that he washed before getting started. It would be a good source for him when trying to clean and refine his ore. Oh, and regular baths, and cooking. He realized then just how lucky he'd gotten to have the river so close. If not for that, he would've had to travel back to town for his water needs until he could dig a well.

After a moment of searching, Rhen located the dungeon entrance. It was a hole in the ground not more than five feet wide, with a ten-foot drop to a rocky bottom. Moss covered the sunless edges of the dark stone, and roots snaked out across the walls. There was a tunnel leading off into the earth on the sunny side, but Rhen couldn't see more than two feet in from his angle.

He was giddy to get inside, but knew he would be tired when he emerged later. If he didn't set up his tent first, he'd be sleeping with the elements tonight. He found a nice flat spot under some trees and made his temporary home.

Rhen really wanted to get in the dungeon, but maybe should secure some more water before going in. He'd be thirsty and hungry after fighting, and would need to be prepared to cook whatever monster meat he found, and he sure as hell wasn't going to eat the defiler with its yellowed flesh.

With water gathered, and tent erected, Rhen looked around at his little camp. Something was still missing.

Ah, a fire pit. He didn't want the whole forest burning down while he was sleeping.

After a good thirty minutes, he'd built a suitable pit for cooking that night. Rhen paused, arms crossed, and glanced about his space.

His space.

Boy, that felt nice.

He turned his attention on the dungeon opening, determination swelling in his chest. He was going to delve the ever-fluffing shi—

A bush ruffled behind him and Rhen dropped into a crouch.

"It is only me," came a familiar rumbling in Rhen's chest.

A watery hand slipped through the underbrush, then Aki's body appeared, carried on a wave between the thick branches.

Rhen stood, his hand resting on the hilt of his crescent moon blade. "What are you doing here?" He tried to keep the accusation from his tone. Aki *said* he was on a pilgrimage, but that didn't make it so.

Aki stopped a few feet away. "You were right about Desedra. I was never going to get to Tertia with them, so I took your advice about a smaller dungeon."

"And you want to try your luck here? I don't even know if this dungeon has enough to get *me* to Tertia, let alone someone else."

"I will do whatever you tell me to do. Please, do not make me go back there. You were the only person kind to me."

Rhen winced. He was playing at his pity, and somehow it was working.

No. He had to resist. He didn't want to be responsible for anyone, plus, the paperwork, and it became so much more difficult to manage the proper delving of the dungeon so early on. There were so many good reasons to send Aki away, even some for his own good.

"There are other more profitable dungeons in the area. I don't have the..." Rhen gestured at his camp, searching for the words. "Anything. I have no inn, no second tent, no baths or food. Nothing."

"I can fish, very well. There is a stream not far. I can also make fires. I can refresh my biosphere with the river water, no bath required. I sleep in three-to-four-minute increments throughout the day, so a tent is also unnecessary."

Rhen scowled. His only argument left was the one he hadn't told him. "It could be very dangerous, Aki. There is no Resurrection node yet; there's not even a Mastery node. If you died or became gravely injured, you'd go back to wherever you last saved your anima profile."

"Then I would return home. I have not made any imprint in the other realms, as is the custom of my people."

Rhen opened his mouth to protest further, and Aki stopped him.

"Please. If you do not wish to have me here, be forward. I will accept your wishes and depart. If your objections are for my safety or comfort, understand that I have been through far worse than a forest camp."

Rhen sighed. "No. It's..."

What was it? A little paperwork wasn't that big a deal. He was aware of the risks. He didn't seem completely incompetent, and survived a week with Desedra. If Rhen got in trouble, having backup would be nice, and Aki's psionic abilities were a wonder. It was a little creepy that he'd stalked him through the forest and just watched him fight, but Aki wasn't really familiar with the common customs, so stalking and creeping may have been acceptable to him.

"Well... I guess you can stay for a while and see if it's profitable here."

Aki fluttered in a circle inside his waterbody, skin pulsing colorfully. "I will make my presence appreciated. I promise."

"Whatever you say. Technically I'm not supposed to let you in the dungeon before your paperwork is signed..."

"I am an adept liar."

Rhen snorted. "Somehow, I doubt that. But it'll be fine. I'll get your paperwork, you sign it, I turn it in. You won't need to lie to anyone, just... don't say anything at all."

Rhen pulled his bag up onto his shoulders and motioned for Aki to follow. There were plenty of stable roots around the edges of the dungeon opening, so Rhen used those to climb down since his rope was currently indisposed. When he reached the bottom, he realized that Aki's body was made of water... and he probably couldn't climb.

"Should I get a bucket for you?"

Aki poured his watery body over the edge and landed with a contained splash at the bottom. He floated around in the bobble of water for a moment, skin pulsing a vibrant pink and white. Then, he reformed his water in the shape of a human and put himself at the top, like a head.

Rhen hadn't given it a second thought before, but realized Aki could move the water into any shape he pleased. There was something uncanny about a cephalopod head at the top of a man-shaped body.

But enough of that. It was time to delve.

"I'm a fighter type. I get close to the monsters with these," he paused and pulled out his crescent moon blades.

"Yes. I've seen you fight."

Rhen scowled. "Oh?"

"The defiler."

"And you didn't think to help?"

"You were not in danger. I would have assisted when necessary."

"Wait, so you watched me set up camp, too?"

Aki's glow faded and he went pale. "I was nervous to approach."

Rhen laughed and patted him on the back with a splash. "You are *definitely* cooking on your own tonight to make up for it. But good, so you know how I fight. What can you do?"

Aki split his watery body in two and controlled the second, half-sized body—making it do a weird little jig. Then his tentacles glowed a bright yellow, and an aurora of color projected from him, winding through the water. It was hypnotizing to watch, and suddenly Rhen realized his hands wouldn't move, nor his legs, or any other part of him. He'd even stopped breathing.

"Kay, got it," he said through his clenched jaw.

"I can control the water, and my Aurora Wave spell has several different Cebrum and Kinse uses. I have five ancilla appended to that one." He dismissed the magic and brought the water back into his body.

Rhen sighed, happy to be free of the spell. "You can be the crowd control. Just try not to get in my way, and I'll try not to get in yours."

Rhen turned to the narrow opening of the dungeon entrance and strapped on his hand drill.

It was time to get to work.

6
NEW NODE

Rhen worked at breaking away the wall, widening the passage so they could stand abreast, while Aki sorted through the raw material. His ability to manipulate water made him especially adept at breaking the harder stone away from the ores and gems they wanted to collect. Aki could also absorb the raw anima out of the stones he broke down by polluting his body with the debris, but that didn't seem to bug him much.

Thirty feet past the initial entrance to the dungeon, the pair came to a wide opening with two new tunnels that diverged. Rhen wanted to cover as much ground as possible, but a nagging voice, weathered and generic from years-old memories, rattled off in his head. *"Never split the dungeon party."*

He trusted the owner of that voice he scarcely remembered. He wished he could hear it more clearly, now.

"I think we should head down the left passage for half an hour, then the right, then call it a night."

"Yes, boss."

Rhen's whole body withered in disgust. "Please, don't call me that. Just call me Rhen."

"But are you not the boss?"

"The owner, and the delve leader, sure. But boss... I don't know. There's something *wrong* about that word."

"I do not understand, but I respect your wishes, Rhen."

"Let's find ourselves a node before we quit, eh?"

Aki fluttered, shifting colors. "Let us do it!"

Rhen smiled. Aki's common tongue was rough since he hadn't learned to use contractions, but his enthusiasm was welcome. They had yet to discover any monsters thus far, but Rhen knew if there was a node anywhere in here, there'd surely be a monster guarding it.

They moved down the left passage, Rhen out in front and Aki providing the minimal light necessary to sneak around. The tunnels had, thus far, been basic caves. While Rhen had been hoping *maybe* his dungeon was more than what met the eye, that it had its own themed chambers, multiple monster and anima types, he would be satisfied with whatever he managed to get. At least he had something.

Just as he was about to give the order to turn back, he heard a growl—*snap!* Some monster feasting on a hapless creature that wandered in from the woods? Maybe an adventurer, delving without permission got caught off-guard? Whatever it was, monsters were a sure sign of a dungeon node somewhere nearby.

"Two monsters around this bend." Aki said it so gently, Rhen barely heard the words.

Aki projected dim light inside the belly of his water body. The silver light took shape as a thick, stocky quadruped. There were sparse details, other than a short, fat face full of teeth, and wide shoulders. It was narrow at the waist, with a stubby tail. Looked almost like a dog, but Rhen guessed there'd be something horrifying to it. Who knew if Aki's prediction was even accurate?

There was only one way to find out.

Rhen sucked down a deep breath, activating the syntial to infuse that breath with magic. He tore around the corner, crescent moon blades in hand and flaming breath spewing heat and light through the cavern. The closest creature caught a face full of fire, dropping the bone it was chewing on. Flame-faced monster and the other one behind it ran for the back wall and scurried behind a stocky boulder.

Rhen blew out the last of the fire and coughed up smoke. Already, he felt the power of Swift Healing going to work on his throat. His eyes hadn't yet adjusted to the darkness, but a deep snarl, right where the little monsters had run off to, caught his attention. Rhen tightened his grip on his weapons and squinted to see better.

The silhouette of a much larger monster bloomed in the darkness, illuminated by the violet glow of a syntial on its back.

Then it was gone.

Not even a blip, or a poof. Nothing. It had disappeared. In its absence, Rhen noticed what it had been curled up around.

A node.

But Rhen knew not to get too excited, to stay on his guard. He put his back to the wall and sucked in another breath. *Light*, he pushed the air out and filled the cavern. The glowing particles of Rhen's spell drifted toward the ground, revealing the outline of a much too close monster stalking him from his left flank. It'd moved so fast and quietly!

Rhen activated Swift Twitch and lunged forward for the first strike, but the creature was ready. It dropped out of stealth and dodged with a sideways prance. Rhen turned and slashed at its hind legs, nicking the exposed ankle tendon. The monster yipped and Rhen kept on the offensive.

He pushed forward, chasing the hound-like creature until it

was cornered. The monster puffed up its chest with a mighty breath, and a red syntial flared to life on its chest.

Shit.

Rhen dodged whatever spell might be spewing from the monster's mouth, but to no avail. The bark pierced the air and rang through his ears. His eyeballs vibrated and his teeth chattered as his jaw spasmed.

Tiny needles pierced into Rhen's calf, and he howled. The unsinged monster had gotten a mouthful of his flesh and growled into it like a beast with its kill. Rhen swiped at the monster several times, missing on account of his vibrating eyes. Finally, he scored a critical hit across the back of the creature's neck with his blade, severing the spinal cord in a single hit. The monster's mouth went slack, leaving Rhen's leg meat flapping, but still attached.

The bigger monster was on him again, chomping at Rhen's face. He rolled right and the hound skidded to a stop. Rhen jumped to his feet—*ouch*—and hobbled with his damaged leg held off the ground. The burned monster approached from Rhen's right and they pushed him toward the cavern wall, slathering teeth bared.

"A little help here?" Rhen asked when he noticed Aki was nowhere in sight.

The small hound dove in for Rhen's damaged calf. Rhen activated Swift Twitch, pulling his leg out of the way just in time. He launched his magic-infused leg at the creature in a powerful kick—*ouch!*—that sent the monster staggering back. The bigger hound took advantage, throwing itself at Rhen's left arm.

A long tube of water splashed against the monster's face, then forced its way down its throat. The hound convulsed, coughing to try to clear the liquid from its lungs. It was no use. The monster flopped to the ground, flailing and wheezing. Then it was still.

The water drained from its mouth, then rejoined Aki's body as he emerged from around the corner.

"A bit savage, drowning... isn't it?" Rhen asked, horrified.

"No more than slicing the enemy's neck open."

Rhen shrugged. "Fair. Hey, where were you when I got my leg half-eaten?"

"I am too vulnerable to—monster!"

The smaller creature Rhen had kicked back gained its feet, snarling deep in its throat. Aki projected a stream of soothing lavender light from his hands, entrancing the creature. Rhen gave it a quick one-two slice across the neck as he had the other, putting it down quickly.

"Come here," Aki said, glowing brightly so Rhen could find him.

Rhen limped over to him. "What?"

"Sit."

Rhen didn't understand why his Prelusk friend was ordering him to the ground, but he sat anyway. Aki swirled his watery hands together into a glowing sphere with his many tentacles.

"As I was saying. I am too exposed. I cannot take damage like you and survive."

The watery orb pulsed with refreshing blue light, and the sediment inside it leached back out into Aki's body. Then, without any warning, Aki splashed the water against Rhen's bloodied leg.

"Dude! Why?" Rhen cried out, cradling the limb.

"To stave off infection. My spell will also increase healing."

Aki pulled the bloodied water back into his body and Rhen cringed. "You just gonna walk around with my blood all over you?"

"There is no alternative water source here, and I need as much body content as I can get, so yes."

"Alright... uh, thanks." Rhen took a moment to inspect his

flappy skin, which was already healing quite nicely. He'd have an interesting scar for later stories, but probably wouldn't have to lose the leg, thanks to Aki.

They riffled through the monster guts until they located the creatures' crystalline cores. They were all a respectable size for being the first monsters they'd encountered. The monsters had nice fangs, but their claws were too brittle to be used for materials. They were hairless, and their skin was much too soft for leather. They'd use all they could, anyway.

Rhen looked to the node at the back of the cavern and licked his lips. Enough fooling around with the dead monsters, it was time to get the real prize of the room.

He crossed the floor, eyes so focused on the node he tripped on the bones the hound had been munching on. He cursed, but kept on toward the crystal. Rhen let his hand linger over the node. This was it. His very first dungeon node. What would it be?

"Here we go." He placed his hand on the glowing stone and light burst from the crystal planes. The room was full of orange sparkling magic and Rhen's skin tingled. Anima surged down his arm, tickling the id syntial on his side.

The light in the room coalesced, then zipped to attention over the node in neat, organized lines of information.

[Congratulations – Rhen Zephitz!]

You have claimed your very first dungeon node, binding this dungeon to you. The Dungeon Owners Guild has been informed of your progress.

In an effort to help you continue your progress on your very first dungeon, the Dungeon Owners Guild would like to offer you a series of quests that will offer a wide variety of beneficial rewards. If you would like to accept this series of quests, place the map gifted to you by the Dungeon Owners Guild in your other hand and say "I accept."

=====

Rhen wasn't sure what possible quests they would offer, nor what kinds of rewards there would be, but if he was going to be mining the dungeon anyway, why not get a little extra? He pulled the map from his backpack, holding it securely in the other hand.

"I accept."

Orange light raced down Rhen's arm and exploded into the map. The parchment glowed with new magical powers, then sprung open, hanging in midair.

Aki read as a line of text appeared at the top. "'Activate your first Control node. Reward, 1% off the first year's Dungeon Owner's Guild dues.' Well, it is something."

"We'll take what we can get. Now, let's figure out what to do with this node."

Rhen focused on the crystal under his hand. The orange light leaked from the center of the node and slipped past his fingers, forming a basic visual display.

[Dungeon Node 1]

Anima Types: Chaos | Dark
Attunement Options:
{Control}
Pour anima into this node to gain spatial control of the area. At level one, the dungeon owner will be able to affect the room in which the node resides. Increasing the level will likewise increase the area it controls and allow for more specialized shaping capabilities. At level one you can craft simple staging

rooms, delver barracks, or a secondary dungeon entrance (provided the room is close enough to the surface). The dungeon is under your command!

[Select] {Yes} | {No}

=====

{Mastery}
Use this node to pull power from the multitude of realms and infuse it into your being through syntials. Adding syntials to your person will increase your body's anima capacity, allowing for more spell casting. Crafting too many syntials on a body that has not achieved 90-100% anima well depth will weaken the anima channels, making spell casting more difficult, and reducing spell potency.

[Select] {Yes} | {No}

=====

Rhen looked at the monster cores grasped in Aki's tentacles, then the glimmer of excitement in the Prelusk's eyes. Rhen *could* activate a Control node and start a barracks. It would be somewhere out of the elements for them to stay, and they'd get the quest reward.

Or... he could activate a Mastery node and get some useful new abilities for each of them. There would be more nodes in the dungeon—probably—but having skills attuned to the dungeon they were delving could be essential for survival. Plus... cool news skills.

Rhen selected Mastery with a thought, and the dungeon vibrated with excitement. The orange light pulsed and shifted to a deeper copper color. The crystal whined as the interior changed shape, preparing itself for its new role in the dungeon.

The noise and light faded softly, and a new image flared to life over the burgundy-colored Mastery node. With a quick assessment check, Rhen saw he was at ninety-four percent anima capacity, which was high enough for an upgrade, and he could use the defiler core to get him a little extra.

He pulled the crystal core from his pocket and activated the Mastery node. The core dissolved in a burst of anima light, then flowed into Rhen's open palm.

[Syntial Additions and Expansion]

Available Options: 4
{Defender's Cry}
Prima I | Active | Mana | Chaos | Cost: 10% Anima
Infuse your voice with the power of the defender's might, frightening your enemies and emboldening your compatriots. Enemies will suffer disorientation and lack of coordination. Friends will have increased strength and courage.
—UNAVAILABLE: Location Occupied—
You already have a Prima Syntial in this location. You cannot apply this syntial before first removing the existing syntial.

=====

{Caress of Night}
Prima I | Active | Enon | Dark | Cost: 15% Anima/Minute
Become enveloped by shadows and disappear in darkness. In very low light situations such as night, or dark rooms, you become invisible. In shaded daylight situations, you will be more difficult to detect while stationary. Variable situations exist in-between—try your luck at your own risk.

=====

{Out For Blood}
Prima I | Passive | Kinse | Chaos | Cost: None
When you are injured, you deal increased damage with all anima spells and attacks. When you are not injured, your passive anima regeneration is decreased by 5% per syntial level.

{Shadow Snare}
Prima I | Active | Enon | Dark | Cost: 5% Anima
Use on a single target to decrease their movement speed for thirty seconds. Movement speed change is determined by percentage of ambient light. A dark room will decrease movement speed by 40-65%. In the shade on a sunny day it will decrease movement speed by 5-10%

=====

It was too bad Rhen couldn't get the first ability. Having experienced it firsthand, he knew it'd be a good one for controlling groups of monsters, but he liked Primordial Breath just fine.

"I would like Shadow Snare," Aki said.

"Oh? Okay."

"I thought perhaps we could strategize, so we do not have overlapping skills."

"Good idea. I liked Caress of Night in any case."

"You will have to learn to be stealthy."

Rhen scowled. "Whaddya mean? I'm as sneaky as they come."

"You ran into the room full of monsters breathing fire."

"I suppose I did, but I was using the element of surprise. I'll do the same with Caress of Night, just differently."

"It is yet to be seen."

Rhen laughed when he realized Aki was trying to joke. "I suppose I deserved that for my comment on your clandestine nature."

"I enjoy our banter."

"Me too, dude."

"Caress of Night is the only viable option for you, and I believe you will put it to good use."

"Alright... Caress of Night it is. I'll show you just how sneaky I can be."

Rhen selected the ability and violet light shot up his arm. The anima surged around to his back, pricking him like needles between his shoulder blades. The dark cavern was filled with the purple light for a moment, then it faded.

Rhen breathed deep in his new power. His dungeon's power.

They were on their way to greatness.

7
BARTERS AND BARGAINS

Aki claimed the Shadow Snare ability for himself and they decided to call it a night, despite still having another monster core. Aki put up quite a fuss, telling Rhen he should use it to increase his anima capacity, but Rhen argued it wouldn't be enough to get him another ability. Not to mention that they'd need to uncover more of the dungeon and activate more nodes to unlock additional abilities. Rhen didn't particularly want Out for Blood at the moment, since his boots were just about totaled and his passive anima regeneration couldn't take the hit.

They got back to the tiny camp well past sunset, and, as promised, Aki went to collect dinner. In a few short minutes he returned with several fish. Rhen started a fire the easy way, flame breath, and sat back as Aki cleaned and skewered the fish for him.

Rhen smiled. What a perfect day.

"What amuses you about my process?"

"Huh? Oh, no. I was just thinking it'd been a good day. Sure we haven't discovered any ecosystems in the dungeon yet, and cave fighting is pretty boring, but it was our cave."

"Your cave."

"Ah, yeah. You still want to work for me, right?"

"Yes."

"Okay, good."

"Why did you doubt?"

"Well, I mean the fight wasn't as sloppy as some that I've had, but we definitely haven't found our mojo. Some people don't have the grit to stick it out and make it work."

"I am invested in making it work."

When the roasted fish was done, Rhen ate greedily. Before he realized, he'd eaten all but half of one. "Did you get enough?" he asked, knowing that Aki hadn't had any at all.

"I ate at the river."

"Raw?" Rhen's face wrinkled at the thought.

"It is the way we eat."

"Oh, right. That makes sense. Your world is just ocean, right?"

"Ninety-four percent ocean, and my people have dominated the majority of it."

"Sorry, I don't know much about Prelia."

"Most outsiders stay on the outside. We let few delvers into our realm."

Rhen picked up the last of the fish. "So, you don't want this, right?"

"Correct."

He finished off the last of the meat and reminded himself that they'd need to buy salt when they went to town next—which needed to be soon. He couldn't keep letting Aki into the dungeon without registering that he'd hired help. If the D.O.G. found out he'd hired help without paying appropriate dues and whatever other dumb stuff he needed to waive the rights to, they could take his dungeon away, and ban him for life.

Stupid D.O.G. rules.

Rhen yawned.

"You can sleep. I will intermittently keep watch and prepare for the delve tomorrow morning."

"What's to prepare?"

"Rope ladder for the entrance, water deposits for pressure drilling, clearing the perimeter to begin your settlement, removing the defiler corpse, and whatever else presents itself."

"I don't think this dungeon will ever need a settlement. It's so small."

Aki hummed. "I do not like being idle."

Rhen yawned again. "Alright. Do what makes you happy. I won't make it another minute."

He kicked off his boots before entering the tent and collapsed onto his bed roll. Within seconds, he was asleep. A blink more, the sounds of the living forest roused him from slumber. The sun was just peeking over the horizon, casting soft pink hues over the canvas above him.

"Hello," Aki said softly.

Rhen rubbed his eyes. "Hello... how did you—" he yawned and stretched.

"I detected the change in your heart rate. I apologize if that was intrusive."

"S'fine, no problem. I'm used to banging pots and shouts for my morning wake-up, so birds and a hello was just fine. Though, if you want to be more appropriate in this realm, we say 'Good morning' instead of 'hello.'"

"What if the morning is not good?"

Rhen slipped on his boots and emerged from the tent. "It's always a good morning for someone, I suppose."

"Is it a good morning for you?" Aki was a sickly yellow color, his fins flapping vigorously.

Rhen nodded. "It is so far. How about you?"

"I ran out of tasks two hours ago."

"And that made you... anxious? I can't tell what this color means."

"I am not comfortable. It is not a good morning. I have wasted time."

Rhen took a deep breath and blew out his cheeks. "We need to teach you how to relax."

Aki went pale.

"But not right now. We have dungeon delving to do."

The Prelusk's color returned to a bright green. "I am ready."

There was a skewer of fish Aki had roasted over the embers of the fire that served as Rhen's breakfast, along with a stale roll from the day before. He used the new rope ladder to get down to the dungeon entrance. It still had defiler bloodstains on it, but Rhen wasn't complaining. Aki had already put in far more effort than Rhen would've.

They went to the Mastery node first, checking the walls for ore deposits. When they found one, Rhen would first give the rock a few good pulses with the hand drill. Then Aki came in with his water and pushed a small jetstream through the rock, blasting the softer stuff away from the metals.

In a matter of hours, they had several ounces of the dull orange mid-tier crafting ore, Lafite, and a few minor gemstones. Though the gems were small, they could be attuned at a special crafter's table to enhance syntial powers and increase body strength. Celinom, a sparkly purple-hued gem, could be used in light armor to increase anima spend efficiency as well as passive uptake, much like the gems that were in the heels of Rhen's boots. Perhaps it was time to not only fix the growing holes in the toe region but upgrade the gems in the heels too.

Rhen had to be careful in not using all the materials they collected. They needed the money to pay their D.O.G. dues and buy better tools for delving as well as building up a more suitable housing situation. He and Aki spent a few minutes dividing up the piles of ore and gems, easily agreeing on how they would be allocated. Then, they got back to work.

Four more hours of drilling into the walls earned them a good pocket of Lafite, which would surely be enough to do everything they needed on their first visit to town, and a few more materials like hakir, a yellow tinged salt that dissolved to create a basic restoration potion. They had to be careful not to get it wet and had destroyed a good half pound of it with Aki's drilling before Rhen realized what it was.

When they were both satisfied with their haul, they returned to the camp so Rhen could sleep. He was eager to get back to town to sell their loot, get Aki registered, fix his boots, and a hundred other things, but he knew he couldn't make the trek through the forest without some rest.

He rose just before the sun and was met with another roasted fish breakfast. He sprinkled a bit of the hakir salt on the fish, discovering it seasoned it quite well, though it was incredibly expensive. The well-seasoned fish eased the aching all over his body, giving Rhen the strength he needed to hack and slash his way through the forest back to Yu village.

The return journey was a little faster since the path had been trodden once before, and they made it into town by mid-morning. The smell of fresh bread made Rhen's mouth water, and so the first stop was at the bakery.

It was a squat, stone building with several tall smokestacks rising from the back. The smoke had calmed in the midday, but Rhen imagined that before dawn, all the ovens were going full speed.

A broad-shouldered woman with bronzed skin and dark curly hair approached the counter from the kitchen. "What can I getcha?"

"What's your cheapest roll?"

"Cheap!" she exclaimed, offended. "I do not make *cheap* food here. If that's what you're wanting, move along—though you'll have quite a ways to go to find another baker."

Aki pulled Rhen aside. "We will soon have the funds to make bigger purchases. Perhaps it would be best not to offend the only baker in town."

Rhen nodded at his companion. Half the work of owning a dungeon was making connections. He approached the counter again with a more professional demeanor.

"My apologies. I'm Rhen Zephitz, the new dungeon owner just out past the Waiting Willow. I've been a delver for many years—"

"That explains your manners," she interrupted, muscular arms crossed.

"Yes, we delvers certainly are at the bottom of society, especially in how we're treated."

The baker's face puckered. After a few breaths, her expression softened. "I'm Fennica Wheatle. Your apology is not necessary. You come from Desedra City?"

Rhen nodded.

"That explains it. We don't treat delvers that way here. You do some of the hardest work that makes our little town thrive. We appreciate that."

"Tell me more about your establishment."

Fennica gestured to a portrait of a man by an old-style clay oven that seemed out of commission. "My mother's father helped found this town, becoming the first baker and providing for the delvers. It thrived under his care, and the village grew, but it's been an age since we've seen any more real profit or growth. I carry on the old recipes, just me. The last of the Wheatles."

"Perhaps you would have use of this." Aki approached the counter and set down the leather satchel of Hakir.

Fennica opened the pouch and peered inside. "Ah, Healer's Salt. Can I sample?"

"Please do," Rhen said, taking a step back from the counter.

Fennica pinched a tiny bit between her fingers and placed it on her tongue. She took a drink from a bottle below the counter, then swished her mouth around. She squinted, scowled, swallowed, then nodded.

"High quality, fresh, no oxidation yet. Going rate is twenty-five marks an ounce and I've got use for an ounce or two."

Rhen balked. He knew the market price in Desedra was ninety dra an ounce, which was closer to fifty marks. But, it could've been more common in the dungeons around Yu, and the price discrepancy may have been warranted. Rhen didn't want to offend Fennica any further, so he conceded with a small barter. "How about twenty-five marks an ounce, and four shelf stable rolls?"

Fennica stroked her chin. "Deal. Where do ya plan on selling the rest of it?"

"We'll find a spot." Rhen turned to Aki. "Or season the fish."

"Best of luck to ya then, and a word of advice... introduce yourself first, talk of your dungeon ownership and let people know who you are. You're not just a delver"—her face puckered—" though you smell like one. You're a dungeon owner. That commands more respect to summa the others."

Fennica pulled four fresh rolls from a warming oven in the back and packaged them up. They exchanged the goods, and coin, then Rhen tipped his head. "Thank you for the advice, Ms. Wheatle. I'm sure we'll be seeing you again soon."

She weighed the bag of Hakir between her hands. "Be sure that you do. You find any father's fennel in your dungeon, be sure to bring it to me first, ya hear?"

"Father's Fennel?" Rhen asked.

"It's a blue-green moss that grows under the bulbous lumps of padreote ore. You'll know it by its pungent fennel smell."

"Can do."

Rhen and Aki moved out to the dusty street, Rhen already digging into the first roll. It was still warm, with a buttery sweetness. Finally, something other than seared fish on a stick.

"Alright, next stop is the dungeon worker registry business. See a D.O.G. building anywhere?" Rhen asked through a mouthful of roll.

He and Aki turned in circles, looking over the sparse buildings of the tiny village.

"I see nothing of the sort."

Rhen sighed. "That's what I feared. We'll have to go back to Desedra."

"Or, perhaps we could forego that formality?"

Rhen cocked an eyebrow. "If they found out, they'd blacklist me from the D.O.G."

"The risk is greater than the inconvenience of returning to the city?"

"Couldn't have said it better myself. Plus, we still have more Hakir to sell," Rhen lowered his voice, "which goes for a lot more than twenty-five marks an ounce in Desedra."

"We should like to sell most of our yield at Desedra, then?"

"I think for now, yes. Until Yu can support a real trade market, we'll be better off going back to Desedra when we feel we have enough to sell."

Rhen and Aki waited a half-hour for a train to arrive, and then spent the two-and-a-half-hour ride to Desedra discussing where to sell their materials. Rhen had circulated among the merchants enough to know which vendors would want what ores and gems, so when they arrived, they made quick work of getting the biggest profits.

With dra coin in hand, they went to the D.O.G. to verify Aki's employment with Rhen. It cost fifteen dra to register him to the dungeon, and of course Rhen had to pay some dues, but when they were all finished, they had four hundred dra and a little over two hundred imperial marks. That was what Rhen made in five weeks—*good* weeks—at Desedra. Their delver wages were completely criminal.

It was nearly sundown, but Rhen found a cobbler willing to do a rush order on his boots and give him a loaned pair until the next day. Rhen found himself giddily heading toward the Down-N-Out when he realized he and Aki had enough money to stay somewhere *nice*.

Hmm, but that money could be put toward better tools, or a new jerkin. Maybe he should save the money in case of emergency, or to purchase some... thing... Rhen found himself making excuses as to why he needed to stay at the Down-N-Out, but when he saw her flowery braided crown of bright red hair and golden flecked skin, he knew the real reason his feet wouldn't stop carrying him toward the delver's inn.

Jakira brightened at the sight of him. "You're back!"

8

ROMANTIC INTERLUDE

"I missed you!" The cute Cadrian threw open her arms and embraced Rhen. "Ugh, and you're just as smelly as usual."

"He is considerably cleaner than last time, however," Aki said behind them.

Jakira pulled away from Rhen, her golden freckled cheeks sparkling in a blush. "Oh, Mr. Aki. It's good that you're back too."

"We're just here for a night, but it's good to see you."

"Why such a short visit? Did you find another inn you like better?" Jakira pouted.

"Nothing of the sort." Rhen couldn't contain his grin. "I'm a dungeon owner, and tomorrow we'll head back to Yu City where my plot is."

Jakira's eyes sparkled and she embraced him again with a high-pitched squeal. "Really? I knew you'd make it! It must be so nice. You have to tell me all about it after your bath." She stepped back and held out her hand for payment.

"This time, I can afford my own."

"Oh, high roller! Have a tip for all those times I covered for you?" She winked.

"You know it." Rhen placed thirty dra in her waiting palm.

Jakira blanched. "Rhen, that's... that's too much." She pushed the money back toward him.

Rhen closed her fingers over the money and held her hand. "You've earned this. You work hard and don't get near enough the respect you should."

"But I could get in trouble! He might think I'm..."

Rhen put a finger to his lips. "If he calls your honor into question, I will set him straight. I'm a dungeon owner now, after all."

"Thank you. Uh, yeah come in. I'll get a bath going for you soon. You too, Mr. Aki?"

"I am not in need of a bath, thank you."

Jakira nodded. "Right, well, we're almost full up for the night so you better find a spot quick."

Rhen and Aki went up to the rickety fifth floor where a few spots remained. Rhen unfurled his bed roll and before he knew it, his bath was drawn. He slumped into the warm water with a deep sigh, letting his muscles relax.

Roughing it in the woods had been worth it for this. Money in his pocket, new boots, a hot bath, decent food, and debts repaid. Jakira played through his mind as he sunk deeper in the tub. Her sparkling cheeks, bright eyes, flowing hair down past her curvy—

Nope.

Rhen dunked himself and shook his head.

There was no time to be thinking of anything of the sort. He had a dungeon to delve and money to make. He'd found a single node, and who knew if there was another in his dungeon? There was a lot still to explore, sure, but it could've been dead ends and blank walls. He couldn't dream of romance with a dry dungeon.

But if the dungeon wasn't dry...

No.

He could think of that when he *knew* there was enough there to support anything more than Aki's wages and a small cabin in the woods.

He scrubbed himself clean in frustration and donned his old clothes. He'd earned enough to have a second set of under clothes by now, though with limited pack space it'd be hard to keep spares on him while he traveled. He'd figure out clean clothes later... it wasn't like he had anyone to impress, and he doubted Aki could smell him.

Aki worked in tandem with the bard that night, showing off his psionic Prelusk skills with ease. He pulsed yellows and pinks, his fins fluttering with excitement. It was obvious to Rhen that he liked showing off, or maybe he liked bringing a bit of joy to the Down-N-Outers. Whatever it was, Aki put on a performance like no other.

In the morning, Rhen lingered in the hall with his roll, waiting to see if he'd catch one more glimpse of Jakira, but she didn't show. It wasn't uncommon for her to be busy with laundry, or kitchen duty, cleaning the rooms, and various other tasks. She worked too hard for too little. Fennica had said how delvers were underappreciated for their hard work, but Rhen knew Jakira worked twice as hard as him—with a little less danger to life and limb, but still.

"Are you ready to depart for the cobbler?" Aki asked for the second time and Rhen knew he couldn't linger any longer.

He nodded and they made their way into the morning market. His boots were done, as promised, and Rhen paid the man his second half for a job well done. The boots were far superior than their previous incarnation. The leather shined, which would dissipate after a few good days in the dungeon, but whatever. They shined.

They made their way toward the train station at the edge of town, a somber air about them.

"Is there something wrong with you?" Aki asked.

Rhen shook his head. "Nothing."

"You have not been the same since last night. You usually talk more and tell jokes."

"I'm just tired I suppose."

"You did have a fitful sleep."

Rhen scowled. "You watched me sleep?"

"I watched our money which was in your bag, under your head."

The bell tolled beside the train heading west, going past Yu City, and Rhen dismissed the oddity. Of course Aki wanted to ensure the safety of their money, and Aki didn't sleep for more than a few minutes at a time, so this made enough sense for him to drop it.

"We better find a spot before the passenger car is full."

They purchased their return tickets and boarded the train, which was already bursting. Morning trains were always packed with traveling merchants returning to their dungeon cities, pockets loaded and trunks emptied if they were lucky. Rhen and Aki had been that fortunate, this time.

With every private box taken, Rhen and Aki made their way to the back of the train with the rest of the overflow.

"Need anything—oh, it's you!" It was the busty fifties-something woman from Rhen's first train ride.

"Yes, I managed not to die," Rhen said with a curt smile. He stepped past her and her overflowing cart of tools toward the open-air boxcar at the back of the train. The door opened with a clank, and Rhen sighed a breath of relief that there was still a good amount of space left.

"Was it not rude to leave her that way?" Aki asked.

Rhen shrugged. "She laughed at me when I told her I was delving my own dungeon, pretty much told me I was going to die."

"Should we not try to make as many connections as we can?"

"Pfft, not connections like her. She's not in it for the love of the delve, just here for a profit. She tried to sell me a broken anima gauge on my ride to Yu, then when I told her it was broken, she tried to insult me to cover her hasty retreat."

The train shuddered, then blasted its departure horn.

"I see. You are right. We must be very selective with whom we allow into your circle."

"Wait! Don't leave without me!" A distant, desperate voice reached Rhen over the noise of the grinding train wheels.

Rhen leaned out the open boxcar door to see a flustered, red-haired Cadrian chasing after them.

"Jakira?"

She grinned and waved. "Rhen! I want to come work for you!"

"But... uh..." Rhen stammered, his head swimming with a hundred thoughts for her safety.

Not only that, but there was also nowhere for her to stay, and his tent was messy.

But he wanted her to come.

She reached in her bag while she ran, then waved around a thin bit of paper. "I already got my work order!"

So that's where she'd been all morning. She'd spent the extra coin he'd paid her on a work order to join his dungeon.

Her eyes sparkled with excitement and melted away Rhen's hesitation. He reached out the door for her hand. "Come on, then. We'll figure it out on the way."

She grabbed onto him, and he pulled her into the train car.

"You purchased a ticket, too, correct?" Aki asked.

Jakira panted, smiling. "I threw some money at the teller as I ran by."

Rhen helped slide her heavy pack off her shoulders. "What's in here, bricks?"

"Thank you." She sighed with relief and slumped to the ground, leaning her back against the wall.

Rhen took a seat too, excited to have Jakira beside him. She wanted to delve *his* dungeon, with *him*.

Aki squished his watery body down so he was eye to eye with both of them. "Why do you want to join us?"

"Do you not want me?" She looked at Rhen, apprehension in her eyes.

"Of course I want you—I mean, I want your help delving the dungeon."

Aki turned yellow and fluttered his fins. "I seek to uncover your intentions. Is this for the love of the delve, or something else?"

She looked back to Rhen, the same fear in her eyes. Then something surrendered in her. "You told me never to change, but I want to. I'm tired of being an inn hostess, like you were tired of being a dungeon delver. I want to be an inn *owner*."

"I think you would make an amazing inn owner."

She blushed, gold sparkling in her cheeks. "I think you make an amazing dungeon owner, which is why I wanted to come delve with you. I'll do whatever you tell me to do; carry ore to the surface, fight monsters, fix your boots—oh, they're fixed. They look nice."

"Yeah, I kept stubbing my toes."

"Rhen, do you find this to be an acceptable purpose to join us?" Aki asked, all back to business. "It is not for the love of the delve."

Rhen looked at Aki and shrugged. "It's for the love of something. What is it?" He looked back to Jakira.

Her blush sparkled brighter, and she looked away. "I really, um, really love helping people, and I'm good at doing everything in an inn. I like cooking too, but I don't get to cook often. It's nice to help people get a good night's rest after a hard day of work.

And it's nice to see them smile and relax, to see that they feel safe and comfortable. And... I really want to help you."

Aki fluttered, his color shifting to green. "Oh, I understand. She is in love with you, Rhen."

Jakira gasped, her cheeks practically glowing. "What? No! That's not it. Rhen is just my friend."

Rhen's heart sank a hair, but he recovered, quickly moving on, so as not to embarrass Jakira further. "It's for the love of helping people who delve. I think that's close enough to the love of the delve, don't you, Aki?"

"Yes, a very acceptable reason to join us. I am glad we understand your motives because now we can trust you not to take all our money in the night."

Jakira crossed her arms and nodded. "Yeah, good. Great. Happy to be understood."

The trio remained quiet for a while, listening to the rattles of the boxcar as the train chugged along. Rhen looked out across the shifting landscape as the towering buildings of Desedra disappeared into a smoggy haze. He liked the trees and how they made the air smell. It was a crisp bitterness that enlivened his senses.

He focused on the scent instead of thinking about Jakira and how she was just his friend.

No, that was fine. It was better that way. Mixing love and business was never a good idea. She would be running an inn for him, if the dungeon wasn't dry.

Oh gods, what if the dungeon was dry?

Anxious thoughts ran circles in Rhen's head until Aki broke the silence to discuss the current state of the dungeon. They filled Jakira in on their progress and what they were hoping to do when they got back. After a while, they started reminiscing. Rhen smiled, forgetting all the issues that had once battled in his mind.

They arrived in Yu and found a few supplies for Jakira, namely her own tent, simple leather gear to protect her, and some bread with sweet cream—something Rhen loved but could never justify buying for himself. When they had everything they needed, they began the hike into the forest.

Jakira was used to walking up and down many flights of stairs, lifting heavy equipment, scrubbing dirty pots, and even chopping wood, so the trek through the forest was easy for her, though she wanted to stop and admire the scenery several times. They made it to the dungeon by midafternoon and got to work setting her tent up not far from Rhen's.

"Where's yours Mr. Aki?" Jakira asked.

"I do not sleep much."

"Oh, but you stayed at the inn?"

"I... do not like to be alone."

"You're scared of the dark, you mean?" Jakira asked, a devious smile on her face. She was trying to get him back for embarrassing her earlier.

Aki pulsed orange and his voice vibrated strongly in Rhen's chest. "My home is the crushing black depths of *Cla'ketre Whri*. I am not afraid of the dark."

"Okay, sorry," Jakira offered and returned to hammering the stakes of her tent corners down.

Rhen didn't have to see the irritated, swift flick of Aki's tentacles to know he was still bothered, and he could feel the tension in the air around him. It was as if Aki was speaking, but there were no words, only frustration. Finally, Aki spoke up.

"I come from a clutch of sixty-eight siblings. I have not seen them in many months. The elders told me I would grow accustomed to the independence, but I have not."

Jakira stopped hammering and smiled kindly. "Well, you don't have to with us here."

Rhen remembered when Aki had asked to work with him in

Desedra dungeon. He'd been a bit cold to Aki, and thought he was being weird when the poor Prelusk just wanted a friend.

They finished with Jakira's tent, and though there was ample time to get in the dungeon, at least for some mining, Rhen wanted Jakira to be properly rested for exploring the other tunnel in case they encountered monsters. So, they spent a few hours showing Jakira how to use the hand drill while Rhen practiced tempering his Tremor Blast ability.

Tremor blast was usually destructive, but when Rhen actively tried to withhold his anima, he was able to make smaller and smaller tremors, or target them to specific areas of his palm. He was able to take out chunks of the wall at a time without cracking the surrounding stone, which led him to a sizable gemstone.

They broke for the night, heading back to the surface to inspect the fist-sized gemstone by the light of the fire. It was another Celinom of very good quality.

"Something this large could be installed in a building," Aki said with wonder.

Jakira gasped. "Like our inn! We could create anima restorative baths by channeling the stream water down here, then make a few pools around this stone."

"That's brilliant." Rhen patted her shoulder.

She grinned. "See, I'll be a great inn owner."

"Never had a doubt."

They enjoyed more roasted fish with their creamy rolls, and then settled in for the night.

"Goodnight guys! Can't wait to fight some monsters in the morning!" Jakira waved and entered her tent.

Rhen smiled back. "Same. G'night."

"Have good sleeps, my friends."

9

DRY DUNGEON

Rhen rose the next morning to the smell of something divine. It was fish for certain, but there was a sweet acidity to the smell, too. He could hear Jakira humming something gently and the grinding of stone on stone.

He put on his clothes in a flurry, and emerged to see Jakira working a rudimentary mortar and pestle. That must've been what weighed her pack down so much... In it, she was grinding a thick purple-red paste.

"Good morning," she said cheerily and jumped to her feet. "Mr. Aki is getting some more fish. I already ate mine, sorry! I was so hungry. But here, try this berry jam I made!"

She pulled Rhen up to the fire and served him a slice of a roll with a smear of sweet cream and a drizzle of her jam. Rhen's mouth salivated at the smell. He didn't hesitate to take an enormous bite.

First, he tasted the dense, salted honey bread, slightly charred from being held over the fire. As he chewed, the cream and the jam mixed, bringing a rich, sweet and tart moisture to the crisp bread.

"Well?" she asked, nervous.

"It's the best thing I've ever tasted." He shoved another bite in, chewing vigorously.

She smiled, cheeks glimmering. "Really?"

He swallowed the huge bite. "Well, you're talking to the guy who eats monster meat soup on the regular, so it's not a hard bar to exceed."

She rolled her eyes with a smirk. "At least I'm beating monster meat, I guess."

Aki surfed down through the brush and sloshed to a stop at the fire. Rhen could feel his smile in the way his skin pulsed from yellow to pink.

"Just learn how to do that, did you?" Rhen asked.

"I have moved quickly through water before when hunting prey, but never have I allowed water to move *me* quickly."

Rhen smiled. "Seems like you've finally had some fun."

"It was exhilarating. I will do it again later."

They finished breakfast and packed up a bit of the jammed bread for a snack in the dungeon. Rhen's stomach tightened at the sight of the dungeon entrance. He paused and watched Jakira descend the ladder while Aki poured himself over the edge, as usual. Why was he feeling nervous to go in?

Jakira would be fighting her first monsters, but he was confident that he and Aki could protect her if she were in any danger —though Aki might wait to the absolute last second to put himself in harm's way...

No, it wasn't that.

What if there were no monsters? What if that was it? There was nothing left in the dungeon. All his dreams, now theirs, dashed, and Rhen to blame for dragging them out there.

"Come on slowpoke." Jakira waved.

Rhen nodded and got onto the ladder. No point in worrying about an uncertain future.

They passed through the empty hall to the fork, and this

time, went right. Rhen took the lead by a good margin, activating Caress of Night as he did. The spell caused a constant drawing sensation from the syntial on his back that spread over his skin like a cool blanket in waves. The continuous drain on his anima from the spell was noticeable, but with his upgraded boots, he could feel that he was balanced. He could maintain stealth permanently without running out of anima.

He would show Aki just how sneaky he could be.

The dungeon tunnel sloped downward and the air chilled on Rhen's face. Aki pulsed brighter, creating a soft yellow ambient light by which to walk. The gray walls darkened, reflecting sheens of blue the deeper they descended. Excitement built in Rhen's chest as he rounded a tight hairpin curve in the tunnel to—

A dead end.

His breathing stopped and he stared at the walls. His fear wasn't unwarranted then. Rhen deactivated Caress of Night and stood from his crouch.

"No monsters?" Jakira pouted.

"It appears that way," Aki said, the disappointment clear in his tone.

No.

This couldn't be it.

Rhen put his hand against the far wall. "Step back a bit."

When the others were out of the way, Rhen focused on channeling Tremor Blast at the lowest possible frequency through the butt of his palm. He breathed slowly, feeling the vibration travel through the rock. It died out abruptly, and Rhen grinned. It was hollow on the other side.

"Time to mine."

Rhen chipped a good hole in the wall to start, then Aki wore it down with his water until a burst of air blasted through from the other side. Rhen moved up to the hole, sucking down a deep breath.

Fire.

He exhaled hard and blew flames into the next chamber, illuminating it brilliantly for a flash. The walls were green and seemed to... slither. When the flames died out, Rhen could hear rushing water somewhere farther into the next chamber.

Nothing tried to bite his face off through the hole, so Rhen focused his Tremor Blast and broke off bits of the wall until there was a gap wide enough to step through. He cast a light breath into the room and saw it well for the first time.

Throughout the room were long, green vines about as thick as Rhen's forearm coming out of the walls. They wiggled, stretching upwards from holds on the walls made by two, three, and sometimes four lumpy gemstones. Right below the stones were tufts of blue-green moss that looked sort of like fur.

Rhen stepped through onto the slick stone on the other side. He pulled a crescent blade from his hip, holding it out toward the green vines that seemed to pay him no heed. They opened large blossoms at their ends that captured trickles of water that came from somewhere above in the darkness. Maybe they were under the river right now.

"Smells like licorice." Jakira wandered toward the bulbous lumps hanging off the wall and ran her fingers through the moss that covered them. "So soft. I bet I could season the fish with it!"

"That must be the Father's Fennel," Aki said.

Rhen sniggered as he understood why. It bore a close resemblance to... well, the tools of fatherhood.

"Jakira, want to collect some? We have a request for some of that from the baker in Yu, Fennica Wheatle."

"On it." Jakira pulled her dagger from its sheath.

Aki moved to the center of the cavern, stepping through stalagmites on the floor. He paused under the drizzle of water and held up his hands. Little ripples cascaded across his body, and he closed his eyes.

"It is mildly acidic."

Jakira cried out and Rhen spun around. One of the thick vines of the father's fennel had wrapped around her wrist. Jakira slashed the dagger across the vine, making little white cuts across the surface but doing very little damage. Rhen waited, despite his need to lurch into action and protect her.

The vine monster pointed its flowery top at her face, and opened its petals to reveal sharp needles lining the inside. The flower snapped at Jakira and Rhen lunged forward with Swift Twitch. He severed the head off the plant, and the vine went limp, gushing milky blood down the padreote lumps below it.

The severed blossom head opened and snapped several times at Jakira's feet and Rhen kicked it away. "Are you alright?"

She stared at the wall, mouth agape. "That plant tried to eat me."

"Everything will try to eat you down here."

She turned to Rhen, wide-eyed. "I think I need some training. Using a kitchen knife on a potato is not the same as a dagger on a monster."

Rhen looked around the room at all the accessible monsters which were, in his opinion, easy pickings. The dangling vine of the monster he'd attacked ceased its bloody gushing and the blossom regenerated, much smaller than before. The vine lifted back up toward the dripping water, replenishing itself.

"Okay, let's practice."

"On these crazy things?"

"They are manageable opponents for us," Aki assured her.

"I don't want to slow you down. Maybe I should go practice stabbing the tree next to my tent," she offered nervously.

Rhen put his hand on her shoulder. "You can do this."

The fear melted from her face, and she nodded. "Okay."

"How did you get it to attack you in the first place?"

She stepped up to the father's fennel tentatively, then pointed her dagger where she'd been cutting. "There's like a root or something that runs over the gemstone, and I nicked it while trying to cut the moss."

Rhen looked at the spot more closely to see the padreote glowing softly below the root of the father's fennel plant. It was drawing anima from it. That's how it must survive! Pure anima and acid rain. What a strange plant.

He pulled on some of the furry fennel gently, then ran his blade across it. The top of the plant didn't seem to notice anything had happened. Then, he poked the tip of his crescent blade into the root nestled around a facet of the padreote. Immediately, the little blossom pointed down as if to look at who had offended it so. It lunged for his hand and Rhen snatched it, holding it still.

"I don't know if you'd be able to behead it like I did, but give it a shot."

Jakira moved forward uncertainly, then slashed at the monster. She made a narrow cut across the newly formed neck of the monster, and it leaked more blood. It wriggled free from Rhen's grasp and pulled away.

Aki moved closer. "Perhaps try stabbing it."

Rhen helped Jakira adjust her grip on the blade. With even more apprehension than before, she stabbed at the monster. Her blade pierced through the base of the plant where it connected to the wall and the monster hissed, then went limp.

"You must've hit its core." Rhen reached into the hole made by her dagger and removed the eyeball-sized core from the milky mess.

"So that's why you're always covered in guts..." Jakira said, finally understanding.

"What, you thought once they died they just spit the cores out of their bodies?"

"I never thought about it."

He handed her the slimy core with a smile. "You earned this."

Her face puckered and she accepted it. "Great."

They killed a few more of the father's fennel plants and realized that once the core crystal was removed, they didn't regenerate. Rhen could see the plants being a decent source of farmable income, especially if the blossoms and furry moss could both be used, so they decided to leave the rest be and move on.

Rhen resumed his place at the front of the pack, donning Caress of Night. They stepped around stalactites and reaching father's fennel until the room opened to a larger cavern lit by glowing green gemstones in the walls. Thousands of father's fennel plants wiggled joyously, tapping the power of the padreote and creating the green ambient glow.

"Mind your step," Aki said, pointing out a circular pit-like drain just in front of them.

The water flowed in from the large cavern as well as the smaller one behind them in little streams that had carved a path over years. The streams flowed over the edge and down, down, down into the darkness before them, creating the waterfall sound Rhen had heard before.

"We'll have to explore that later," Rhen said as he walked through the stream to get around the hole. They didn't have enough rope, or the right equipment for spelunking like that.

A soft whooshing of air Rhen had barely noticed before made itself much more apparent the farther he moved into the cavern. It sounded almost like... breathing. Then, he spotted the large, stalagmite-covered boulder at the center of the room as it moved up and down with the rhythmic whoosh.

Rhen stopped in his tracks. "Shh."

Aki dropped low to the ground and pulled up beside Rhen. "I am sorry I did not detect it. The ambient noise and movement is creating confusing signals."

"Quiet, or *it* will detect *us* before we can murder it in its sleep." Rhen moved forward, walking heel-toe and dodging rocks and streams. He was stealth incarnate, and this monster would have no idea what hit it.

As he edged closer, Rhen could see finer, more terrifying details, like the fact that the monster—while lying prone—was six feet tall. Its wide, muscular back was lined with sharp spikes of varying length. Those spikes created a hard shell down the monster's spine up to its short, stubby face. It was one of the hounds he'd fought before, and its clawed paws were coated in milky-white blood.

The hound cracked one massive eyelid to reveal a bright green glowing eye. Rhen held incredibly still, but his confidence waned when the monster's breathing pattern changed. Its dark-green pupil shimmered purple as it pinned on Rhen.

Perhaps he was not stealth incarnate, after all.

10

BONES FOR DAYS

Rhen exhaled a small breath of fire into the monster's face, hoping to blind and surprise it. The creature roared and reared back, blinking madly.

"I thought the plan was stealth!" Aki taunted.

A brilliant aurora of purple and teal surged past Rhen's feet like a river. It washed across the floor and rushed up the monster's thrashing body, entrancing it.

"Hurry! It is strong, and I cannot hold it!"

Rhen charged forward with Swift Twitch, bounding off the cavern wall and slish-slashing the hound's massive throat. Blood rushed down its chest and it broke free of the charm. Rhen was batted out of the air by its enormous paw. He sailed backwards and smashed into Jakira.

Rhen scrambled to his feet. "Run, Jak!"

The hound opened its mouth to bark, but a hoarse exhale was all that came out. Rhen deactivated Caress of Night and used the added anima for another Swift Twitch while the monster was still confused. He leapt up and blasted the monster's face with a cloud of acid, burning his own mouth as he did.

Aki pulled the aurora of colors back into him. "Shadow Snare!"

The monster swiped at Rhen in comically slow motion. Rhen ran his blades down the monster's arm until he gained purchase, then he climbed it. The creature slowly chomped at Rhen, getting a mouthful of water instead. Rhen climbed up to the monster's back to see Aki, cradled in Jakira's arms, with just a tiny bubble of water surrounding him at the back of the room.

The hound coughed, expelling the fluid before Aki could drown it like it had done the other. Rhen held tight to one of the spiked plates on the monster's back and used his other hand to slash the back of the beast's neck. The cuts split several inches into the beast's hide, but it wasn't enough to get to anything vital.

"This won't work either!"

The beast tossed itself toward the wall. Rhen jumped from its neck and rolled out of range. The monster smashed its plated back against the wall and the cave trembled. A stalactite dropped from high above them and shattered against the floor.

Even at a slowed speed from Shadow Snare, half blinded from acid spray, and bleeding out, the hound was staying on the offensive. It lunged forward and Rhen dodged left, snatching the hound's lip with his crescent blade like a fishing hook. He yanked, ripping the beast's cheek open to expose even more teeth.

The hound kept charging, its wide-open mouth aimed at Rhen's friends. The hound would get to them before he could do anything, before they could even move, unless he did the unthinkable.

He had to.

Rhen reached out, summoning the forbidden spell that could save them: Piercing Detonator.

Hot power surged down his arm and into his palm, culminating in a ball of liquid anima that took everything from him. A vicious vibration erupted from Rhen's palm as the projectile blasted forth. The shot pierced the hound's back and imbedded deep in its muscles with a splash of blood.

Explosions rippled against the beast's back, shattering the many hard plates and exposing its spine. Liquified guts splashed out the hole he'd made with the projectile and the hound collapsed. It slid across the floor and Jakira leapt out of the way with a yelp. The monster's face smashed into the back wall, the exit covered. Rhen jumped on its back, punching his blades into the exposed spinal joints until the beast finally stopped moving.

Weary, Rhen slid off the monster's back and leaned against its side. His hands trembled with weakness, his anima totally drained.

"That was *incredible*! What was that spell?" Jakira asked, elated.

"Tremor blast," Rhen lied, and gave her a weak smile. "I'm just glad we didn't die."

"Same for me." Aki pulled the water from the ground and made himself a body, then swam out of Jakira's cradling arms.

The deceased hound's stomach rumbled, then it let out a long, whining fart. Despite his lack of energy, Rhen couldn't help but laugh.

"Ugh, gross! I need some air!" Jakira ran for the blocked exit. She pushed on its massive face. "Oh gods, it smells! Help, please. I have to..." Jakira retched. "Have to get out!"

Aki's watery hands glowed a soft yellow and the water in the cavern came to life at his command. The streams changed course, surrounding the beast until it hovered just a hair off the ground. He slid the body backwards a few feet and Jakira rushed through the gap, gasping for air and making horrible burping sounds.

Aki released the spell on the enchanted water. The beast dropped to the ground, splashing water across the cavern and pushing Rhen over on his side. Rhen moaned in protest, but couldn't find the energy to get up.

"Do you think she will be all right?" Aki asked as Jakira's retching receded up through the cave tunnels.

"She had to get acquainted with the rigmaroles of death eventually. She'll be fine, and if not, we'll give her some money to get back to Desedra."

It was really starting to smell rank in there. Rhen sat up. "We need to get the core. I've got ideas for this thing's bones too, but I'm sure it'll take some effort to get them out before the dungeon consumes the body."

"Then we had better set to work."

After a few more minutes of letting his anima regenerate, Rhen was able to stand and help Aki with the nasty business of stripping the monster meat from the bones. Rhen cut away the hide and tendons while Aki used the stream water to power blast the bones clean.

Deep in the rib cage, they found the core. It was an incredible thing, three times the size of Rhen's head, but a deep crack ran through it from where Rhen's piercing detonator spell had struck true and leeched the power needed to kill the monster.

"How did that happen?" Aki asked.

"Dunno, must've been the force of Tremor Blast. I put all my energy into it."

"Interesting."

Rhen looked around the room, desperate for a deflection. "There has to be a node in here. This beast was too big to be guarding a cavern full of father's fennel."

Aki cast an aurora of light across the walls, revealing another tunnel opening at the other end, but no nodes. Rhen scowled at all the sparkling green padreote. Not a single node.

"Perhaps it is in the next room?"

"Yeah. We have to finish up with this beast before we explore. I want *all* the bones."

"Why for?"

Rhen grinned. "You'll see."

Jakira returned a shade lighter in the cheeks. "I'm ready to help."

"Your tummy okay?" Rhen asked sarcastically.

"I will shank you," she threatened, whipping out her dagger.

Aki paled, his tentacles wiggling uncomfortably. "Would you bring the cleaned bones to the surface?"

"You got it," she said with a chipper smile. She stuck her tongue out at Rhen and sloppily sheathed her dagger.

When Jakira left with the first pile of bones, Aki cut his water blast and looked to Rhen. "Should we not tell her to leave?"

"What? Why?"

"She threatened to harm you!"

"She's not going to stab me. She was just joking, buddy."

Aki pulsed yellow at the use of the friendly moniker and calmed. "How do you know?"

Rhen remembered that Aki was not familiar with the common language, nor the common culture. "Hmm. I guess it was the tone of her voice, and the way she stuck her tongue out at me."

"I understand. Do you think she threatens to harm you because she cannot admit her true feelings of affection?"

"I don't think that's how women work."

"And you know all women well?"

Rhen frowned. "I didn't say that, I just... it doesn't seem like something that they would do. I don't know."

"What if it is a specific Cadrian woman behavior? Do you know many Cadrian women?" Aki asked, fluttering with excitement.

"I don't, but the Cadrians have been merged with the

common society longer even than my people, the Shin'Baran, so I doubt she'd have many, uh, native tendencies? Why don't we just... get back to cleaning some bones."

"Of course, buddy."

They got halfway through cleaning the monster bones when the discarded flesh began to sparkle a soft orange and melt into the floor. The dungeon reclaimed deceased bodies after a time, fueling itself with more anima from the consumed matter. Rhen wondered if it was the crystal core inside them that kept them safe from the dungeon eating them, too.

They rushed the remaining cleaned bones to the surface and left the rest to be reclaimed by the dungeon. Rhen flopped down in the grass next to the cluster of bones, panting. The sun was just past its apex, and Rhen's stomach howled in protest of more work.

Jakira got out the creamy, jam sandwiches for them, and Aki retreated to the river for a meal of his own. Rhen couldn't stop staring at the massive monster core, thinking about all its possibilities. If they fed half of the anima to the Mastery node, who knew what kind of abilities would be unlocked?

"So, what's the plan for all these bones?" Jakira nudged a femur with the toe of her boot.

"I had a few different things in mind." Rhen grabbed one of the long canine teeth out of the pile and placed it spike-side-out on his shoulder. "Armor upgrades for one. We can bring some of these materials in to get custom affixed to our gear. A good crafter will be able to bring out the material's natural strength with different syntials."

He rolled one of the thinner straight bones toward him. "This could be a flute. Again, a skilled weapons crafter could make a bard's instrument unlike any other. With its natural power of that howl, Defender's Cry, the instrument could produce the effect when played correctly."

She picked up the femur. "And this could be a club!" She gave it a few swings. Her balance was good, stance nice too. The weapon seemed a little more natural in her hands than the dagger.

"Want to spar with that, see how you like it?" Rhen asked.

Her cheeks sparkled. "If you want to."

"Yeah."

Rhen smiled and jumped to his feet. He picked up two of the shorter, smaller bones to accommodate his fighting style. Jakira walked toward the grass closer to the tents and took a timid fighting stance.

"My anima is still low, so go easy on me." Rhen bowed, then put his weapons up to rest on each shoulder.

She chuckled nervously. "I don't think I'll be landing any hits."

"Don't discredit yourself so quickly. Now, come at me like you want me dead."

Her forehead wrinkled and she grimaced. She licked her lips, gave a few heavy exhales, and then put her battle face on. She charged with a roar, swinging her club hard from the shoulder and leaning in. Rhen turned into the strike, blocking with his escrima-style bones. Her strike trembled up through Rhen's arms and he shoved her club back.

The force of his parry pushed her off balance, and she turned her back. He could've given chase and whapped her from behind—a killing strike—but he refrained. He didn't want to damage her confidence so quickly.

"That was a strong hit, but you leaned forward for the strike." He leaned forward, holding his little sticks like her club. "When you put too much weight in the front foot and lean your upper body, you become less stable in your balance. Try that move again, but instead, try to keep your shoulders over your hips."

Jakira nodded vigorously, and took up her offensive stance again. She charged and he parried over and over until his shove no longer threw her balance. She used the momentum of his push to bring the club back up to her shoulder and went in for a second, overhead swing. Before she could complete the move, Rhen dodged left and smacked her belly with his escrima. Jakira *oofed* and slammed the club into the dirt.

"Be mindful of your opponents' weapons. I have two small weapons. My arms can move independently and much faster."

"Got it," she gasped, leaning on the handle of her bone-club. "I think I'm done for now."

"Practice is essential for growth," Aki said.

He had gotten back from the river, several fish clutched in his tentacles. They were surrounded by auroras just like Aki had cast on the hounds in the cave, immobilizing them, but keeping them alive.

Jakira sighed. "A few more, then."

She attacked again and again, sweat gathering on her dark brow and messing her fiery braided crown. Her speed was slowing, and she was getting sloppy, but Rhen could see the determination in her eyes.

"Come on. Hit me!" Rhen urged.

Jakira growled, swinging up from the hip. Rhen turned and blocked, as usual, and pushed her away. She swung the weapon up to her shoulder and Rhen went in for a belly slapping kill. Jakira changed her grip, moving her hand to the ball-end of the femur, then pulled the bone to her chest to block.

She pushed Rhen back and swept the bottom of her weapon upwards at Rhen's head. He leaned back to avoid the swipe and Jakira changed her grip again, meeting the other hand at her shoulder.

The weapon flowed easily from one pose to the next as Jakira swung from the shoulder. Rhen used both escrima to block, but at his awkward angle, the force of her strike pushed his weapons down against him. His shoulder throbbed from the hit and he stepped back, rubbing the painful muscle with one hand.

"Ouch."

Jakira rolled her eyes. "Liar. You *let* me hit you."

"I would never."

"It's okay. I mean, it felt kinda nice to finally get you back." She rubbed her stomach. "Still, I'd like to do it on my own."

"I saw every move in great detail," Aki said." Your grip change surprised him, and he was not prepared to dodge the strike. His wrist positioning would not allow him to put more strength into the parry, and so in fact, you did hit him all on your own."

She crossed her arms. "Sure, but if his anima wasn't so low he could've used one of his abilities to blow acid in my face, or duck super fast."

"You'll get abilities like that, too," Rhen assured her. "We just need to explore more and level up the Mastery node."

"And you will get stronger with practice."

Jakira chuckled. "Okay. Thanks, guys. But no more practice for now. I think my stomach is bruised, or I'm hungry... not sure which."

Rhen cringed. "Probably both. Why don't we head down and feed half of this jumbo core to the Mastery node, then give ourselves a boost? I bet with all the work you've done at the inn you're well at your anima capacity already, Jak. You could get a syntial without having to use any of the monster cores."

"You think so?" she asked, giddy.

"Let's find out."

11

CELEBRITY DUNGEON OWNER

Jakira had only ever received an identification syntial; the small, binding tattoo that would reveal to anyone who inquired, exactly who one was and what they'd done with their life.

"How does this all work?" she asked, approaching the node cautiously.

"Well, as far as it's been documented, there are four primary anima types. Kinse is related to body spells, Cebrum is mind spells, Mana is matter control, and Enon is space and time control. Within those anima types there've been five registered distinctions: Light, Dark, Life, Death, and Chaos. These were all divvied up and categorized by guild officials of course, so while some things will make perfect sense, others will seem a little off.

"The dungeons use information in our id syntials that translates the information stored within the node to present to us in a readable way. It leans on our own language and understanding of the world to find meaning, so, not everything looks the same to everyone, either.

"Still with me?" Rhen stopped for a breath.

Jakira nodded.

"The Prima syntials are the basic, big ones that can be built upon and specialized. Syntials keep your anima inside you as it grows. Using your spells and absorbing monster cores will grow your anima capacity over time. You can really only grow to a certain point without applying a syntial to exceed it. Your body does not allow for the additional pathways to be created, something about self-preservation."

"So what happens when the anima comes out?" she asked, chewing her lip.

"Weeeell, in a channeled way, through the syntials, it'll come out in the form of a spell, whatever's been inscripted. But if you grow your anima capacity beyond what the syntials can contain, you'll start having outbursts of power from where your body's anima shield—the syntial layer—is weakest. And it'll come out in completely random ways, but sometimes it's destructive to both you and whoever is near you."

"Why hasn't this happened to me or anyone else without a syntial before?"

Rhen shrugged. "I didn't really get any lessons on that in delver school."

"It is just what Rhen said about self-preservation. The body will not grow its anima capacity if it will put itself at risk. But as soon as that safeguard is bypassed by the first Prima syntial, the body cannot prevent anima growth. This is true of all species across every realm we have investigated," Aki added, suddenly a font of information.

"You've been studying us?" Rhen scowled, amused.

"We are curious about our reality, and every realm it touches."

"Yet you don't ever let anyone leave, and you have special accords with the Imperial Kingdoms to keep people out..."

"We are also a wary species. Our history is wrought with conflict."

Rhen hummed thoughtfully. "Any more questions, Jak? Aki seems to know everything."

"I think that's it." She took a deep breath and placed her hand on the Mastery node to receive her first prima syntial, Defender's Cry. A second later, she howled and ripped her hand away.

"Is it supposed to be so painful?"

Rhen gently guided her hand back to the node. "You'll get used to it after a few inscriptions. Some people even like the way it feels."

"Can't imagine what kind of minds *enjoy* pain." She steeled herself, taking a sharp inhale through gritted teeth. "Continue," she said to the node, and the orange light flared to life under her tan-colored shirt right on her diaphragm.

Jakira groaned, grinding her jaw side to side. After a few moments the syntial completed, sealing in her burgeoning anima and allowing her to channel it into the Defender's Cry. She exhaled hard and pulled her hand from the node. Her cheeks were sparkling, flushed from her racing pulse.

She touched the mark, smiling. "I can feel it, the power. I feel... contained. But not caged. Cradled, maybe? Guided."

She sucked down a deep breath and the orange syntial came to life. "*Whooo-hooo!*"

Her anima amplified voice echoed through the room, invigorating Rhen. He felt like he could take on two of those massive hounds himself.

Aki pulsed a bright pink, his tentacles wriggling. "The effects are amplified through my water. I have so much energy!"

"I feel it too, like an eagerness to fight," Rhen said, his hands itching for his crescent blades. "Aki, you go next."

The Prelusk pulled one of the small father's fennel cores from under his mess of tentacles and approached the Mastery node. "I hope to infuse their regenerative abilities into my

Aurora Wave, to create a spell that will heal many wounds at once."

Pronouncing one's wish to the Mastery node was an effective way to guide the node into finding the right way forward. Words held much power, though it was a mystery to Rhen as to why. The nodes were anima channeling crystals, much like the cores of monsters. They retained power, held and transferred information, but were they more like a thinking being?

Aki placed several of his tentacles on the node and closed his eyes. The green core of the father's fennel plant dissolved and flowed into his body. That green light traveled through his body and into the Mastery node, then appeared at the top in the shape of an information page.

[Syntial Additions and Expansion]

Available Options: 2
{Soothing Aura}
Ancilla I | Active | Cebrum | Light/Life | Cost: 5% Anima/Minute

Append to your Aurora Wave. When active, you project an aura of light that creates a calming effect on friends and foes alike. Reduce the chance that enemies will target you and anyone within your aura. Increase the likelihood of friends and neutral targets to be more amenable to ideas they may not have been previously.

=====

{Radiative Regeneration}
Ancilla I | Active | Mana | Light/Life | Cost: 12% Anima

Append to your Aurora Wave. When casting Aurora Wave, you may infuse it with regenerative properties, allowing anything that steps into the stream to have increased healing and anima regeneration speeds. This spell cannot differentiate between friend and foe.

=====

"These are both excellent options." Aki's skin pulsed yellow.

Rhen held up the huge core from the mega-hound. "So, get both."

"What if there is not enough anima left for you?"

"Look at this thing, there's plenty to go around."

Rhen could feel Aki's elation. "If you insist."

He placed a tentacle on the hound's core and agreed to add both ancilla syntials. Purple power was drawn from the hound core and pulled through Aki's body into the Mastery node, then with a burst of blue-green, it flowed back into Aki. The prima syntial glowed on the back of his head as two new petals were etched into the mandala design. They flowed like smoke, just like his aurora did, and Rhen marveled at the way the likeness of the spell was represented in the syntial.

Aki stepped away from the node. "Do you have a spell you are wanting to add?"

Rhen thought for a moment. He had good speed, and passive regeneration increases, a cloak of darkness, magic breath, and a high-powered vibration ability. What would complement his quick, not-yet-stealthy nature?

"Something to keep my enemy unaware of my presence."

"Isn't that what hiding in the shadows with Caress of Night is for?" Jakira hefted her bone club over one shoulder.

"Yes, but the enemies have more than eyes with which to detect me. I want to be quieter, I suppose."

Rhen placed his hand on the Mastery node with that intent.

Anima from the hound's core flowed through him and into the node, lighting it up with neat purple rows of information.

[Syntial Additions and Expansion]

Available Options: 9 {Expand? Y | N}
Recommended Options: 1
{Dark Hush}
Ancilla I | Passive | Cebrum | Dark | No Anima Cost
Append to Caress of Night. When in the shadows, reduce the chance that enemies will detect your footsteps, breathing, or heartbeat by 5%. Effects increased by 20% when stealthed by Caress of Night.

=====

Jakira hummed. "It amazes me how you can ask for what you want and get it."

Aki fluttered happily. "Dungeon nodes are powerful things that bridge realms, impart magic, and even resurrect the spirit. They are quite a wonder beyond the ability to seek out the dungeoneer's request."

This was exactly what Rhen had asked for, but he felt some disappointment. Not in the node, but in his lack of imagination. There was still a good amount of anima in the hound's core, so he decided to make one more request.

"What about something to prevent enemies from casting spells?"

Purple anima surged into the Mastery node from the hound's core, sucking the last of it dry and dissolving the crystal. Rhen stared with bated breath as the neat lines of information rearranged themselves.

[Syntial Additions and Expansion]

Available Options: 10 {Expand? Y | N}
Recommended Options: 1
{Curse of Anima Rot}
2x Ancilla I | Active | Anima | Dark/Chaos | 20% Anima
Append to Caress of Night with a sister ancilla linked to Tremor Blast. Choose one: Infuse your Tremor Blast with the black curse of anima rot. Anything in the path of your blast will be afflicted by reduced anima regeneration and increased anima costs when casting spells. Or, infuse your physical strikes with the black curse of anima rot when you are stealthed by Caress of Night. Landing a hit directly to an opponent's syntial will prevent anima flow to that syntial for 15 seconds.

*Warning, this ability will permanently link Prima Syntial Caress of Night to Prima Syntial Tremor Blast, altering their effects.

**Warning, this ability will take up *two* ancilla slots, one on each Prima Syntial.

=====

Now that was a cool ability. Dark Hush was good, and would certainly help him with the sneakiness, but Curse of Anima Rot was too good to pass on. If he could sneak up on an enemy, he could infuse his blades with the curse and disable their syntials before they knew what was happening... but that required him to be able to sneak. For now, he could open combat with an infused Tremor Blast. A good hit and a nice curse at the same time.

"I accept Curse of Anima Rot."

Purple and pink light swirled up Rhen's arm, settling on his left hand and his mid-back. Sharp, stabbing pain poked at him in both places as the boxy ancilla were added to the Prima syntial. A vibrant pink line shot up his arm and over his shoulder, linking the two ancilla.

Rhen willed his id syntial to display his spell information in the Mastery node.

[Rhen Zephitz – Full Assessment]
[Spell Assessment]

Number of Syntials: 7 | Highest Syntial Level: Ancilla, I
{Prima II: Swift Twitch}
{Ancilla I: Swift Healing}
{Prima II: Primordial Breath}
{Prima I: Tremor Blast}
{Ancilla I: Curse of Anima Rot}
{Prima I: Caress of Night}
{Duplicate - Ancilla I: Curse of Anima Rot}
{Prima I: Identity}
Syntial Build Analysist – Rogue/Fighter Type, High Damage

[Anima Assessment]

Anima Capacity: 1% *Use your abilities and absorb monster cores to increase your capacity.
{3x Kinse – Light, Life, & Chaos Alignments}
{2x Mana – Chaos Alignment}
{1x Enon – Dark Alignment}
{1x Anima – Chaos Alignment}

=====

Rhen expanded both Caress of Night and Tremor Blast to see that the shared effects were not to their detriment. Tremor

Blast would have increased damage potential and a lower anima cost if it was cast from stealth, and Caress of Night now had the added benefit of reducing his vibrations—very similar to the Dark Hush ability. It seemed he was able to get everything he wanted.

Jakira yawned, then apologized. "I'm used to working long days; I don't know why I'm so tired."

"You are not used to sleeping in a tent and eating only bread and fish. That has something to do with it, I am sure."

Rhen nodded. He wasn't feeling at the top of his game either after emptying his anima well completely. "What if we head back to Yu and stay at the inn for the night? We could sell some monster bones and bring Fennica the herbs she requested."

"And I could have a hot bath." Jakira sighed at the thought.

"It would be nice to play with the Sephine bard again. I enjoyed her melody."

"It's settled then. Let's mine a bit, get a few more materials to bring into town so we're making the most of the trip."

Jakira went topside, preparing several of the bones and ore for transport while Rhen and Aki mined out some of the padreote from the deceased father's fennel plants. The gemstone removal was quick when the plants were dead, and in a short thirty minutes, they had a fair amount of the moss and the gems.

The hike back to Yu was getting easier every trip as they continued carving their path through the forest. The sun was nearly set by the time they arrived, and Fennica had closed up for the night, so they went to the inn for the evening.

The Sephine bard had already moved on, it seemed, and so Aki took to the stage alone. He hummed an enchanting tune and clicked the beak tucked away under all his tentacles. It was not the usual lute and song, but it was beautiful music all the same. When Aki had the attention of the crowd, he released his Aurora Wave spell in purples and greens. Rhen's muscles relaxed, and he knew the spell had been infused with the magic of radiative regeneration.

The others around the room sighed with relief, rubbing their hands and feet as they all felt the magic doing its work. When the performance was over, many of the delvers approached the stage and dropped a mark or two for Aki, who did his best to refuse the money to no avail.

"He's really great," Jakira said, watching him with a serene expression.

Rhen nodded. But Aki's presence was temporary. When Aki achieved his tertia syntial, he'd depart for the next realm on his pilgrimage. At their current rate of progress, that would just be a few short months.

Jakira placed her hand on Rhen's shoulder. "You're great too, ya know."

Rhen chuckled. "Why do you say that all of a sudden?"

"Well, you looked kinda sad, like maybe I didn't think you were great."

"No, that wasn't it."

They helped clear the tables and chairs to the sides of the room. Rhen had been adamant about Jakira getting her own room, though ten marks was steep. He used the excuse of all their wares needing a safe place behind a locked door, and that seemed to satisfy her. She bade them goodnight and Rhen unrolled his sleeping gear among the thirty other dudes.

It wasn't so bad really.

Aki gave one last aurora performance, layering the group with a soft lilac blanket of light that made Rhen's eyelids droop. He laid back on his lumpy backpack-turned-pillow and drifted into a dreamless sleep.

Rhen awoke to the dulcet voice of his favorite Cadrian and the scent of honey and licorice.

"Fresh bread for everyone," Jakira said, closing the door to the inn behind her. She carried two heaping trays of green-tinted buns that had been folded over and over to create a flaky texture. Rhen hadn't seen anything like it before.

He jumped up and met her at the door, taking one of the trays from her. "How did you make these? Where, more importantly?"

"You said Fennica wanted those herbs we collected so I went to her bakery this morning. The sun shined right into my window and woke me up so, I couldn't help myself. She showed me how to make these breads. Try one!" Jakira pulled a roll off the plate and stuffed it toward Rhen's mouth.

He took a big bite, then passed his tray off to the other delvers who were just rousing. Each layer of the crispy bread was coated with green, crystalized honey and the licorice was mild, almost smoky tasting. Shaved almonds provided a bit more crunch, and a salty balance to the sweet.

"Well?" Jakira asked his approval.

"Wonderful. So unique. How did you do it?" Rhen crammed the rest of the sweet and smoky bread in his mouth.

She grinned. "It took about an hour to layer all the dough, but it was simple. Thin dough coated in the father's fennel infused honey, baked for just a few minutes. I won't be able to replicate it until we have a proper kitchen, but Fennica said I could come bake with her anytime."

"Hmm, right. I did want to get started on a real inn for you, part of my plan for those smaller, uncraftable bones."

"How's that?" she asked, puzzled disgust pulling her mouth into a grimace.

Rhen chuckled. "You won't even know they're there. We'll dry them, roast them, crush them into a powder, then mix that with some stream water and a few other ingredients to make a mortar paste. It'll help seal the inn, which will be primarily crafted from wood and dungeon rock."

She cocked her head, now amused. "How do you know all this?"

"Well, I was raised in a delver's school. My whole life was dedicated to fighting, crafting, and using everything that was available to survive."

"Oh, so... your parents?"

Rhen shook his head. "I've never known them."

"That's sad."

Rhen shrugged. "It's just different. Like Aki growing up in a brood of sixty-plus siblings. I'm sure his parents rarely had time for him with so many children. I honestly don't know anything about his culture."

"I guess that's true, but you've never felt like, I don't know, you wanted parents?"

Rhen laughed to shrug off the knot growing in his chest. "What does that feel like?"

"Well, loved, unconditionally, and supported."

"I had many mentors impart all the knowledge they had for me, wishing the best for me, pushing me to achieve greatness."

"Sure, but that's not the same. It's knowing that if you fall, someone will be there to pick you up."

The knot tightened across his stomach. "When I fell, it was my responsibility to pick myself up, and that made me who I am."

She looked down at the tray, her eyes glistening. "I... right. I'm sorry. I guess I'm not explaining it well. It's a wonderful thing to have parents, that's all I was trying to say and so now I realize how stupid I was to have pushed the subject."

The knot in his stomach twisted and a feeling of guilt spread. "Sorry, I didn't mean to—"

"I better pass these out."

Jakira hurried away with her tray, moving among the groggy delvers.

Rhen groaned. He should've seen the signs sooner that he was upsetting her. Why did he have to argue? Why did he feel threatened by this idea of having nice parents? Why couldn't he just have said, "Yes, I wish I had," and leave it be. He rubbed his eyes in frustration and set about rolling his bed back up into his backpack.

"Don't you have enough for a private room by now, or is that *profitable dungeon* dryer than you'd thought?" a burly voice accused from behind him.

Rhen sighed and turned to face Welsh. He looked uncomfortable surrounded by the dirty delvers in his nice, buttoned-down vest, and clean slacks. "I do have enough, but I'm not better than sleeping on the floor, amongst the delvers."

Welsh scoffed, a feral grin pulling his lips wide. "You're *not* better than them, are you? How old are you, again?"

"Does my age have anything to do with this?" he deflected.

Welsh puffed up his chest. "Oh, I think it does."

Rhen's palms grew sweaty, and his heartrate picked up. "Are you trying to figure out whether I'm an eligible bachelor for your daughter? Sorry, I'm not interested."

"You would be so lucky!" He snatched Rhen by the collar of his shirt and pulled him close.

The silent tension in the room was palpable. Jakira and Aki stood ready to pounce, but Rhen shook his head. He could handle this.

"There's something fishy about you, *Mr. Zephitz*. You look about twenty-three, five if I'm giving your little chin stubble credit. How is it a boy of your age, with no friends, no family, and no meaningful connections, came into enough money to buy a dungeon plot?"

Did Welsh already know his secret? No... the age on his id syntial wasn't *that* old. If Rhen had resurrected several times, it could've pushed his looks back... there were excuses that explained the discrepancy. He just had to evade, and play it cool.

"I think you mean, how can a man so distinguished as I remain so youthful looking."

Welsh barked a laugh. "You maintained that cocky mouth of a twenty-something, too. I have smart people on my side, boy, and we're going to get to the bottom of this. Don't get too comfortable here."

Peter turned and strutted off, leaving Rhen shaken. He had to stay calm, keep cool. No one knew anything. Neither Jakira nor Aki had taken note of the forbidden Maddox spell, Piercing Detonator, that he'd used on the mega-hound. There was no reason for anyone to suspect he was someone other than Rhen Zephitz, as claimed on his id syntial.

"What did he want?" Aki asked.

"I've become a minor celebrity, it seems. Not the good kind."

"What does that mean?" Jakira scowled.

"It means he's going to try to make trouble for us. But we have more important things to focus on than some insecure prick who's trying to threaten us. We won't be bullied by the big fish in this small pond. He's no Desedra, and the D.O.G. is not lenient on small-change like Mr. Welsh."

"Would that not mean the same for you? Would the Dungeon Owners Guild care if we were sabotaged?"

Rhen chuckled. "Rule-breaking means fines. The D.O.G. loves money. We're safe; don't worry so much.

"Now, we have materials to sell and weapons to craft."

12

FLOATY IDEA

Rhen made his way outside with Aki on his heels, his mood soured from all that had taken place so early in the morning. Jakira escaped the inn amid many sweet farewells from the delvers, all of them begging for her to come back tomorrow with more flaky rolls. Rhen wanted to be happy that they were making a positive impact on the little town of Yu, but couldn't help feeling... angry, instead.

He'd finally found his place in the world after fighting and scraping a living that *he himself* had earned, and Welsh was trying to threaten it.

Jakira hefted the bone-sack with a smile. "Where to first?"

"Weapons crafter." Rhen narrowed his eyes and glanced around at the signs on the main street. After a moment, he saw the telltale mallet and anvil of a blacksmith on a road sign pointing to the east. That was a good place to start.

Rhen took off in that direction, trying not to overanalyze what he was feeling, and instead focusing on what they needed to do. They'd need to bring back some more materials and tools to get started on their inn, not to mention the baths Jakira wanted to build.

When he turned off for the blacksmith, he saw another sign, for Wyland's Weapons and Dungeon Gear. He veered off for the shop, which looked in ill repair. Two of the windows out front were cracked or broken, covered in a dark cloth. The door was askew on its hinges, and whined loudly when Rhen opened it.

Inside wasn't much better. Towers of broken junk filled the room, and a haze in the air gave it an antique smell. There was a narrow path on the dusty wood floor that led to a well-lit room in the back.

"Wyland, are you here?"

The crazy old man appeared around the edge of the door. He wore some large metal contraption on his head with mutli-colored lenses, and another metal contraption on his arm. "Who's that? Gerald?"

"It's Rhen, sir."

Wyland rolled his chair through the open door and stood. "Oh Rhen, yes. New dungeon owner. Finally realized my worth, did ya? Come in!"

Rhen made his way down the path to the back. The towers of junk swayed at his passing, giving Rhen more doubts at Wyland's claims of worth.

"What're you here for?" the old man asked. He flipped up the glasses to look at Rhen better.

"We have materials for sale. I wanted to offer them to you first, but also, we'd like to make some upgrades, perhaps add a syntial."

"Hmm." Wyland pulled off the metal arm attached to his left shoulder and scratched at his scarred nub while he thought. "Where's the weapon?"

"Jakira?" Rhen motioned her forward.

She pulled the bone club from the pack, holding it hesitantly as she looked at the one-armed man.

Wyland strapped the metal attachment back on and a syntial

lit up on his shoulder. The metal pieces clicked and clacked, coming to life with the orange anima flowing through him. He reached out with both arms, the fake metal one moving just as if it were his own.

"Hmm, nice femur. It's fresh, good. The syntial can take better when there's still marrow inside."

Rhen opened his mouth and Wyland cut him off.

"Don't ask me why, it just is. Okay, what do you want to infuse this thing with?"

Aki's fins fluttered. "My good sir, first we need to know your rates."

"Rate depends on whatcha want." He winked.

Jakira pulled one of the little green father's fennel cores from a satchel at her side. "These have regenerative properties. I wonder if you couldn't use that?"

Wyland reached out with his metal arm like lightning and snatched the core. He flipped down a yellow tinted eyeglass and peered into the core. "Hmm. Yes. Not bad. Come back in four, no, six days, I'll have something."

"But, the cost?" Rhen asked.

"And what do you intend to do with it?" Jakira followed up, arms crossed.

"You can trust me. I've been doing this a long time. It'll be a hundred marks and you'll have a club like no other."

"A hundred!" Rhen protested.

"I know my worth."

Rhen pulled up one foot. "These anima restoration boots were only twenty marks!"

"And little booties ain't the same as a weapon, boy! Now, you best be learnin' my worth, or take your business elsewhere."

That seemed to be the growing theme in Yu. The price was the price, and if he had a problem, he'd have to crawl back to

Desedra for a better one. Rhen pulled in a deep breath to calm himself.

"What about trade? We could give you a few of these bones for crafting and you could knock off fifty marks?" Rhen asked.

"You think you got the gods' given bones in that sack, then? Fifty is a slap to my face."

"Forty off, and we'll give you a pair of these quality monster cores, too. Maybe you could add them to a few of your other wares to create saleable weapons..."

Wyland scowled, then looked around at the leaning towers of junk. "I suppose that would do."

"I'm glad we could agree. Now, other things we need. A wheelbarrow, two hundred-foot lengths of rope, two large buckets, two axes—"

Wyland laughed. "Slow your roll, Gerald. I don't have a wheelbarrow, first off, but let me get to my stuff for the rest."

The old man turned and headed into his office, which was, unsurprisingly, a complete mess.

"It's Rhen, and if you don't have a wheelbarrow, what do you have that's comparable?"

"I've got a one-man boat," Wyland said with a kookie smile.

Rhen turned to Aki to express his exasperation when a thought struck him. The river ran from the Waiting Willow all the way to their dungeon. The path to the waiting tree was flat enough to roll the boat to if they could get a few wheels under it.

"How much for the boat and you add some wheels to it?"

Wyland laughed. "You saw my nifty chair, did ya? I could add some wheels to the boat, got a few lying around I'm sure... twenty-five marks."

"Fifteen, and we'll need it by midday. If you can do that, we'll have no reservations."

"You're gonna work me hard, eh?"

"Seems the only work you have at present," Aki said, gesturing to the empty shelf labeled "work orders."

"That's an old system. Keep all that up here now," he said, tapping his temple. "Still, I can manage fifteen and midday if it means I prove my worth. I get it; can't take anyone at their word these days."

Wyland hurried to the back of his cluttered office where another door sat, closed up tight. He fiddled with the lock for a moment, then looked at Rhen. "I'll have it to ya. Just come back at noon ready to pay up. I'll have your buckets and rope and axes too, in the boat I'm guessing?"

"Yes, sir."

"Y'always were a smart one, Gerald. Off with ya, now." He disappeared into the dark room without another word.

"Why does he keep calling you Gerald?" Jakira asked.

Rhen shook his head. "No idea. Crazy old man."

"Do you trust him?" Aki asked.

"Don't have any reason not to... yet. Come on, we've got more to do."

They departed, keeping in mind the bones and gems they'd promised to Wyland, and made their way to the apothecary next. Rhen traded some of the father's fennel moss and plant petals in exchange for the acids and minerals he'd need to make the mortar. They managed to get out of it with a small surplus of coins, which was a pleasant surprise after getting gouged by both Wyland and Fennica.

Next was a small jeweler who practically squealed at the sight of the knuckle bones. "Perfect for divination, they are! Please, your price?" the Sephine hissed in common.

Rhen thought of how he'd traded two of the larger bones and two gems for forty marks, but divination bones were specialized tools that could sell for quite a sum in the right place.

"What if I sold it to you for half of the profit? You craft the divination bones and on our next trip to Desedra, we'll sell them for you."

The Sephine stroked her colorful scaled chin. "How can I know you will return and share the profit?"

"I'm Rhen Zephitz, and my dungeon is just outside of Yu. If I don't give you your appropriate dues, you can report me to the guild of your choice."

"It's a pact, then?" the Sephine asked, holding her hand out for a shake.

"It is." Rhen gripped her claw-tipped fingers in his, and their anima went to work, binding them to their word.

A new, yellow oval bloomed on Rhen's id syntial with a single hash. If anything were to go wrong in the transaction, either could report the other and have a record of the agreement burned into their flesh. It was nearly impossible to fake a pact, and so they were usually evidence enough for the guilds to take action against them. Any guild would do, the crafters or the dungeon owners. Word would spread and the offender would be punished accordingly—with a fine too, of course.

It paid to keep your word.

There was still an hour before midday, but they'd already managed to sell all the bones they'd brought. They still had a few of the father's fennel monster cores, aside from the ones owed to Wyland, but decided to keep them in reserve. They could always use them to activate dungeon nodes, or level up their anima capacity.

What was left were a few more ounces of Lafite and some padreote gems, so they headed to the blacksmith. It was a good-sized building on the outskirts of Yu, with several forges, but only one that was active. There were several empty racks around the room, and not a single assistant in sight.

The bored young man who emerged from the back looked

over Rhen's ore with little interest. Just as Rhen thought he'd have to hold onto all of it for another trip to Desedra, an older man—obviously an older brother and not a father—appeared. He weighed and assessed the materials, then offered five marks an ounce. It was significantly less than he could get at Desedra, but he haggled up to eight and called that good enough.

The padreote went for criminally low at twelve marks an ounce, but Rhen wouldn't always be able to return to Desedra to sell. He had to consider the train ticket price, the time spent traveling, the accommodations and food. After taking all that into account, he'd only lost about ten marks an ounce, which wasn't horrible.

Finally, the sun reached its apex. Rhen, Aki, and Jakira returned to Wyland's shop to see the old man standing out in the street with a boat, barely big enough for one person, standing on two-foot-tall wheels.

"Well?" Wyland asked, gesturing grumpily at the boat.

Rhen inspected the axles and how it was affixed to the boat. He'd used some kind of quick drying tar and washers to cover the holes made by the nails, keeping the boat watertight. Wyland had done this without prompting... he must've known about the river leading to Rhen's dungeon.

He stepped into the boat, then rocked side to side. The wheels creaked, but nothing wiggled. Good quality work. Rhen stepped out and pulled the fifteen marks from his bag.

"Five more for the equipment." Wyland pointed to the gear piled up at the door to the shop.

Rhen checked the axe blades, then tugged on the rope. He didn't have time to measure them, they'd need to be on their way to get back to the dungeon before dark, but Wyland had been honest so far. He tossed Wyland the extra five and dumped the gear into the boat-turned-wagon.

"Jakira, the bag?" Rhen motioned for her to drop it in.

Deathless Dungeoneers

She gingerly set the pack into the boat. Rhen rooted around in it, then removed two of the nicer, arm-length bones and two monster cores. He passed the materials to Wyland.

"We'll be back in six days for the club with your sixty marks."

"It'll be ready!" the kookie old man said with a wide grin.

"It better for *that* much," Jakira mumbled.

Rhen and Jakira pushed the boat-cart along through the town, up into the forested hills, and onto the path to the dungeon. Once they reached the river, Rhen felt a mischievous feeling stir inside him.

"Aki, want to race? You with Jakira and the boat, me on land."

The Prelusk pulsed from yellow to pink, fins flapping excitedly. "This sounds like a challenge."

"How about a wager on top. Losers make dinner."

Jakira scoffed. "*Losers?* So, you've already written us off, have you?"

"Ready, set, go!"

Rhen activated Swift Twitch, continuously pouring his anima into the skill. He blasted into the trees, feet flying over the depressed tall grass. The path had been worn enough times now that he knew the fallen trees, the twists and turns.

"You're not beating us!" Jakira yelled from far behind him.

Like heck he wasn't.

Rhen turned his palms to the ground and triggered Tremor Blast. The vibrations smashed into the ground, kicking up dirt and propelling Rhen over a narrow ravine. He landed with a whoop, feet pounding against the earth.

"You're gonna burn out!" Jakira's voice was even more distant, and the wind in Rhen's ears made it hard to hear her other taunts.

It was another good mile and a half to his dungeon, but if he kept up his current pace, he'd be there in less than ten minutes.

He pushed harder, feeling the drain on his anima and the slow siphoning replacement of anima through his boots.

"We're catching up!" Jakira said, closer now.

Rhen didn't spare a glance. He knew that areas of the river narrowed down to a trickle, and navigating the boat-cart through wet sand would be a challenge. They might pass him now, but he would catch them again.

Jakira cheered and the boat rocketed past Rhen on a wave four-feet tall. Aki glowed bright blue from the front of the precession, pulling the water along with him as he swam.

"Psionic abilities are cheating!" Rhen called.

"You failed to set the conditions before departure," Aki taunted back.

Rhen gave himself another burst from Tremor Blast to vault over a tall boulder. His feet slapped against the moss-covered rocks and loose branches faster than before, but he was still losing them. Visions of jabbing a spear into the water to catch fish filled Rhen with dread. No! He wasn't losing!

Except he was...

Rhen arrived at the dungeon in just eight minutes, but Aki and Jakira were already relaxing around the empty firepit.

"I'd like three fish, please, with a salt and father's fennel rub," Jakira said, kicking her feet back.

Rhen collapsed to the ground, panting for his life and dripping sweat. "Sure. Thing. How about you two... do some foraging. We need to... ugh, need air. We need to start finding the forest's... natural resources... and exploiting them."

"I think it would be prudent if I taught you to fish," Aki said. "Otherwise, I fear we will all go hungry tonight."

"Much... appreciated."

When Rhen could stand without feeling as though he would pass out, they made their way to the river. The banks were soaked from Aki's cheating. Rhen pulled off his boots, letting his feet squish into the mud. The cold felt nice, despite his reduced anima regeneration.

Rhen sharpened himself a spear and Aki instructed him on how to strike. Aki's people didn't use tools for collecting prey anymore since their psionic abilities were far superior, but his knowledge of the water, how it displaced the prey, and how the fish might move were all important points of guidance.

After thirty minutes and only four fish, Aki decided to take over. Rhen watched in awe as the Prelusk dropped into the river, his watery body disappearing.

For the first time, Rhen really saw Aki.

His humanoid shaped water body and placing himself up at the head position made Rhen associate him more with a bipedal creature, but he really was a multi-tentacled master of the sea.

Aki darted this way and that, snapping up fish in his suckered grasp. He flung the fish out of the water into Rhen's waiting buckets. The terrified creatures landed with a plop and flapped about madly.

Rhen did at least know how to clean a fish, so he set to work doing that and spearing them for roasting. At Jakira's behest, Rhen seasoned several of them with hakir salt and father's fennel. He wasn't sure that combination would be any good, but he wasn't going to let any of it go to waste either way.

By the time they had all the fish prepared, Jakira had a fire going. They roasted the fish and ate happily. Rhen's weariness seemed to dissolve with the fish, leaving both his body and his anima feeling refreshed.

Now, it was time to get to the *hard* work.

13

GODDESS FRUIT FUN

After many hours, Rhen had dug out most of the foundation for the inn. It would be six rooms to start: the kitchen with a small basement pantry, which still needed to be dug, the entertainment room, and three bedrooms. Though Aki didn't sleep, Rhen felt it would be nice for him to have someplace to put his things.

Rhen stood up straight, his spine creaking as he did. "I shouldn't feel this old yet," he complained as he rubbed his lower back.

"How old *are* you, anyway?" Jakira asked.

Damnit, she must've heard that fluffer Welsh talking about it. Who could blame her for being curious, but... Rhen couldn't tell her the truth. He couldn't tell her a lie, either, for if she said anything at all to Welsh or his goons, he'd know he could act on his suspicions.

"Not old enough for my bones to sound like a rusty door, that's for sure."

"Oh, avoiding the question?"

A flicker of fear shot through him. "No, it's just, not important."

Jakira hummed, carrying the dirt-filled buckets to the boat-cart. "Maybe you're just not as young as you think you are."

Rhen rolled his eyes, feigning calm annoyance. "I'm old enough, but not so old."

"Well, you have the personality of a twelve-year-old."

"Just because I have fun doesn't mean I'm immature. What do you call this?" he said, gesturing at the inn foundation. "That, right there, is maturity."

"No, it's capability. You're a very capable twelve-year-old trapped in a fifty-year-old's body."

Rhen laughed. "That sounds about right."

"C'mon. Tell me or I'll find out for myself." Jakira reached for his jerkin.

"Don't." Rhen snarled and jumped back, hand pressed against his side.

Jakira's smile melted. "Whoa, I was just messing around."

Rhen pulled down on his jerkin, securing it. "Yeah, who's twelve years old now?"

"Both of us, I suppose." She scooped more dirt into the buckets and carried them to the boat.

They cleared the dirt in silence for a few minutes. Rhen's reaction played over and over in his mind. Her sad expression, how he snapped, and the distrust that was now growing between them. But he couldn't tell her... the truth could undo him, and the lie on his id syntial wasn't as believable as he wished it were, even with the excuses he could craft.

He didn't *know* Jakira and what she could be capable of for money. Aki, too, who was dying to get on with his pilgrimage. Or perhaps he was being too arrogant. What were the chances the delver's school was still looking for him after all these years? They had to have assumed little Maddox died by now.

"Are you okay?" Jakira asked, timidly.

"If you're truly my friend, you won't press this."

She nodded. "I won't. Just know that you can share anything with me, when you're ready."

Aki emerged from between the trees with all-too-conspicuous timing, though he didn't comment on the exchange. His watery body was bulging at the center with a variety of berries he'd collected.

"Have you seen these before, Jakira?" Aki held out a few of the variations.

Jakira looked at the berries by the firelight. "Poisonous... poisonous... Oh, I'm pretty sure these are Kelimynew." She held up the green pod with gold flecks, scowling at it. "How many of these did you find?"

"Only a single plant. I collected twenty of the fruits."

"They any good?" Rhen plucked one of the berries from Aki's arm and tossed up, mouth open.

"No!" Jakira snatched the berry out of the air. "Just because I didn't say *poisonous,* doesn't mean you should eat it! Kelimynew is the unprocessed plant for goddess fruit."

"I do not understand. What is the danger?"

"It's for divination rituals, communicating with other realms, spirit seeking—"

Rhen scoffed. "And for Desedra goons that want to cut loose. It's drugs, Aki."

"Drugs? I do not know this word."

"It's only drugs when misused, Rhen."

"Will they not be profitable if they are used in important rituals?"

Rhen sighed. "Yes, but we can't guarantee that's all they'll be used for. I've seen what too much of this stuff will do to your head, and profit or not... I don't want to be part of that."

Aki collected all the Kelimynew in his hands. "Then we will not grow it."

He tossed the berries into the fire.

"No, no, no!!" Jakira dove for his hands, splashing into them and catching only a few of the pods.

The berries landed in the fire with a sound like popping corn, and the flames turned green. Golden smoke lifted from the pit and surged toward them. Jakira ran, mouth and nose covered. Rhen stepped back too, covering his face. She coughed a few times, and Rhen's throat was tickling.

After a few seconds, the green flames burned off.

Rhen's head swelled, feeling too heavy for his neck. "Great. Just great, Aki."

"What have I done?"

"You gassed us." Jakira's horns were growing and wiggling like father's fennel plants.

"I'm going to tent." Rhen said, stumbling toward his white canvas triangle.

He tripped on a fish and splashed into the dirt. He rolled over, eyes finding the sky between happy trees, waving their farewell. He accelerated into and then past the clouds, the light of stars whipping past his vision so fast his stomach turned. He slammed to a halt beside a green cloud full of glowing light. His body was weightless in the black, and he couldn't catch his breath.

Aki swam past the nebula. "Are you unwell?"

"I'm in the heavens."

His body careened sideways, colors blurring past his face. Nausea rippled through him and Rhen rolled to his side to vomit. Purple smoke filled the starlit sky until Rhen was emptied. The cloud of purple collapsed in on itself, exploding in brilliant light. Rhen tried to shield his eyes, but his arms were gone, his body—gone. He had turned into stardust.

The light dimmed, revealing a massive star, encircled by twelve shimmering planets. Anima roots snaked through the system, connecting the planets to their star, and the star straight up into... Rhen.

He fell backwards, arms pinwheeling as he screamed. Hundreds of years and a second later, he landed back in the dirt beside the low embers of the fire. Rhen clutched at his thundering chest. What in the absolute fluff had just happened?

A purple strand of light so fine it looked like a hair wiggled between Rhen's fingers and shot off toward the dungeon.

The trees waved hello, and the wind whispered, *"Come find me."*

Rhen grabbed a coil of rope and stumbled toward the dungeon, following the thin purple light coming from his chest. He slipped down the ladder and turned to the cave. It glowed with otherworldly purple like his heartstring, inviting him in. He staggered down the hall, his hands gripping the strand coming from inside him like a wayfinder string.

"Down here," the dungeon wind said.

Rhen dropped to his knees. Water wet his pants and flowed into the gaping hole that glowed with the light of a new star. Rhen leaned over the edge and shielded his eyes. The cavern opened below to a massive lake, filled with all manner of monster. Deep within the lake was a node...

"Nexus node," Rhen whispered.

"Yes."

"How do I get you?"

"Give of your anima and open the way. Connect the roots. Grow the Tree of Being. Save Life. The alignment will fade in twelve cycles, and this chance will be lost."

"Twelve cycles? Roots?"

Water swirled up around Rhen, cocooning him. The water cocoon jerked him away from the hole, from his node.

"No," Rhen mumbled, reaching for the crystal as the purple light faded from his chest.

"What are you doing? Trying to die?" Aki asked, his skin flaring bright orange.

Rhen's senses returned to him like popping the air from his ears. Suddenly, he realized just how completely stupid he had behaved.

"It's the goddess fruit. It makes you do stupid things."

"Yes, I realize now. Jakira has not once, but three times attempted to jump out of the trees and fly! I cannot climb and my vertical water control is limited! I have been chasing her all over the forest."

"Where is she now?" Rhen asked.

"I have tied her up in her tent." Aki set Rhen down, leaving him soggy and cold.

"I suppose that's the best thing for her until she's better." Rhen's stomach growled, mad with hunger.

"Oh, yes. And I have spent several trips to the river cleaning your vomit."

Rhen chuckled weakly. "That's your punishment for drugging us."

"I did not realize... I did not understand what a drug was."

"Now you do. Let's go get some more fish. Jakira will be hungry, too."

Aki turned away for the dungeon entrance, his fins fluttering madly.

"Here."

Rhen spun around, eyes affixed on the hole in the ground. It must've been a trick of Aki's receding light, but Rhen could've sworn he saw a purple glimmer wink out down in that hole. He shook his head and followed Aki. What the heck had that goddess fruit done to his brain?

When they emerged, Rhen could see the first light of dawn on the horizon. Had he really been blacked out for so long?

"Not funny, guys!" Jakira cried from her tent.

Rhen jogged across the grass and stopped at the opening to her tent. "Can I, uh, come in?"

"Yes, get in here and untie me!"

Rhen pulled back the opening and ducked down into her tent. Poor Jakira lay on her side, flopping like a fish out of water. Aki had hog-tied her, and the wet rope had expanded as it got warmer, making the knots tight.

"Are you sure you're not still high?"

"I'm very, *very*, aware of myself and my present situation," she said through gritted teeth. "I'm also very aware of the Prelusk right outside whose ass is getting kicked as soon as these ropes are off!"

The glow from Aki's body dimmed as he walked away from the tent. Rhen struggled with the tight ropes, but they didn't budge. Finally, he pulled his crescent blade from its holster at his hip. He didn't want to waste the rope, but didn't want to leave her tied up another moment.

With delicate care, he cut the rope from her wrist, and untangled the rest from there. Jakira rubbed her wrists, her face flushed with gold flecks. She eyed the tent exit, her teeth gritted.

"You were jumping out of trees trying to kill yourself."

Jakira glared at him. "And would I have been if Aki hadn't thrown the Kelimynew in the fire?"

"No, but he didn't know. I said I didn't want anything to do with them, so he... disposed of them."

Jakira growled, her frustration having no target. "Fine. You're right. It was an innocent mistake that almost cost me my life, or limb, and you"—she sniffed—"Blech! what happened to *you?*"

"I threw up on myself... probably a lot."

"Smelly delver, as usual," she said, the anger fading from her voice. "Ugh, I have to get away from you."

She flipped open the tent opening and breathed deep the fresh air.

The wind blew past their camp and Rhen felt something stir inside him. A memory of something just outside his reach. Purple strings, crystals, huge monsters. What was it?

"Did you have a dream?" Rhen asked.

Jakira scowled, eyes closed. "I think so. It's so hard to remember after waking up thinking I'd been abducted." Her eyes snapped open, fiery gaze pinned on Aki.

"I am sorry."

Jakira laid into him, but Rhen couldn't focus on what she said. The wind blew away her words and replaced them with a deep pulsing, like a beating heart. Purple light glowed from the dungeon opening.

"Time is running out. Twelve cycles."

Images flashed through Rhen's mind: an exploding star, planets rich with life, strings connecting him to the dungeon, monsters swimming, biting, shocking. Rhen's stomach dropped as he realized what it all meant, remembering his trip to the sky.

"There's a Nexus node down that drain."

Jakira stopped mid-rant. "What?"

"The hole in the ground in the dungeon that was too dark and deep to see down, I think there's a Nexus node there, but not for long. There's an alignment, the strings, roots, whatever they were coming out of my chest..." Rhen pressed a hand to his sternum.

"Are you sure you are well?" Aki asked.

Rhen grinned from ear to ear. "Absolutely. Come on!" He gathered up the cut rope and dashed toward the dungeon.

Jakira gasped. "Rhen, did you divine something?"

"I think so. goddess fruit might not be so bad after all... if it proves right."

14

NO NODE TOO DEEP, NO MONSTER TOO BIG

Rhen pulled on the rope at his shoulders, then at his hips, ensuring the knots were as tight as Aki's had been. Next, he tested the simple crane he had put together from bones. The hole was situated in a fairly narrow passageway, so Rhen had designed the crane to brace against the walls in a triangle shape. He grabbed the other end of the rope then lifted his feet off the ground.

The bones creaked, much like his own had the day before, but they held his weight. He bounced side to side, stress testing it.

"This should work for now." He tied the rope in a loop right above him.

Jakira grabbed the slack he would use to lower and raise himself and twisted it around her hand. "What if the bone breaks? What if the rope slips? What if... you're too weak?"

"The crane is like this so if I can't pull myself up, you can grab this end and reel me in. Plus, it'll be a brief trip down. Just far enough in that I can use my breath to light it up. I'll get a lay of the area, so we know exactly what we need, and then come back up. Promise."

"And if he falls in, I will follow. Water is my natural habitat."

"Right, so why isn't Aki going again? He weighs a lot less and can make a lot more light."

"Well, because..." Rhen shook his head. He didn't have a good reason. "Because I was only thinking about how cool it would be to spelunk into my own dungeon and find a Nexus node. But now that you mention it, Aki, hop on my back and make some more light for me."

"Wow," Jakira huffed.

Rhen understood, she wanted to keep him safe. He'd made the crane himself, and tested it. Everything would be fine as long as the crane didn't slip and fall in with them. As for his muscles giving out, he doubted it.

Aki's suckered tentacles latched onto Rhen's neck and shoulders as he let most of his watery body drain into the pit. It was weird having water lapping against his back, but he'd get over it once they were being continually dripped on.

Rhen positioned himself butt-first over the pit, belay end of the rope gripped tightly in both hands. "Ready?" he asked with a glimmer of excitement.

"Completely."

Jakira groaned. "Okay, fine. Good luck, seriously."

"Thank you," Rhen said with a cocky smile, then dropped them over the edge with a little bounce.

They descended a few feet at a time, the walls of the tunnel getting narrower and wider at random intervals. Aki projected a brilliant green aurora around them, causing a tiny rainbow wherever the water from above slapped against rock. The stone was black, and coarse, perhaps some kind of volcanic. Rhen could see the drainage outlet and a soft yellow light glowing from beyond it just a few more feet below.

Aki sent his aurora zipping through the opening. Rhen braced his feet on the wall and looked down in awe. The lake was even larger than he remembered from his fever dream. He couldn't see the edges of the lake to the left, but not far below him and to his front he could see a rocky outcropping from the wall and a sparkling white beachhead.

The ground glittered like shattered glass, and magnificent crystal stalactites held fast to the ceiling. He lowered himself on the rope a little more.

"Can your aurora reach the water?"

"I will try." Aki reached one of his little glowing tentacles out past Rhen's face, as if that much distance would help.

The aurora swooped low over the lake, but couldn't reach all the way in. Rhen strained his eyes to see any traces of the megamonsters he'd remembered from his dream. The water rippled from the drips from above, making it even more difficult to see.

Then, something poked out of the water. An antenna. It was gone just as fast. Rhen held his breath, and all at once, a massive creature with a wide-set jaw and thousands of teeth rocketed out of the water at the aurora. It snapped at the light waves, four massive claws coming from either side of its face closing around the thin air, trying to shove the light into its mouth.

It smashed back down into the lake before Rhen could glimpse any more of the horrifying gigafish. The waves from its impact slapped against the walls of the cave, making it tremble. Stalactites dropped from the ceiling and crashed into the water, revealing a feeding-frenzy of smaller creatures that were still likely huge in their own right.

Some of the smaller fish had wide wings that they used to propel themselves out of the water, catching the crystals before they were swallowed up in the dark. Other silhouettes he could see beneath the water looked like oversized shrimp, thousands of little legs and antennae coming off them.

"Why is there always a giga-monster?"

"Because the dungeon is protecting itself?"

"Sorry, buddy, that was rhetorical."

The lake lit up with bright purple from a point far below them, casting a glow through the water.

"The Nexus," Rhen breathed in awe.

The ripples of light shone across the whole lake, revealing its gargantuan scale. It looked like an ocean.

Some of the smaller creatures near the dropped stalactites glowed with the Nexus node, and all at once Rhen saw them grow in size. The stalactites fed the monsters anima.

"I've seen what I need to see for now. Ready to go up?"

"Very."

Rhen pulled down on the other side of the rope, slowly raising them back to the surface. He braced his feet on each side, stepping up with every pull, slow and steady. When they breached the top, Jakira grabbed onto Rhen's shoulders and hoisted him out. Her face was pale and hands shaking.

"You want to go next?" Rhen teased.

Jakira looked like she would throw up. "Killing monsters is one thing, dangling over a pit like bait is another."

"You saw the monster?"

"Barely, but I heard it. Sounds like a beast."

"It'll have an incredible core, for sure."

"Like we're ever getting past that thing any time soon."

Rhen tapped his chin. "With enough people, I think we could."

"But why rush it?"

"The dream, the feeling... it said time was limited, twelve cycles. I don't know what that means. Twelve moon cycles? Twelve years? Days? I don't want to just sit on my haunches and let this opportunity pass us by. A Nexus node to a new realm would be... we'd be kings—and queens," he added hastily.

"You really think we can do this in twelve days?"

"We have to," Aki said.

"We *can* do it, but not alone. It's time to grind."

They grinned at one another, determined. Aki's fins fluttered and his skin pulsed from yellow to blue. Rhen set each of them to task mining out the areas that were still profitable, while he went back to work on the inn. There was so much to do.

He cut down the trees closest to where he wanted the inn so that it would have enough space to grow when needed. Those trees became the foundation poles for each corner of the building, and the interior supports. Next, he ran the boat-cart back and forth from the river, collecting big, smooth stones that would make up the floor and base structure.

At midday, his brain was getting hazy, so he stopped for a deep drink from the river and a quick cooling splash. Jakira and Aki returned, buckets full of gemstones and ore. They devoured a quick meal of just edible berries and bread. Rhen looked at the wood poles and pile of rocks, resolved. He was going to get that foundation laid, gods and goddesses be damned.

Rhen laid the first layer of stones a few inches into the dirt, then mixed a big clay mud-puddle near the river. He carried bucket loads of the river mud down to the inn, then hacked and slashed at the tall grass, adding it to the mud. He applied liberal coats of the primitive mortar to the spaces between the rocks at the bottom. Then, blasted it with his fiery breath to harden the clay.

The sun was already getting low and Rhen finally stopped to review his progress. It was a large building, but he'd gotten every support and the exterior wall foundation started. He grinned, happy with the progress.

Jakira crawled toward the camp on hands and knees, her hair a mess and skin coated in layers of dirt. "I... need... bath."

Aki was looking filthy too, his water clouded by black particles.

Rhen was exhausted, his throat itching from the use of his

fire breath, but he knew they needed to relax. "Aki, you up to helping me with something?"

"I would not be elated, but I will help."

"I'll take a reluctant yes. Let's go."

He led Aki down to the river. "When I was getting stones for the foundation, I noticed a closed off space where the water flows into and out of slowly. It's clean, but cold. If you can pull the water out and move it around, I can heat it up. Maybe not bath temperatures, but warm."

Aki hummed. "Let us try."

Aki lifted the water from the little river outcropping in streams, pulling it past Rhen as he blasted it with fire. After a few minutes, Rhen dipped his hand into the pool. Certainly not bath temperatures, but warmer. "Just a little bit more."

After another five minutes, Rhen felt it was sufficiently hot for bathing in. He still had a tiny nub of soap left that he offered Jakira. She crawled her way to the pool. She was so exhausted, Rhen feared she'd fall asleep and drown. At his request, she let Aki and Rhen stand guard not far off with their backs turned.

Rhen felt the inconsiderate urge to glance over his shoulder as he heard her clothes hit the ground, but kept it at bay. She was his friend, and that would be a friendship-ending glance if there ever could be one.

"Aaahhh yeah, that's the stuff," Jakira moaned, splashing water as she got into the pool.

Aki leaned closer to Rhen. "I could not help but notice you and Jakira argued yesterday. Is it resolved now?"

Rhen sighed. "It wasn't important, I'm sure everything's fine."

Rhen hoped the goddess fruit helped her forget her curiosity in the first place. His age was a loose thread on a careful lie he'd woven over the last eleven years. A little tug could undo it, and him. He prayed she would forget.

Aki hummed and looked across the camp. The sun's last

vestiges spread red and pink across the cloudy sky, giving the whole camp a warm hue. Rhen eyed the inn, thinking of everything he needed to do tomorrow. He'd need to build a ladder, and a smaller step stool, cut more trees—saplings too. He'd have to start roasting the bone for the stronger mortar, and collect even more river rocks. Was he going to have enough time to do it all?

"Is it because she likes you?" Aki asked.

"What?" Rhen said a bit too loud.

"I'm fine!" Jakira called from the pool.

Rhen lowered his voice. "We weren't arguing because of that."

"Well, perhaps the content of the conversation was not her affection for you, but I believe the intent was. She is very taken with you."

"You'd know all about it, wouldn't you?"

"There was not much to do while mining. We talked."

"What about?" Rhen asked a little too eagerly.

"How you met. She said she noticed you for many weeks before you ever truly spoke to one another. A clear indication of her interest."

Rhen rolled his eyes. "Give it a rest, Aki. If she wanted anything more than friendship, she'd tell me."

"Are you so sure? You have a very... confident presence. I too was nervous to reveal myself and ask for your friendship."

"But you did. And she will too, if it matters enough to her."

"I suppose that is valid."

They stood quietly for a few more minutes, listening to Jakira splash and enjoy herself as the sun set. A chill settled in once the sun was gone, and Rhen's discomfort—though he wasn't sure of what—intensified.

"I'm going to go start a fire. You've got her, right?"

"I believe she has herself, but yes, I will continue to stand watch."

Rhen retreated into the woods, looking for felled trees. His muscles ached, and the mud caking his legs and arms was starting to sting, but he chopped away at the dry wood he could find for what felt like forever. Jakira emerged between the trees with a wave. Her hair was wet, but she was dressed in fresh clothes. She'd been smart enough to bring a second set...

"Your turn, Smelly," she said, reaching for the axe.

Rhen took a whiff of himself. Licorice and earth were all he could smell, but he relinquished the axe and helped collect the wood. He set a fire for her before he left, and brought his sleeping blanket with him to the pool. He hadn't brought extra clothes, something he'd remedy in a few days when they went to get Jakira's club.

He stripped down and slid into the warm water with a sigh. That *was* the stuff. He cleaned himself, and then his clothes, while Aki fished for their dinner. Finally, he was sitting by the fire with his clean clothes hanging to dry over the bone crane he'd built, stuffing a roasted fish in his mouth.

He'd gotten used to eating the same thing over and over, but there was something better about repeat roasted fish in the camp outside his own dungeon. Maybe it was the setting, or the company, or the father's fennel, but it made him feel less stuck than the years of monster soup he'd consumed to survive.

It was hardly twilight, but Rhen and Jakira agreed it would be better to sleep early and rise early for work.

"What can I do while you sleep?" Aki asked Rhen.

"Do you think you could move some river rocks?"

"Alas, rocks are heavier than water. It would be quite difficult for me to move ones of the size you require."

"Okay, could you... collect some straw for the thatching? Can you braid? I'll need a lot of twine for the rafters."

"I see this is not where I am best suited to help you. Jakira would be. I can continue to mine out the small chamber with the Mastery node. We will need a lot of profit to hire help."

"Sounds good, buddy. We'll see you in the morning, bright and early." Rhen checked his clothes, still a bit damp, so he went to bed wrapped in his blanket.

The next morning, Rhen put a hash in the dirt beside his tent. He didn't want to lose count of how much time might be left. If only the gods, or the berries, whatever had given him the vision, had been a little clearer about what twelve cycles meant.

His body ached, every muscle sore from the work of the day before, but he refused to slow down. Aki blessed all of them with a cooling wave of radiative regeneration that seemed to help while they ate breakfast, and then it was off to work.

Rhen directed Jakira on how to braid the twine for the rafters and helped her construct a ladder and stool. He roasted the bones for the mortar and crushed them into a fine powder with a few good stones he'd selected.

Aki returned from the dungeon with a bucket only half full of Lafite ore. "It seems that room may be running dry."

"No biggy. I've actually got something for you. Follow me." Rhen led Aki to the river again.

"Another bath?"

"Nope. I want you to help me cut these huge stones into flat flooring. I'll use Tremor Blast to crack them, and you direct the flow of the water to cut them in half. How about it?"

Aki flared yellow. "This I can help with."

The hours flew by, and by midday, they had enough stone for the entire inn floor. Jakira had collected all the roof thatching, made of about two hundred feet of twine from the tender sapling bark, and helped crush the bones.

"This is doable. We can do this. In three days, we'll head into town after finishing the rough construction, and we'll stay at the Bustling Brood—with a real bath."

Jakira shrugged. "I don't know, the river pool was honestly pretty nice."

Rhen smiled. "Glad we could accommodate. Hopefully soon we'll have a Nexus node and one of the busiest dungeons in the realm. We'll be setting up river baths for all kinds of realm-renowned delvers."

"I can see it now," Jakira said, jumping to her feet with excitement. "The Zephitz River Retreat! Restore your anima, revitalize your body!"

"Enticing statements," Aki fluttered.

Rhen nodded appreciatively. "You're really good at talking to people, too, Jak. We're going to need your help convincing the delvers to come fight that insane monster with us."

"I'm sure the coin will do more convincing than I could," she said sheepishly.

"No, really. You have such a bright smile that people can't ignore. It's like you're a magnet, or something."

"Oh, thanks." She sat, the gold in her cheeks sparkling.

Rhen sighed, tossing his fish bones into the fire. "Back to work. This inn won't construct itself!"

15

WELSH IS THE NEW DESEDRA

It.
Was.
Done.

Rhen plopped into the dirt, his body weary. He marveled at their creation. Was it perfect? No. But it was a respectable-sized inn for such a small dungeon. Aki had helped test the roof by dropping a steady downpour over it; not a single drop fell inside. They had layered the mud and mortar with impeccable speed and skill.

Jakira dropped down beside him with a sigh. "I didn't think we could, but then we did."

"But then we did." Rhen smiled.

Sure, the interior was completely unfurnished, and the kitchen barren, but they had an inn. All things started somewhere.

"It is time for us to depart," Aki called from the boat-cart. It was full to the brim with ore, gemstones, father's fennel, and buckets of berries—not goddess fruit...

Aki was psionically tapped out from all the mining, so he hitched a ride on Rhen's shoulders while they pushed the boat up the path. They made decent time, arriving in town just before the shops shuttered their windows.

They were able to get Fennica to buy up most of the father's fennel, and brought the rest to Perry, the inn keeper of the Bustling Brood. Rhen was able to get an order in with the tailor for some more shirts and pants to avoid any more naked blanket situations, and then the Sephine jeweler—Gwhan—bought up several of their gemstones and handed over the completed divination bones.

"Don't sell these for less than three hundred marks, yes?" The Sephine grinned, revealing her menacing teeth.

"We'll get four," Rhen said with a confident smile, and took the bones.

The smoothed knuckles and sharpened claws glowed with otherworldly light when Rhen touched them. Images of the Nexus node, the boss monster, and the star suspended in purple haze connected by a thin line to Rhen's dungeon flashed in his mind.

Gwhan hissed a laugh. "You've been at the berries in the forest?"

"We have, unfortunately." Rhen shot a glare at Aki. He shrugged his tentacles sheepishly.

"You have a connection to that dungeon, Zephitz. The binding done to you both is at the spirit level. That crystal is powerful, and time is running out."

"How do you know about that?" Jakira asked, hand on the hilt of her dagger.

"I see many things behind your eyes."

Rhen leaned forward, excited. "How much time?"

"That is difficult to tell."

"The voice said twelve cycles, but I don't know what that means."

Gwhan tapped her chin, then curled her finger at Rhen. "Come with me."

She led him through a beaded veil that obscured the pungent scent of burnt goddess fruit. Rhen covered his mouth and nose instinctively.

"It will enhance my connection to your vision," Gwhan said, gently pulling Rhen's hand from his face. He did as instructed but breathed shallowly.

Gwhan chanted in her native tongue, and her eyes came alight with silvery anima. Rhen couldn't look away from her, omnipotently experiencing his entire goddess fruit trip as her eyes bore into him. Rhen covered his mouth to hold back vomit.

Gwhan laughed. "Go, get a meal. It will make things better."

Rhen swallowed back bile. "How long?"

"I believe 'cycle' in this instance will refer to one thing: the flow of anima through the Tree of Being."

"The Tree of Being, that's something else the voice said. So, it is another realm!" Rhen said, excitement pushing through the nausea.

Gwhan nodded. "The anima flow cycles once every four days in this realm, every seven days in my home realm of Hapthar, and so on."

"How do you know this?"

Gwhan chuckled. "It is what I am paid for." She held out her hand expectantly.

Rhen scowled. He hadn't agreed to pay her... but his vigor was made stronger by the news. At least they knew.

Forty-eight days. Well, forty-four now.

That was a lot more than he'd thought previously, and it made the whole thing feel more doable.

He placed a few marks in her hand. She looked at them as if disappointed but hurried them away to her purse all the same. She showed them out, bidding them happy delving.

It was too late to sell any more, so the rest of the wares they stored in Jakira's room at the Bustling Brood under lock and key. They enjoyed a long, hot bath, and two heaping portions of rabbit stew with fat bread rolls. They must've looked like savages, as the rest of the delvers wouldn't stop staring at them. Finally, a young woman with hair like straw and brown freckles across her nose approached their table.

"You're the Zephitz crew, right?" she asked.

"We are." He stood and held out his hand. "I'm Rhen Zephitz."

She grinned and accepted the handshake. "Olliat Nilson. Could I sit with you?"

"Please do. This is Aki, and Jakira."

Olliat grabbed her bowl of stew and set herself at the table next to Jakira. Her legs bounced under the table as she surveyed the Zephitz crew.

"Is something the matter?" Aki asked Olliat.

"No, uhm, not really." She glanced over her shoulder at the other delvers. "So, how is the dungeon?"

"Good. We just finished the inn." Rhen talked past a big chunk of bread in his mouth.

"Oh, so you're preparing to host delvers?"

"We are. Everyone with a love of the delve is welcome," Jakira said with a kind smile.

Olliat nodded, looking to Rhen. "And the rates?"

Rhen looked between Aki and Jakira. "That wasn't something we'd discussed yet, but I think we all agree that delvers deserve more than a measly ten percent divided between you."

"Ten!" Olliat laughed, then covered her mouth. "What dungeons have you been delving, Mr. Zephitz?" She leaned in and whispered, "Mr. Welsh gives us a tiered flat rate, rarely more than five percent."

"That's criminal," Rhen barked, his heart hammering.

The room quieted, delvers glancing their way, some with less than courteous stares. Rhen could tell that a couple of the delvers looked a little better off; nice clothes, recently bathed, a nice flagon of beer at their table. Must've been some of Welsh's goons. Dungeon owners always had goons.

Olliat whispered, trying to calm Rhen. "It's just the way it is here in Yu. The Yu dungeons went dry ten years ago, and Welsh was all that was left... but lots of us had made family here already. Pickin' them all up and moving to Desedra wasn't possible."

Rhen gritted his teeth. "That doesn't give him the right to exploit you."

That damned Welsh thought he could be the next Desedra and treat his delvers even worse. Rhen would show him the power of capitalism against a poor business practice. The delvers here didn't have any other choice before, but now, there was another plentiful option. Those anima crystals in the lake chamber alone could level every delver in the Bustling Brood three or four times over.

"Keep your voice down, Mr. Zephitz," Olliat whispered. "Those men are his."

"I'd gathered as much by the daggers they're staring at me." Rhen locked eyes with one of the bigger men. His lip curled back in a snarl, then he buried his face in his beer mug.

Olliat leaned in farther, whispering so low Rhen could barely hear her. "When can we join you?"

"How many?"

"Five."

"Builds?"

"One bruiser, two fighters, a mage, and a mule."

"Like an actual mule?" Jakira asked.

Rhen chuckled. "Packrat's what they call them in Desedra.

Enon syntial bags for days, they have huge carry capacity. How many node boss fights?"

Olliat winced. "None for me, but the other fighter, my brother Eli, he's seen one."

"Seen, or fought?"

"Um, well..."

"It's fine. What's your syntial level?"

"I'm Prima I, just the one. Eli is Prima II, the bruiser, my father Joseph Nilson, is Ancilla II, Eli's mother, Valine, is Ancilla III mage, and our mule, my uncle Bort, is Tertia I."

Rhen nodded as the prospects improved. An Ancilla II bruiser could be a good tutor for Jakira, and help with the makings of two delve teams. Eight was a good-sized party, but two teams of four would be better for their current mission in the dungeon. They weren't ready to take on the lake room yet, but there was hopefully plenty more down past the father's fennel farm.

"We need to make a trip to Desedra to sell our materials and wares, but we should be back within two days. If you meet us here again, paperwork ready to go for everyone, we'll take you to the dungeon."

"You will!" Olliat squealed, then covered her mouth again. "You will. Wonderful, Mr. Zephitz."

"Stop with that; just call me Rhen. We can discuss payment on our return, but I can promise it'll be better than what Welsh enslaves you with."

Olliat nodded, her smile bright and unstoppable. "Then we eagerly await your return. Until then."

She picked up her bowl and returned to her family's table. Rhen spotted Joseph the bruiser easily. He was twice as wide across the chest as Rhen was, and nearly a foot taller than him. His hair was darker than Olliat's, with a smattering of gray, but he sported the same freckles on his nose bridge. He was scarred up and down each arm, and across his face. It must've been an age since he had to resurrect.

Joseph gave a courteous nod in Rhen's direction and raised his beer. Welsh's goons in the corner took notice of the motion and scribbled something on a bit of parchment. Rhen hoped he wasn't dooming this poor family with his agreement... he'd do what he could to protect them until they were part of his dungeon crew.

"I think it might be a good idea if one of us stays in town."

"I will stay and keep the peace," Aki said, his presence growing friendly as a pinkish hue surrounded his watery body. He took to the empty bard's stage, ready once again to entertain the crowd. He was damned good at it, too, and with his abilities, he might just be able to subdue the Welsh goons without a fight.

As the dark outside the inn deepened, the Welsh goons departed, same as Olliat's family and a few others. Jakira retired to her room early to organize the wares, and Rhen stayed up to spur on Aki's performance. Aki molded and transformed the water of his body, creating interesting spectacles as the light passed through the orbs of water.

The enchanting display soon put Rhen to sleep right where he sat, and he was roused by the gentle hand of a fellow delver. They moved the tables and chairs aside, and within seconds of hitting the floor, Rhen was fast asleep again.

Jakira woke Rhen in the morning with a shake. She handed him a fresh roll and sat next to him on the floor.

"I've been thinking... you should stay here while I run the merch to Desedra."

Rhen felt a flicker of fear. What she had in that pack must've been worth close to five-thousand marks. If anyone had a whiff of what was in there, she'd have wolves descending at every second.

"Don't you think I should escort you?"

"You have a lot to do for the inn, and I'm sure Aki wants you here to help with those goons."

Rhen scowled. "Are you sure you can manage with all that? What if..."

She smiled. "Oh, don't worry about my safety. Look," she flexed her bicep. "I'm getting stronger every day, and plus, I have that Defender's Cry. I'll kick them all between the legs and make them throw up."

He'd forgotten how much strength she'd gained. "Yeah. Okay. Just never open the pack in front of anyone. Come to a vendor with what you want to sell in your second pack, your smaller side pouch."

Jakira chuckled. "Oh, so it wasn't my safety after all, but the profits."

"No, that's not it! I just mean..." he leaned closer and whispered, "If you open the bag and people see inside, they'll know how much you have. They'll come after you."

She stood, pulling on the straps of the bag. "I promise, I've got it. I'll be back tomorrow afternoon, everything sold."

"See that you do, or no bonus for you."

"I'm getting paid? I thought this was a charity dungeon."

They shared a smile that lightened the tension. Rhen didn't really care if she lost all the loot—save for the knuckle bones he had a promise riding on. He didn't want to see her hurt. He didn't want to see Aki hurt, either, and those goons were more likely to make some sort of move now that Olliat had done her business in the open.

"Well, you better get to the train," Rhen stood, reaching out for a handshake.

Jakira pulled him into a hug. Rhen tensed, surprised. After a second, he relaxed into her. He wrapped his arms around her back and squeezed, feeling his worries melt. How long had it been...?

She pulled away. "I'll be fine. See to it that my inn is ready when I get back, or no bonus for *you*."

Rhen saluted. "Yes, miss."

She gave him one last wave and a smile, then disappeared into the cool morning air.

"And you say she does not have affections for you." Aki appeared from nowhere, startling Rhen.

"I don't know what you're talking about," Rhen said, rolling up his blanket.

"Oh, come off it," an older delver with a shaved head chimed in. "We all saw the way yous was lookin' at each other."

Everyone but Rhen laughed.

"Aki, don't we have more important matters to attend? Like an inn, and a dungeon?"

"Aye, I heard her threaten'n you about that inn," the shaved man said. "Need a hand with it? I've done a fair share of carpentry in my day. Barrek's my name." He held out his hand for a shake.

Rhen went to grab it and the man pulled back a hair.

"You're not gonna hug me, are ye?" He grinned wide then gripped Rhen's hand with a hardy shake.

Rhen shook his head. "I can appreciate a joke, but I don't want her too embarrassed to come home... she has all our money. The miss already declared we are friends, so that's it on that matter."

"Eh, what's a wife but a friend you share a bed with?"

"If yer lucky!" another man piped in.

"Lucky for the friend, or if yer sharin' a bed?"

"Either?"

"Both!"

The room roared with laughter, and this time Rhen joined

in. He didn't know if it was the infused bread rolls, Aki's aurora, or perhaps seeing the prospect of a new dungeon that had them in such high spirits. Rhen was happy to be surrounded by the laughter all the same.

Rhen cleared his throat. "All right. Who can build furniture?"

16

THE ULTIMATE GAME CHANGER

In a matter of hours, Rhen's camp was host to five new visitors: Barrek, his wife, Leslie, two of their friends, Caleb and Gil, and Gil's wife, Patti, who all promised to get the inn ready for patrons. They agreed on five marks each an hour, which was a reasonable rate for the work given the circumstances.

They had filled the boat-cart on the way out with hammers, nails, pots, pans, plates, utensils, blankets, and so much more, leaving Rhen with very little money on his person. That was fine, because they all knew Jakira would be returning with their wages in a few days' time.

When Rhen saw the carpentry team had chairs and tables under control, he headed off into the dungeon with Aki. He'd spent the last week building an inn and was itching for some monster battling action. They made it past the drain, now covered by the bone crane with a sign reading, "Warning, death below."

With the newcomers inbound, Rhen didn't want any accidents, especially before he'd found a Resurrection node. But he hoped that they were about to fix that. He knew his quest from the Guild wanted him to activate a Control node, and he wanted to find one, but if he was going to safely take on that Nexus boss, he wanted a fully operational Resurrection node first.

Rhen dropped into stealth and skipped ahead of Aki, who projected a broad, green aurora. The opening at the back end of the large hound room split three ways. The left tunnel angled down, and Rhen hoped that tunnel would lead to an easier way into the Nexus chamber. The forward and right tunnels stayed relatively flat for as far as he could see.

"Going right," he whispered to Aki, then crept into the darkness.

Aki's light was just enough for Rhen to navigate, but soon, another light shone ahead. It waved and lapped, as if a bright moon were shining down through layers of calm water. Rhen kept close to the wall until the silver pouring from the opening ahead was so bright, he thought he might be blinded.

A singsong whistling drifted down the hall and the drain on Rhen's anima ended. His body appeared below him in full view. How strange. Was the light so bright that Caress of Night could not be used?

"There is a creature ahead. I cannot see it. The shape is shifting."

The singing whistle blasted louder, vibrating Rhen's stomach. Aki's aura dispersed, as if blown away by an unfelt wind. Nausea threatened him and Rhen realized it must've been something akin to the Defender's Cry, but with a spell-canceling effect like Anima Rot. Jakira was going to love this ability.

"I'm going in."

Rhen charged forward, one hand out for a Tremor Blast laced with Anima Rot, and the other pulling his blade from its holster. He squinted as he rounded the corner, seeing nothing but bright silver. Without a visible target, Rhen decided to wide-blast the room with low vibrations, trying to hit everything.

The vibrations shot out of his arm and bounced around the cavern. Lights flickered and died as wet *thwaps* hit the stone. The creature lying before him looked like a cross between a bird and a jellyfish, with translucent leathery skin, wide wings, a sharp beaked face, and hundreds of tiny tentacles coming out the bottom. The light inside it faded as a black smoke snaked through its body.

A whistle cut through the air like a knife and Rhen doubled over from the nausea. The back of his neck stung as if he were being stabbed by thousands of tiny, hot needles. Something slimy wrapped around his throat, then his arms. He took a deep breath before the airway was cut off and he looked up.

A dozen of the luminescent jelly-birds had wrapped him in their grip and were taking off. Not if he had any fire to breathe about it. The air in his chest burned as he activated his Primordial Breath. When he couldn't stand to hold it in another second, Rhen belched flames all up the creatures' bodies.

They whistled and flailed, losing their grip on his neck. Rhen gasped for air, then triggered another anima rotting Tremor Blast. The attack hit several of the creatures above, knocking the brightness down to non-blinding levels. Rhen fell to the floor and Aki rushed in beside him.

He used his water like a wrecking ball, slamming into the flying jelly-birds and knocking them out of the air. Rhen targeted the plummeting monsters and gave them each quick, narrow blasts laced with Anima Rot. Wet splats sounded all around them and the light in the cavern dimmed.

"Hold off," Rhen said when only five of the creatures remained circling at the top around the prize: a node.

The creatures whistled, but without the combined power of all their voices together, the sound hardly ruffled Rhen's hair. He scratched at the back of his neck, the skin there swollen and irritated.

"I think they're venomous. We may be able to use it for potions or coat my blades. It doesn't feel very powerful, but if it could be distilled..."

"I understand. You would like to keep these as 'farming' monsters. I will capture them."

With the light so low in the cavern, Aki was able to activate Shadow Snare, slowing the monsters until they descended like petals on a breeze. He cocooned the monsters in auroras of lilac light, and they went completely docile, as if asleep. Their wings fluttered gently, but the tentacles dangled motionlessly.

Rhen wasn't sure how he'd cage them and extract the venom, but he did know with them out of the way, he could access the node. "Hold them still for a minute while I do this."

Rhen jogged across the open cavern and stood under the node. It pulsed faster at his presence, as if inviting him to activate it. The walls were dry, so Rhen scaled them easily. However, once at the top, he had no real way of getting to the node. It was a good six feet from the back wall, and Rhen wasn't about to climb upside down with no support.

Or maybe he didn't have to climb...

Rhen gauged the distance from the node again, then glanced down. The fall wouldn't kill him, but he'd no doubt be walking with splints for a few days. Days he probably didn't have if he wanted to claim that Nexus node.

"What are you thinking?" Aki called from far below, the jelly-birds floating beside him on lilac light.

"I can jump it and hold onto the node to activate it, but I don't think I could make it back."

"Do we not have five skilled carpenters up at camp?"

Rhen grimaced. "Yes, but building a ladder will take time, and I don't think we can have them in the dungeon without proper paperwork."

"You had me in the dungeon without paperwork."

"Yes, because you promised to keep your gob shut about it. That's five people we hardly know up there, we can't trust them yet... and plus, I want to see what the node is now."

"I too am excited to discover its possibilities, but you are putting yourself in unnecessary danger. Jakira would not stand for this."

Rhen sighed. He was right. It wasn't worth it.

Unless it was a Control node.

Rhen could rearrange the cavern with a simple command, lowering the ceiling and making it safe to drop down.

"Rhen, I can feel your heartbeat. Please, do not do this."

If it wasn't a Control node, he could use Tremor Blast to slow his descent—as long as Aki wasn't too close. His forearms were starting to get tired from holding the lifted pose, so he dropped to a long-armed hanging position.

"We can build a ladder."

"It'll take at least an hour to get everything set up down here, and that's an hour lost on inn work. Trust me, I can make it. Just, maybe don't stand directly below the node in case I need to break my fall with Tremor Blast."

Aki moved away from the node, giving Rhen his space. "Good luck."

Rhen pushed with his legs, angling himself out from the wall and toward the node. He did this a few times, breathing deeply with each practice move. He sucked in one last breath and lowered to his haunches, then set his sight on the node.

Swift Twitch activated at a thought, and Rhen blasted off from the wall with all his might in an explosive dynamic move. He twisted, turning himself to land on the node, hugging the base of the stalactite. What a terrible time for him to realize that this stalactite might not be able to hold his weight, that he and the node might come crashing down to the ground, both broken.

It was too late now.

Rhen opened his arms and reached for the node, fingers splayed and flexed. He touched its glassy surface and latched on. Adrenaline surged through him as his chest hit the node, his legs swinging wide. Rhen muscled himself up the node's shaft, scrambling for purchase until he reached the rough stone of the stalactite. He wrapped his legs around the node and sighed with relief.

"That was incredibly irresponsible, and heroic looking."

"Thanks," Rhen said, trembling from the adrenaline.

He exhaled slowly to collect himself, then reached down and touched the glassy surface of the node. Light poured out of the crystal and formed words... upside down.

"What does it say?"

"Congratulations, first Dungeon Owner's quest complete. This is only a Control node. Do you wish to activate it?"

Rhen strained his arm to keep contact with the node. "Yes."

"Would you like to edit the chamber layout now?"

"Yes," he grunted.

Rhen fell backwards into a black void, nothing to hold onto, nothing to catch his fall. It was like being sucked into the sky by goddess fruit again. His descent slowed until he was floating in a gray nothingness, with no horizon, no ground, just gray.

Silver text materialized in front of him along with a map of the explored areas in his dungeon. Dark blobs sat on the entrances to the two other tunnels they had not taken, and another dark blob covered the drain hole in the father's fennel farm room.

[Dungeon Owner's Map Synced!]

Your Dungeon Owner's Map has now synced to this Control

node. You will be able to view the entire dungeon you have explored from this control center, or from your map.

*Check your map for a new quest from the D.O.G.

**Bring your map into the nearest D.O.G. headquarters to activate your discounted tax rate for the next twelve months!

=====

[Welcome to Dungeon Editing, Owner!]

You may edit any area of the dungeon you control by way of node, or monster clearing. Editing the dungeon can reveal hidden levels, allow you to stage your raids, provide homes for your delvers, or makes a great party room!

Use voice commands to make broad adjustments to the dungeon, and hand gestures to fine-tune those changes. If you need help, you may ask any questions while within this space. Information within the node is limited, so be sure to ask your question a variety of ways to see if it has an answer for you.

Best of luck, and happy shaping!

=====

Well, that was neat.

"Display Control node chamber." Rhen's voice sounded far off, like his ears were deep in a cave, and his mouth was on the outside of it.

The map shifted, showing a three-dimensional view of the cavern. It showed every creature in a basic, gridded outline, and the topography of the cavern was revealed with colors from red to green. Rhen's outline was still clinging to the Control node, Aki and the five jelly-birds were standing on the ground not far off, and nothing was moving. Was Rhen... suspended in time?

"Tell me more about this place I'm in now."

[Control Command Center]

This is the center for controlling your dungeon layout.

=====

Well, that wasn't very descriptive.
"Where is the Control Command Center."

[Error – Query Not Refined]

Unable to provide an answer, too many answers exist. Query needs to be refined for specificity.

=====

Rhen scowled. "Too many answers... Am I inside the Control node? I mean, is my mind, my thoughts, inside the Control node?"

[Control Command Center]

This is the center for controlling your dungeon layout.

=====

Rhen sighed. He wasn't getting anywhere with this thing. First his question is too broad, then too narrow. Maybe it couldn't give him anything more than this?
"Is this a Cebrum spell that I'm under?"

[Reply – Yes]

"Interesting. I would like to edit the dungeon layout by bringing the ceiling closer to the floor in this chamber."

The map shifted, creating a room that was only ten feet tall, but another thirty feet wider in all directions. A black blob appeared on the map to the left of where Rhen was, and another one on the far end of the wall to the right. Those must've been new tunnel openings revealed by the shift! Incredible.

Rhen used his hands to make a few minor changes; slightly taller ceiling, wider opening, and other tweaks. It was strange at first, like playing with clay. It had haptic feedback that startled Rhen at first but became more natural the more he used it.

Then he moved the Control node down to the ground and crafted a stony chair beside it. Rhen wasn't certain if he was still holding on for dear life outside the control center but didn't want any collapsing incidents to occur while he was making adjustments.

Finally, he was satisfied with what he'd made. "I'm done with this and would like to change the dungeon to fit this form."

[Dungeon Editing]

Cost for current adjustments: 1,200 anima points
Current chamber allotment: 6,892
Pending absorption from deceased creatures: 480
Would you like to utilize the current chamber allotment to make these changes? {Yes} {No}

=====

"Yes, I would."

Rhen was sucked backwards through the gray void, away

from the map and into the black. His stomach lurched and he smacked his head on something hard, then flopped to the ground. He was upside down, holding onto the base of the Control node which was now on the ground, next to a horribly malformed stone chair. He'd need to practice more.

"That was... I do not have words to describe it."

"Same, buddy." Rhen climbed to his feet and looked around the chamber. It had reflected all his changes perfectly, and exposed several deposits of ore and gemstones as well as the two new tunnels.

Rhen smiled. "This is the ultimate game changer."

17

FARM, FARM, FARM

"Don't ease up, almost there," Rhen said from behind Olliat.

Flecks of stone pelted her leather apron and metal face shield as she punched away at the stone with her hand drill. The flecks turned to sparks and Rhen tapped her shoulder.

"See that? Lafite!"

Olliat cut the drill and inspected the hole she'd made. "Nice vein."

"Nice *work*." Rhen patted her on the back.

He moved on to the next mining station that was excavating some more padreote—these gems were even more potent for their lack of father's fennel leaching the power out. They were in a rush against time, Rhen told them as much, but as for why, he kept the details sparse. "There's an opportunity that won't be available forever," was all he'd say. But he paid good wages—thirty percent of whatever they pulled out divided amongst them—and provided syntial upgrades without restrictions.

They'd discovered a few new abilities from the jelly-birds, an ancilla add-on to Defender's Cry like Rhen had assumed, and a venom sting Rhen set his sights on. If he could combine that with Anima Rot, he'd have a powerful physical attack that would debuff the enemies' anima use and poison them with a painful blinding effect.

"Rhen, ready to go?" Jakira asked, her green-glowing {Bone Club of Life Drain} hefted over one shoulder. The damn thing was a masterful piece of equipment, and Rhen would never doubt Wyland again. He probably should've paid more for it than he had, but the trade benefited Wyland better in the end. He was able to sell a few new weapons to some of the delvers that had joined Rhen's crew, and that suited him fine, too.

"Ready as ever."

Aki and Joseph met them at the tunnel entrance down to the unexplored chamber to the north. It was a bit overkill to have two bruisers on the team, but Jakira needed to learn somehow. With Aki serving three purposes, control, damage, and healing, Rhen was certain they could take anything the dungeon had to throw at them—except maybe the gigafish guarding the Nexus node.

Not their objective today, in any case. They were on the hunt for a Resurrection node, something Rhen was adamant about finding before they took on the Nexus boss. He wouldn't have anyone forever-dying on his watch.

Rhen took the lead, shrouded in shadows. The go-between tunnels from chamber to chamber rarely had monsters, but it was good to be prepared just in case.

The tunnel sloped down, and the air grew thick with fragrant moisture. The darkness was punctuated by spotlights coming from white crystals lining the ceiling of the tunnel. Rhen stopped to inspect one.

He touched the smooth surface and felt the anima surge below it. It must've been the same kinds of crystals as those in the lake chamber.

"We might be able to harvest these," Rhen whispered to the party.

"Scout ahead. Less gawking more stalking," Joseph said in his rough, poetic way.

Rhen smirked. Bruisers were de facto delve leader in most cases, so Rhen fell in line with his order. "Yessir."

There were a few precipitous drops they were able to navigate with some anchored ropes Jakira put down, and the humidity increased again. If it hadn't been for the warmth and floral scents, Rhen would've thought they were nearing the lake chamber.

The tunnel widened more and more, the light growing, until at a final turn they were released into a thick jungle. Broad green leaves unlike the ones up top at the camp, hanging vines, bright pink, yellow, blue, and purple flowers, whistling noises of birds —perhaps more jelly-birds, and sounds of insects. Finally, they'd found an eco-chamber.

A chamber with its own closed ecosystem was one that was rich indeed, and one so full of life as this would undoubtedly hold a Resurrection node. Eco-chambers regenerated anima, materials, and creatures over time. As long as he kept the balance, this chamber would never run dry.

The broad leaves provided enough shade from the glowing crystals far above that Rhen could steal from shadow to shadow, remaining hidden. Tall trees with pale bark and thick pink and blue fruits peppered the landscape. Streams of glowing silver water carved a path through the underbrush, and fragrant bushes weighed down by berries and flowers filled the spaces between.

The heat from the crystals above felt good on his skin, almost like it was regenerating his anima. Rhen could see himself being in this chamber a lot for relaxation.

A low *click-click-click* caught his attention, and he stopped, hunkering down in the shadows. A response *click-clackackack* in a higher pitch alerted Rhen to the danger he'd so eagerly snuck himself into. He looked back to see Joseph a good thirty paces behind him, scanning the forest.

A hazy outline of something bigger than Rhen, on two legs, with clawed hands blurred into view. Another creature, larger still, parted the leaves ever so gently and emerged beside the smaller one. They were cloaked in the same stealth Rhen had used to get this far.

They weren't looking at Rhen though, and that gave him the advantage. The monsters divided, one to each side of the path, waiting for Joseph and the others to bumble into their ambush. Too bad Rhen had an ambush of his own to unleash.

The smaller monster clicked, nodding at the larger, and Joseph stopped the team with a raised hand. The larger monster held still, but the smaller one moved forward. While the larger was distracted, watching the little one move in to execute a sloppy ambush, Rhen snuck up behind it.

Rhen targeted the creature's lower leg, going for the hamstring, and gave it two quick cross-slashes. Instantly, the monster curled back and snapped at Rhen. He triggered Swift Twitch, dodging backwards just in time to not lose his face. He deactivated Caress of Night and pulled in a deep breath for a blast of flames.

The monster revealed itself, too; nine feet of sharp beak and beautifully vibrant feathers. It looked something like a big, colorful chicken, aside from the razor clawed hands and feet. Behind the larger monster, Rhen heard Joseph engage the smaller.

The ache in his lungs was too great, so Rhen lowered his weapons and exhaled hard, releasing the fire. The terror chicken —terrocken, Rhen decided quickly—spread its arms, fluffing out the brilliant feathers and threw back its head. The wings pulsed with anima and the beast *click-clacked*, chanting as green magic swallowed up Rhen's fire.

The flames guttered and the last of the energy flowed into the beast. That same green magic flowed through the monster's feathers and down into its bleeding ankle. The flesh mended itself before Rhen's eyes, and he stared, mouth agape.

Rhen looked up at the terrocken and saw a gloat in its stupid beaked face. It had seriously just sucked up his spell like it was nothing and then *used* it to heal itself.

Well, that nixed most of Rhen's syntials, then. He'd have to go blow for blow with it.

The terrocken clicked and stalked forward. Rhen activated Swift Twitch and lunged forward. He dodged under the creature's swipe and slashed across its belly. The blade slid off the feathers to a sound of metal on metal, his blade completely ineffectual. Rhen stepped back, but too slow as the monster whipped its fat ass around at him, hip-checking Rhen's shoulder.

Rhen bounced into the underbrush and rolled to his feet. The terrocken advanced on him, snapping its long beak. Rhen moved both blades to his right hand and held up his left, unleashing Anima Rot laced Tremor Blast in a narrow beam directed at the monster's face. The vibrations hit the creature's eyes and it staggered back, blinking.

Rhen swapped back to his blades and moved in, targeting any area not covered in the magical feathers—of which there were few. Under the creature's arm, next to its beak, its lower legs and... that was it.

A loud screech turned the terrocken's head. Rhen glanced to see Jakira landing an undoubtedly killing blow against the smaller monster, smashing its skull with her massive bone club. The larger monster turned, whipping its tail into Rhen's gut and knocking him to the ground again.

Rhen gasped for air and crawled to his hands and knees, then charged after it. "Look out," he tried to shout but wheezed instead.

Joseph swung in from the side, smashing his axe against the terrocken's shoulder and throwing it off course. It staggered, right arm hanging uselessly at its side, but didn't take its gaze off Jakira. Aki's lilac magic surged toward the monster, but with a flare of its feathers, it absorbed the anima. Its dislocated arm snapped back into place, and it shrieked.

Rhen slammed his hands against his ears to block the noise that shook his eyes and turned his stomach. Damn, every creature had Defender's Cry! Rhen finally caught his breath and gained his feet.

"Screw you, too!" Jakira screamed back and the terrocken flinched. Her voice carried through the forest, hitting Rhen with an invigorating wave of power. He triggered Swift Twitch and leapt up onto the monster's back. He squeezed his legs under the terrocken's arms and pinned them back, then laid his head against its feathery neck and held on tight.

The beast bucked and kicked, but Rhen held fast. It turned its head to snap at Rhen's shoulder, sending a lance of pain down his arm and up to his neck. There was a loud *clunk* and the terrocken staggered sideways. It collapsed, tossing Rhen to the ground onto his bleeding shoulder.

Rhen cursed, dragging his legs out from under the monster. Jakira and Joseph whacked at the terrocken's head, ensuring it was good and truly dead.

"Sit still," Aki said, coming to Rhen's side. Blue-green infused light poured from his tentacles and wrapped Rhen's bleeding shoulder. Like he'd seen with the terrocken, the flesh mended itself before his very eyes—to a point.

Aki went in for another round of mending, but it seemed the wound wouldn't stitch any further than it had already. His own

Swift Healing was going to work on it, and the bleeding had mostly been stopped, but it still hurt like the gods' fire.

"We need those feathers," Rhen said through clenched teeth. "For armor."

"You are being impatient. Give it a moment, you are injured."

"I'm fine. We have to pluck as many of those as we can before the bodies disappear into the dungeon."

Rhen staggered to the bigger terrocken, inspecting the feathers, claws, and beak. Endless possibilities laid out before him as he catalogued the monsters. The feathers weren't metal, but something the terrocken had done had made them resist piercing damage. Wyland would figure it out for a few hundred coin, Rhen was sure.

Some of his flesh dangled from the monster's hooked beak. Rhen gingerly touched his shoulder at the thought of it. The beaks were raptorial, curving down and sharply ending in a point. They could make interesting fist weapons for Eli, if he so wanted.

The claws were a bit less useful, but Rhen removed them anyway, storing the bloodied stumps in Jakira's large pack. They dug out the cores next, and while Rhen wanted to take some time to claim the bones as well, he knew they needed to keep moving forward.

He looked around at the forest. It was as if he were outside. The cavern ceiling was so far away and shrouded in mist, he couldn't see it. The trees towered thirty feet up or more, and the vegetation was thick. There were sure to be more of those creatures in here. He'd get their bones yet.

Jakira touched his uninjured shoulder. "You okay?"

"Fine, like I said." Rhen gave her a smile to set her at ease, but it seemed to do the opposite.

Joseph and Aki moved on through the path in the underbrush, leaving Jakira and Rhen some distance to speak.

"Aki is right. You're rushing. What's going on?"

Rhen shook his head. "We don't have time to waste. That Nexus is going to close, and then... What if the dungeon dries up?"

Jakira smiled kindly. "Not for a long time. Look at this place. Even if you don't get the Nexus node, this dungeon will be profitable for a while. You can buy another plot, a bigger one."

"But Nexus nodes are so rare. And if the vision was true, and there's another realm on the other side of it, this could be the only chance to connect. An eighteenth realm, Jakira... there could be another sapient species, but even if not, there's so much to discover and explore in a whole new realm. Think of all the inns you could build."

She smiled and shook her head, sighing. "Okay. Let's keep doing our best, but really... you're going to get yourself killed if you keep going like this."

"Once we find the Resurrection node, that won't matter so much." Rhen grinned.

Jakira rolled her eyes. "Lead on, fearless dummy."

They spent all afternoon in the rainforest chamber, hunting terrockens and finding other small prey type creatures that would be delicious in stew. Rhen hoped there was a predator for the scary chickens too, because so far, his dungeon was not revealing a lot of new realm-shattering abilities.

They didn't manage to find the node before having to turn in for the night, but Rhen stopped at the Control node on his way out to see all they had mapped. There were quite a bit of black blobs still obscuring the rainforest chamber.

Pressure, like a tight band, snapped around his head. There was *so* much left that was unexplored, and too few delvers to take on the gigafish even if they did find the Resurrection node. He needed to move faster, fight faster, recruit faster.

He needed to return to Desedra.

18

BURIED TRUTHS

The train bumped along into Desedra City. The tension in Rhen's head had mounted to a full-blown migraine, and his nerves were frayed. They had thirty-eight days left to activate the Nexus node, and too few prospects for recruiting.

Rhen had to be selective. He couldn't risk bringing in someone who—once they knew the potential wealth—tried to blackmail Rhen into surrendering more than he could afford. And he most certainly couldn't bring anyone in who would sabotage the delve for a payoff from Welsh... which was likely, at this point.

Welsh would do everything in his power to prevent Rhen from making competition for him, and bribing rival delvers was a good tactic. Rhen had seen it before. That was, if Welsh didn't uncover his dark past first, which would be much more catastrophic for Rhen than false negatives and stolen goods.

"Hey, you okay?" Jakira touched Rhen's arm, jerking him from thought.

"Why do you ask?"

"If your scowl could kill, everyone on the train would be dead."

Rhen took a deep breath and felt the creases in his forehead. He relaxed and gave her a smile. "Better?"

"You can talk to me about anything. I'm your friend."

"I'm worried about Welsh manipulating anyone we bring in, and I'm not sure we'll even find enough good quality delvers to get this done... that's all. I don't want any mercenary types; they don't play well in groups and charge too much."

"You've made that pretty clear," Jakira said with a giggle. "Trust me, I know scum. I've seen a lot of it. I'll make good choices, and with both of us on the hunt, I'm sure we can get, like, at least ten people."

But what if they couldn't?

And what if Welsh pulled back the wool, revealing Rhen for the little wolf he was?

"There's that death-scowl again. Come on, what's going on, really?"

"I'm just concerned about the time we have left, and the quality of people we can recruit... and Welsh."

"Keep your secrets, then." Jakira sighed and looked toward the window.

The train slowed as they entered the city proper, tooting its arrival horn several times. They disembarked and while Jakira went to the market to sell wares, Rhen went to the delvers guild first to review the delvers looking for different employ.

He sent request messages to each of the candidates he liked, informing them of where to meet that evening to discuss: the Silver Mark. It was a mid-tier inn, not too fancy, but showed Rhen had money. He offered to pay for their night's stay whether they agreed to join his raid party or not, which should've been enough to reel in every one of the prospects for the pitch. He just hoped they'd check their messages daily.

That alone had taken him three hours, and Rhen was getting hungry. He took to the market district, his gaze scanning every face in the crowd as he hunted for Jakira. He found her pitching some of the terrocken claws at a weapon's dealer and stood back to let her work. After a few minutes of haggling, Jakira got him to buy eight claws for ten marks.

"Want to get something to eat?" he asked.

Jakira jumped, startled, and turned to face him with her hand on her club's hilt. "Oh, Rhen! You're done already?"

"I narrowed my search to help ensure we were only getting quality delvers. We need to make a stop at the Silver Mark to reserve several rooms—it was part of the deal I offered the recruits."

"Yeah, I could definitely eat. This pack is still a bit heavy. I haven't been as persuasive this trip as I was last…"

"Maybe we should send Aki?"

Jakira laughed. "How would he hold the bag?"

"Good point. Let me take the bag for you," he offered, reaching out for the pack.

"No, I'm fine." She grabbed his hand. "So, where's this inn?"

Rhen looked down at their joined hands, a wave of confusing thoughts washing over him.

Jakira smiled, her cheeks sparkling. It wasn't the sun making her gold flecks brighter, the haze from Desedra core processing plants had long since blotted that out, so it had to be… embarrassment? She must've been worried she'd get lost in the crowd.

Rhen shrugged it off and headed toward the Silver Mark, pulling Jakira along. "It's just a few blocks this way. I've only seen inside once, but it was nice."

"Will we be able to afford several rooms?"

Rhen dodged some arguing barterers and headed toward the main road. "For one night, yes. But it will be a serious expense. Hundreds of marks."

"Ouch, what a waste!"

"We have to prove that we have a profitable dungeon and spending flagrantly is a good way to accomplish that."

"I guess that's true. Couldn't you just offer to buy them all weapons from Wyland? Or something?"

"I needed to prove our profitability before even meeting them, to incentivize them to come. They'll review my record before coming and see that I just purchased my plot. Sure, they'll see the dues I've paid the D.O.G. and know that there's *some* worth, but this will prove our confidence in what's down there for the raid. Only an absolute fool would spend this much if they didn't have anything going for them."

"Okay, you convinced me."

They finally made it to the road. Rhen released Jakira's hand and walked beside her. Motorized wagons blasted by, and people on bicycles chimed their warning bells as they passed. He could see most of the downtown buildings—monstrous things that towered hundreds of feet tall, crafted from ore mined in Desedra I. Rhen yearned to see his own little town flourish outside Zephitz dungeon.

"It's just up here," he said, pointing to a long cluster of signs that steered the onlooker down the side street that was only for foot traffic.

A vehicle sped by with a loud *bang* from its anima engine and Jakira jumped, then latched onto Rhen's arm.

"Sorry," she said sheepishly, and released him.

She must've been on edge being back in the city, worried whether her old boss would try to pull something shady and get a mark on her record. He grabbed her hand and looped her arm back in his. She smiled up at him, face glowing with gold.

The side alley wasn't nearly as busy as the market, and Rhen was relieved to be out of the noise. The Silver Mark was a clean building crafted from stone and wood, keeping that rustic look while affording the amenities of the big city, like electricity.

They stepped into the inn, cool air blowing past them into the warm street. There was a second door, and beyond that, the air was even colder, almost too cold. At the front desk sat a Cadrian man in glasses. He used an anima display pouring from a crystal behind the desk, reviewing patron accounts and daily openings.

"Ah, a room for the happy couple?" he said, lowering his glasses down his nose bridge.

"No!" Jakira pulled her arm out of Rhen's and took a half step back. "I mean yes, but I need a room for myself."

Rhen chuckled and approached the counter. "We need several rooms, actually. My name is Rhen Zephitz. I'm a dungeon owner who will be hosting several delvers tonight to discuss raid rates over dinner and a night's rest."

The man smiled. "Very good, Mr. Zephitz. Have you stayed with us before?"

"No."

He turned and picked up the crystal, then placed it on the counter. "Just need to scan your id, and then we can talk rates."

"Yes, is there a discount for buying several rooms?"

The Cadrian chuckled, his cheeks shimmering gold like Jakira's did. He cleared his throat and regained his composure. "No sir, I'm sorry but there is not."

Rhen cringed. That must've been a pretty fluffer thing to ask in a place like this. He put his hand on the crystal and the anima flowed into him, activating the syntial on his side. His information displayed a second later and the Cadrian nodded.

Rhen reserved just the two rooms to start and asked the Cadrian to hold a few until the other delvers arrived. He gave the attendant all the prospects' names and asked that he tell them whenever they arrived.

They were shown up two flights to their individual rooms that overlooked a small, fenced-in garden with a pond. It was idyllic. No wonder they were a hundred and twenty marks per room. But Rhen didn't plan on staring at the pond all day; he had contracts to draft up. He didn't know if he wanted to maintain all the delvers after the raid, so he'd need special paperwork to ensure that once the raid was complete, the delvers were no longer under his employ, unless they all agreed otherwise.

That absolute nonsense took him another two hours, even with a D.O.G. representative helping him. He tipped the rep with five marks, to which she turned her nose up, scoffed, and stormed away. Rhen still wasn't used to the high-rolling status...

It was closing in on dusk, so Rhen bathed and made himself very presentable with a nice set of clothes. A black button-down shirt that he tucked into black pants, secured by a dark belt with a silver buckle. After smoothing back his curly hair for what felt like the hundredth time, he left his room and walked to Jakira's.

He knocked on the door. "I'm heading down to the tavern."

"Oh, wait for me," she said, excitement muffled by the thick wood door.

There was a bang and an, "Ouch!" then some more ruffling around, until the door opened. Rhen's jaw dropped. Jakira wore a heavy chainmail shirt over her clothes, a high waisted belt that sported her glowing club prominently, leather leggings with metal guards for her shins and knees, and heavy boots.

She stared at his chest, her mouth agape. "I obviously didn't understand what *dress the part* meant!"

She tried to close the door and Rhen stopped her. "No! This is perfect. You look like an experienced bruiser, and I look like an established dungeon owner." He tugged on the belt holding up his nice pants, then smoothed his tucked-in shirt.

Her cheeks practically glowed. "You really look... different. Like a Desedra."

Rhen smirked. "You told me you wished I'd change, so, here I am."

"Yeah, just don't go acting like a Desedra too, and we'll be fine. Smelling good suits you, though."

Rhen grimaced. "*Good* is in the olfactory of the beholder. I smell like candy."

She laughed and he stepped back from the doorway to let her out. They walked to the stairs, still chuckling from his stupid joke. Jakira jingled a lot, and her boots clomped like death was coming. She'd certainly give the recruits a fuzzy feeling.

The tavern of the inn was just off the atrium, through a side door. It had a secondary entrance on the street, but this private back entrance gave them access to the exclusive tables. The air was thick with the smell of beer and the sound of laughter, the music just getting started.

Rhen hailed a barman as he walked by. "Is anyone waiting for Zephitz?"

He shook his head and moved on.

Rhen shrugged and found his way to one of the open tables for the Silver Mark customers. He and Jakira settled in, ordered a flagon, and waited. There was some kind of fight on display in rippling anima, in every corner of the tavern. It was a battle of bruisers in a white, cordoned-off ring. The display projected from a tiny crystal in the ceiling that had a pulsing anima string connecting back to a Communication node somewhere under the bar. Rhen inspected it idly, since he'd hardly ever seen communication nodes used in that way—or in any other way, for that matter. Such advanced tech was scarce in the lower delver circles where he spent most of his time, saving his marks up for the dungeon plot.

He watched the fight for a while and listened to the commentary over the din of the tavern goers, trying to keep himself entertained. The beer on the table was getting warm, and after forty minutes of waiting, Jakira poured two drinks.

"It's rude to pour before your guests arrive."

She rolled her eyes. "They teach you that in delver school?"

"No. My sponsor did."

"Look, they're late. That's rude too." She pushed his beer across the table and raised her glass to him. "To finding the help we need and blasting open that Nexus node to a new realm."

Rhen raised his glass and took a tiny sip. He was never very fond of beer, nor the aftereffects. Ten minutes later it was apparent Jakira was perfectly fond of it, pouring herself another glass while Rhen nursed his.

"Drink up, we can order more when they get here," Jakira said with a smile.

Forty more minutes and the barman started getting a glare about him. Jakira's cheeks were glowing brightly, and she started talking about old gossip from when she worked at the Down-N-Out.

Rhen ordered a plate of food to help level her out. The last thing he needed was her telling tales of Rhen's days sleeping in a room with thirty other dudes. He needed to be a respectable dungeon owner to these prospects.

"Are you listening?" Jakira asked.

Rhen blinked. "No. I'm sorry. I was thinking—

"I don't think they're coming."

"I'm gathering as much too, but why?"

She shrugged, then took another pull from her mug. The flagon was empty.

Rhen stole a bit of bread from her plate, chewing angrily. *They* were the ones in search of work, and Rhen offered to host them a night in a decent inn, pay for their meals, just to talk... How could they turn down such an offer?

"Do ya think it's Welsh?" Jakira hiccupped.

"How?" Rhen growled, stuffing more of her food in his mouth.

"What if he, like, told everyone your dungeon isn't profitable?"

"But anyone would be able to see the dues I pay the D.O.G. and know it's a lie. I wouldn't put it past him to try something like that..."

"Whatever it is, it's scared *eeeveryone* off. Look, everyone's been staring at us, but no one is coming over."

"Because they haven't been invited. It's a private table."

"Hey, hey, I know. What if we just forget the delvers and go to a school! We could become sponsors."

"I'm not engaging in child slave labor," Rhen snapped.

Jakira sobered. "I didn't mean... I meant we could do what your sponsor did. He paid your debt and like, freed you, right? We could do that."

Rhen was quiet. They were teetering too close to the truth he had to keep buried.

"That's what happened, right?"

"I asked you not to bring this stuff up. This is *not* the right time to talk about it."

"Will you two be wanting anything more, or can you release the table?" the barman asked, holding his hand out for payment.

"Yeah, we're done." Rhen pulled out twenty marks and slapped them down on the table, then stood.

"Rhen, I—"

"See you in the morning, Jakira."

Rhen's heart pounded in his chest and the blood rushed in his ears, blocking all other sounds. How could she be so ignorant? With her parents' love, and her obviously sheltered upbringing it was no wonder. She would never understand what it was like.

He stormed into his room and slammed the door. He gritted his teeth, fingers fumbling with the tiny buttons on his shirt.

"Stupid..." he grabbed it by the collar and ripped it off, panting.

His reflection glowered back at him from the mirror at the end of the bed. The light pink scar around his id syntial screamed *liar, cheat,* and Rhen pushed his palms into his eyes to stop the tears.

"Don't let'em tell you that you haven't earned this. You've more'n paid your debt to them, to me. You don't owe nobody nothin'." His voice was calm at the end. How could he have been so calm cutting open his own chest?

Rhen dropped to his knees, the lump in his throat threatening to strangle him. The Nexus node was so close, but just out of reach. And it seemed everything he tried to do left him one step farther away than he was before.

"I don't want to do this. I don't want you to die!" Rhen heard his little voice echoing in the dark cavern. Tears streamed down his cheeks now just as they had then, hot and fearful.

"Ain't no stopping my death, but through it, you can have your freedom. You're strong, Maddox. I know you can do this, son. Show the realms just how great you are."

Rhen breathed deep and pushed away the tears. He climbed to his feet, looking at his reflection. "Be the man he knew you could be."

He couldn't go to a school, he wasn't old enough yet to go unnoticed there... but maybe there was something else, another way forward. Rhen sniffed back the last of the tears and donned his delving gear.

It was time to expose the devil.

19

SLANDER AND SLIGHTS

Rhen dozed in and out, the train home rocking him to sleep after a night of hard work. He clutched the inflammatory leaflet he'd gotten from the Delver's Guild on the Zephitz dungeon.

"Young. Inexperienced. Foolhardy. Don't delve with Zephitz," read the title of the pamphlet. Welsh must've spent at least two hundred marks getting this pushed to the front page of the delver's digest.

Of course, Rhen had gone to the D.O.G. and the Delver's Guild to do just the same, to find what he needed to put Welsh in his place: off Rhen's back. He'd found just that in the tax archives, as he knew he would.

The Welsh cluster was dry, save for one dungeon going on its fifth level. He paid lower and lower wages each year, approved by the Delver's Guild only because of a signed petition from the delvers themselves requesting to allow it. Welsh had used the "small town spirit" against them.

He must've tricked the delvers into signing it somehow, or maybe they hadn't signed it? Either way, he was bringing that proof back to Yu, and posting it on every quest board he could find. Rhen hadn't wanted to stoke the flames of Welsh's anger, push him to dig any deeper into Rhen's past, but he wasn't going to roll over and let the Nexus node slip through his fingers.

The Yu delvers were good people, from what he'd seen so far, if not a bit underpowered. If he could get at least half of them out of the Welsh cluster and into his dungeon, he'd have what he needed to take down the gigafish.

The train bumped hard, and Jakira startled awake. Her eyes were red and the skin around them puffy. She squinted, groaned, and covered her face with her arm.

"Too much beer?" Rhen asked.

"Uh-huh."

"Why'd you keep drinking it if you knew you'd feel like this?"

"I've never had it before." She groaned and resituated the pack behind her head.

"Any alcohol?"

"Nuh-uh."

"I find that hard to believe given your line of work."

She pulled her arm away from her face, glaring at Rhen. "Are you calling me a liar?"

"No, just, you were surrounded by it for years. Never got curious?"

"Never could. Leery watched all us maids like a hawk; she portioned our food and drink so we wouldn't get too fat and made sure we were presentable every day before dawn."

Rhen was stunned. He never imagined that an inn maid would be under such strict control. "So... why did you decide to try it last night?"

"Because I wanted to have a good time." Jakira sighed, apparently annoyed with him.

"Okay." Rhen sat back and looked out the window.

He thought of Jakira looking down at a small plate of food,

hardly enough to fill her howling stomach after a hard day of tending to the inn. It made him angry.

Jakira growled. "We've been working *so* hard, and you're stressed out! I've seen the people who drink beer being all smiles and laughs, having the best times of their lives. I just wanted that for us for a night."

Rhen leaned forward and scooped her hands up into his. "Thank you, Jak."

The creases in her forehead smoothed, and her eyes glossed with tears. "You're welcome."

"I want to have fun too, but now isn't the time. We have a Nexus node to unlock, and thirty-seven days to do it."

She sniffled, nodding. "I know."

"We can't get experienced delvers with specific power sets, so we're going to need more people." He placed one of his hastily drafted up leaflets in Jakira's hand.

Her brow furrowed as she read. "The Welsh Cluster is dry, but your wages don't have to be. Rhen, is this slander against Welsh? Isn't this dangerous?"

"It's not slander, it's all true. Look," he said, pointing to the body of text that explained the decreased tax dues year over year for the last five years.

"What's this about a Desedra deal?" Jakira pointed to the juicy bit in the middle.

"Wyland told me that Welsh was working on a merge deal with Desedra for the other four dungeons because they were too big and profitable, that he needed more professional delvers there. I found no such records of any deals in the D.O.G. archives, so it's obviously false.

"That combined with the tax information, it's obvious he's about to dry up. He's setting himself up for retirement, working the people of Yu to the bone while he makes land purchases in Shin'Bara."

Jakira scowled and set the paper aside.

"What? This'll get at least half his delvers to defect and work for us. Half is all we need."

"What about your secret?"

"What do you mean?"

Jakira raised an eyebrow and crossed her arms. "How you've vehemently guarded your age, no one sees you shirtless—ever, and how you wouldn't answer me when I asked about your emancipation."

The breath caught in Rhen's chest.

"Rhen, I would *never* do anything to compromise your freedom, no matter how you got that id, but I have to know... did you kill him?"

Rhen sighed, the fear binding his chest releasing him.

The jig was up.

"No. I loved him like my father."

Realization donned on her. "Your sponsor."

Rhen nodded. "His illness was uncontrollable and... it came back, even after resurrections. It was as if the universe were telling him his time was up, at just twenty-nine years old. That was eleven years ago."

"And you've been pretending to be him all this time, Rhen."

"I had to visit the same dungeons he had, get the same syntials and learn his fighting method. It was a long journey and a lot of sneaking around. I sent a small payment and a letter of apology to the training school stating that I, that Maddox, had died. They didn't believe me and demanded full restitution of my debts, five thousand marks, and a loss of expertise fee of ten thousand marks.

"Seems I was worth more to them dead, but after a few years of running, they gave up. It wasn't worth their time to try and hunt Rhen down, so the Delver's Guild put a mark on his record and we all moved on."

"But if the delver school ever discovers you, Maddox, are still alive and it's Rhen that's dead…"

"My five thousand marks of debt's been accruing interest for eleven years. They would take everything from me, oh, and not to mention there are serious fines that come with impersonating another delver. The D.O.G. would have a riot with me, fine me into oblivion. I'd be working Desedra for the rest of my miserable life, all my wages garnished."

The train tooted their arrival at Yu and the speed decreased.

Jakira snapped her fingers. "If you found a new realm, no one would be able to touch you no matter the crime."

"That's the hope. I'll be rich enough to pay off whatever debts mar my record… Rhen's record."

"You wouldn't want to be Maddox again?"

Rhen watched the village pull into view. "He's dead."

"But you aren't!"

"He never even lived! I was Maddox for thirteen years. It was a name assigned to me by the school. I fought, trained, delved, and died for them as Maddox the slave. Rhen is who I really am. Never call me anything else, please."

She took her dagger to one of her horns and cut into it.

"What are you doing?" Rhen grabbed her hand.

"Making the most binding promise I can." She cut away a sliver of her horn, wincing as tears filled her eyes and blood trickled down her forehead. She handed the piece to Rhen. "I promise I'll never betray you, Rhen."

Rhen looked at the other crack in her horn with new eyes. "You've made a promise like this before. Is it a Cadrian thing?"

She chuckled. "Yeah, it's a Cadrian thing."

Rhen remembered the Cadrian guard, hornless… what had she promised?

He dismissed her from his mind. That Desedra lifer was of no importance when Jakira sat here right in front of him, bleeding. He opened his bag and ripped off the bottom of the button-down shirt he'd planned to salvage. This was a better use for it, anyway. He stood and tied the cloth around her wounded horn, then handed her the rest to wipe the blood away.

She looked up at him, eyes wide and sparkling. "Thanks."

He smiled. "It's no problem."

The train hissed to a stop, jostling Rhen back into his chair.

Jakira cleared her throat. "So, what are we going to do?"

"We're going to spread these pages all over Yu and steal Welsh's delvers. I'll suffer whatever consequences come of it after we've unlocked that Nexus node."

"And if they come sooner?"

He held up the chunk of her horn. "We'll figure it out together now, right?"

"We would've figured it out together sooner if you'd just let us in."

Rhen imagined Aki on the outside of the secret now, unaware and unable to help.

He handed half of the letters to Jakira. "Let's get these distributed quick, then get home."

Jakira went to the market side of town while Rhen went to the crafter side, starting with Wyland.

"I knew it! I tried to tell 'em!" Wyland's bushy brow nearly climbed off his face. "That damn Welsh, he ruined my business when it was all true after all!"

"What happened?"

"He called me an incompetent, irresponsible, blight of the Yu community. He commissioned an order from me for somethin' well outside his delvers' anima capacity. He used it anyway, killin' a girl and seriously wounding her father." He removed his hat, grimacing.

"Killed, like *kill* killed?"

Wyland blew a raspberry. "No, Welsh resurrected her, of course! He didn't want *his* reputation tarnished, just mine."

"What was it? The thing you made for him?"

The old crafter moved to the locked back door and motioned for Rhen to follow with a conspiratorial glimmer in his eyes. Rhen followed. Through the door and down a set of stairs Rhen found himself in an immaculate workshop, everything in its proper place, everything clean. Tools he had no name for lined the walls above workbenches covered in intricate machines.

"Whoa," Rhen gasped.

"Far cry from above, eh?" Wyland knocked his arm, then hurried over to one of the many armoires that lined the far wall. He pressed his hand on a glass panel on the front of the cabinet. It glowed to life, drawing anima from Wyland's body. There was an audible *click* and the door popped open.

Inside was a skeleton of metallic wings, folded up and attached to a thick harness.

"Anima glider, for crossing big fissures. They're only supposed to be used for short bursts. Like I said, *glider*, not flier."

"So, the man tried to fly?"

"No, he was usin' it to ferry the delvers across instead of building a permanent structure like I told him to. The man he picked to do it ran out of anima mid-glide... *Boom*." He slapped his hands together. "Miracle the man survived, not in good shape, a'course. Years of recovery, vicious scars."

They stared at the wings in silence for a moment.

"Well, thank you for showing me this. There's several more stops I have to make before I head back to the dungeon for the night, so..."

"Ah, sure. Don't need any more of this old kook's stories."

Rhen turned to him. "You're not a kook. You're brilliant."

Wyland grinned. "That's what I've been tryin' to tell ya. I'm always lookin' for work if you're willin' to pay my prices."

"I know where you sleep," Rhen said, pointing to the bed in the corner covered by a small curtain.

"Ha, so ya do! Good luck out there, sonny!"

Rhen showed himself out and he got on his way. The other businesses allowed him to post the message on their door for a small fee, and Rhen met Jakira at the inn.

They jogged home, using their abilities as they went to help train. Rhen was getting quite fond of using Tremor Blast jumps, no matter how much it hurt his feet to land. Maybe he'd sneak back into Desedra and get that Vibrational Dampening after all.

Aki was mining when they returned but came up to the inn at Rhen's beckon. They let the crafting team take a break from building out the pantry and sat Aki down by the warm hearth.

"Give us a minute?" he said to Jakira.

She nodded with a kind smile, then closed the door behind her.

Rhen took a deep breath through his nose, steeling his nerves. Aki deserved to know.

"I have something important to tell you."

"If it is about your affection for Jakira, it is fine."

Rhen waved him off. "That's not what it's about. It's about me... my, uh... gods be damned."

He fell silent and Aki waited patiently.

Just spit it out. I'm not Rhen. It's that easy.

"I knew that already," Aki said, fins fluttering.

"You... I'm sorry, you knew what?"

"That your name is not Rhen, but Maddox. You said it twice, very clearly, the first time we met."

Rhen's heart beat faster. "No, I'd thought it."

"There is no difference to me."

"No, thinking is inside my head." He tapped his temple. "And no one else but me can hear that."

"I do not have a mouth to make words like you. I use my

psionic abilities to communicate directly into your mind. I *hear* the words you say before you speak them."

Rhen suddenly felt very stupid.

"I did not understand at first, the lie of your name. The more time I spent near you, the more I realized who Rhen was. You dream of him and his kindness often. You miss him."

"I do."

Aki moved closer to Rhen and wrapped his tentacles around his neck in a slimy hug.

"You are not alone."

Rhen patted Aki's side, not really knowing how to hug him back. "Thanks, buddy."

Aki released him, then pulled the residual water off Rhen's face and back into his body.

"So, you knew *the whole time*?"

"Not the entire time, no, but before I came looking for you here. I knew exactly who you were."

"But you hid in the bushes and let me duke it out with the defiler on my own?"

"As I said, I feared your rejection."

"Can't you read my mind?"

"Yes, but not the future. You are welcoming on the surface, the words that you say, but on the inside, the words you think, you distance yourself."

"Force of habit, I guess."

"It is time for new habits."

Rhen chuckled. "That's yet to be seen. You and Jakira both could make a lot of trouble for me."

Aki hummed. "That would not serve either of our end goals."

"Wow..."

"I am just speaking logically for myself. My only chance of

continuing my pilgrimage is with you. However... I am not sure I want to continue it."

"Why not?"

"It is complicated, and I do not wish to speak of it at this time."

"Believe me when I say I understand. You can talk to me whenever you're ready, and whatever the decision is, you've got my blessing—though it'd be nice if you stayed."

"Oh, why?"

Rhen shrugged. "Well, just speaking logically for myself, it wouldn't serve my goals for you to leave."

Aki paused for a moment, then fluttered and pulsed yellow. "I see what you have done. You made my accidental insensitivity into a joke."

Rhen facepalmed. "Yeah, it's not funny anymore if you explain it."

"I will refrain from explaining the joke in the future."

"Good. Now please, remember that my identity is—"

"You do not have to say more. I understand the severity."

"Okay, okay." Rhen stood, chuckling as he headed for the door. "Too much of me is rubbing off on you, I think."

"If only the opposite were true." Aki pulsed between hot-pink and yellow, his fins beating gently against his sides. That smug little fluffer thought he was the new jokester in town.

"I am learning from the best this realm has to offer."

"I don't know if they're going to *want* you back in your home realm with a smart mouth like that." Rhen opened the door to see Jakira guarding it.

"One of the many reasons I am considering staying here, among the degenerates."

Jakira spun on her heel, pointing at Aki. "I'll degenerate your face."

Aki leaned close to Rhen. "That is a joke, yes?"

"Maybe..." Rhen grinned.

"Is there not work to be done? We should be working, I think." Aki skirted past Jakira toward the dungeon.

Jakira shouldered her club and swaggered after him. "Come on, Dungeon Owner. It's time to grind."

20

GET YOUR GRIND ON

Rhen used Tremor Blast below the terrocken junior's feet, tripping it up. The monster's feet sunk into the earth. It wobbled to the side as it tried to free itself, then collapsed. Jakira was on it in a second, bashing the side of its skull in. Her club flared green, leeching some of the life-sustaining anima out of the monster's body and into hers.

"Look out!" Olliat yelled.

Terrocken senior hadn't liked what Rhen had done to its companion—the usual behavior they had learned. The sharp-beaked vulture lunged at Rhen's face, snapping. Rhen used Swift Twitch and ducked low, slashing the area just below its beak where the feathers didn't grow.

Blood gushed from the strike, but the terrocken didn't stop coming. It picked up one massive, clawed foot and raked at Rhen. He rolled out of the way, narrowly avoiding a rending strike.

Jakira dashed forward with a heavy, underhanded swing that shattered the monster's beak with a *crack*. The terrocken flailed its arms, staggering. It must've been seeing stars, because it didn't see Rhen's next attack.

He pressed his hand against the monster's chest and triggered Tremor Blast. Its ribcage shattered, and Jakira came in for the killing blow. The monster squelched from its busted beak and dropped to the side, dead.

The second junior terrocken lunged at Aki. Olliat used her curved sickle to hook the monster's neck. She yanked hard and the creature's legs flew out from under it, kicking dirt into Aki's watery body. Aki called up the shadows of the broad leaves above them, snaring the monster and slowing its speed. With the creature incapacitated, it only took a quick stab through the eye from Olliat's offhand dagger to put it down permanently.

They'd gotten good at de-feathering the terrocken by now and were able to harvest all the feathers, the claws, and a bit of the tasty thigh meat before the creatures dissolved into the dungeon. Bort, a lanky man with a shifty gaze, slunk out of the shadows and dropped his small pack. He opened the cinch and began arranging the harvested materials.

One by one, he'd stick his arm into the small bag all the way up to his elbow and deposit the organized items. Enon syntial bags were a wonder of magic. Something so small, just the size of Rhen's head, could carry all the materials from this encounter and the three before.

They'd been exploring the rainforest chamber for two days, and Rhen was worried they'd never find the node hidden there. He pulled out his dungeon owner's map and flipped it open. His anima flowed into the parchment, activating the syntial that connected it to the Control node back in the upper chambers.

Colorful ink spread across the page, showing everywhere they'd been, every encounter he'd had, and the many dark blotches on the map that showed unexplored territory. Rhen was simultaneously excited and annoyed that the rainforest chamber was so large. If they weren't in a race against time, he'd be elated, but the Nexus window was closing in just thirty-three days, and they still didn't have an operational Resurrection node.

The good news was that another delver team had joined their cause: the Faust family. Rhen was learning that most delver crews were families out here in Yu. He supposed it made sense, but it certainly gave the campfire cookouts a more *familial* feel. It only took a few days for the Nilson family to warm up to Rhen and realize he wasn't trying to trick them or manipulate them.

Rhen had offered all the delvers thirty percent of what the dungeon pulled, split evenly among them. It was necessary for him to emphasize that the inn crafting team was just as important as the mining teams, who were just as important as the delving team.

Everyone shared, including Rhen, and the rest went back into building the dungeon village, crafting interior elements, and even putting power into the nodes for new ability discoveries. He was reserving a large amount for the Resurrection node too. He wanted to make absolutely sure that there was enough anima to resurrect everyone in the raid team, just in case no one made it.

Bort finished cleaning up and tied off the bag. He stuffed it in a larger backpack, then strapped himself in. "About an hour of anima on the bag."

Rhen nodded. If the Enon bag ran out of anima, the spell that allowed for near-infinite storage capacity would end. The bag would explode, feathers would fly, and then the dungeon would reclaim its energy. It would take about twenty minutes to get out from here, so they still had a little time.

"We'll head back soon. There's one more little nook I wanted to check."

Rhen's finger traced the map until he found the opening in the retaining wall he'd marked the day before. It may have just been a tunnel into a new chamber, which would be great of course, but not helpful *right now*. He needed that Resurrection node.

"It's about ten minutes away—"

The gold light around them dimmed, shifting to orange. Every tree in the forest simultaneously shuddered, their broad leaves vibrating. The birds' songs ended, and suddenly, all was very quiet.

"What... was that?" Jakira held her bloodied club up to one shoulder, ready to swing.

Rhen looked up. The glowing crystals that provided warmth and light had shifted from white to gold over the hour before, but the shift was gradual, and the trees hadn't moved.

"The dungeon would not perform this activity if it was not useful for sustaining this ecosystem. The light shifts must play an integral role for the plants."

"It may be dangerous to stay, Dungeon Owner," Olliat said, her wide eyes apprehensive.

"Okay, you guys head back to camp. I'll go on and check in that nook."

Jakira scoffed. "Like hell. I've been hunting this damned node same as you, and I want to find the bugger."

"I, too, will accompany you, to round out the party," Aki said.

Bort was already pointed toward the exit, marked by two tall palms that could be seen between the thick branches of the canopy. Olliat waffled.

Rhen patted her back. "It's okay, you're not abandoning us. Go back."

She nodded. "Yes, Dungeon Owner."

Rhen would have to break them of these blind habits soon, but for now, the obedience served him, and her. Rhen had a months'-old anima save back in Shin'Bara, and Aki had one back in his home realm, but Jakira...

"You should go back too, Jak. You don't have a res profile anywhere, and if you die, that's the end."

"But I—"

"Please. Olliat and Bort may need protection on the way out."

Jakira puckered her face in frustration. After a moment of looking like she might protest, she sighed. "Okay, let's get out of here guys, double time."

She led Olliat and Bort toward the exit, bone mace ready to smash anything in her way. But the forest was still. There were no predatory clicks and clacks, no bird calls, no insects, just the quiet rustling of leaves from the cycling air. There was no time to worry and watch them go.

Rhen motioned for Aki to follow, then took off at a jog through the forest. Aki propelled himself forward in a ring of water, perpetually surfing. He kept pace, and they made it to the tunnel offshoot in a few minutes.

"Aki, light my back." Rhen stepped into the shadowy tunnel and dropped into stealth. A soft blue glowed behind him as he sped down the tunnel.

Please, be something more than just a dead-end cave.

The tunnel sloped upward and opened to a cavern about as big as Rhen's inn. Huddled at the back in a cluster of nests made from dead leaves and mulch were five adult terrocken and at least twelve of the younglings.

Rhen slowed and Aki's light diminished.

It was near total darkness in the cavern, but the terrocken's feathers pulsed softly from anima flow, creating just enough glow to see them. There was no node, no nothing but the damn oversized chickens.

Dread pooled in the pit of Rhen's stomach.

If the apex predator of the forest was hiding, whatever was happening outside was not going to be good.

Rhen slunk back from the cavern. "We have to go, now."

"I was thinking the same thing."

Foregoing stealth, they rushed to the cave exit. Out in the rainforest chamber, the orange light had faded to deep red, giving everything an eerie aura. What that meant, Rhen wasn't sure, but he was starting to doubt whether staying behind was a good idea. The tree outside the opening shivered, the leaves trembling and the bough leaning toward them. Or was that just a trick of the red light?

As they ran, the ground trembled under Rhen's feet. Roots pulled up out of the dirt and Rhen tripped. He fell into a roll and gained his feet once more. When he looked back, the roots were snaking toward Aki. They went straight through the watery ring, but reached up for his cuttlefish body.

"Grab on!" Rhen reached for him.

Aki abandoned his water body, keeping only a small, sustaining bobble around himself. He wrapped his tentacles around Rhen's shoulders and flattened himself. As soon as Aki was secure, Rhen activated Swift Twitch and Tremor Blast, leaping into the air and out of the way of reaching roots.

He hit the ground hard and made himself speed incarnate.

Vines snapped out of the sky and reached for him. Rhen was panting too hard to infuse his breath, so he let the vines have it with Tremor Blast. Red anima exploded from the vines and sparkled up into the heavens.

"Get behind me!" Rhen heard a voice through the crashing of trees.

"Left twenty degrees. They are in danger."

Rhen dodged a dropping branch trying to obstruct his path, then leapt over a felled tree. Another branch cracked over a thick trunk ahead, and Rhen realized that not all the attacks were aimed at him. A tree with tan bark and green vines whipped at a tall palm, wrapping its vines tightly around it. The palm strained under the tan tree's tugging, until finally, it snapped. The top of the palm smashed into Rhen's path, and he vaulted it.

"Rhen! Aki!" Jakira screamed, her call desperate.

Rhen pushed himself faster, blasting branches out of his way as he exploded through the warring forest. In a small clearing beside the main stream of the chamber, Bort crouched at the center of a maelstrom of blades and green anima. Olliat used her daggers to slash at stray vines and Jakira batted away branches with her club.

"What the hell is happening?" Jakira roared, triggering Defender's Cry as she did.

"The trees are mad!" Rhen leapt into the fray, cutting down a vine reaching for Olliat.

"Why can they even move in the first place?" Olliat's cry was loaded with incredulity.

"I believe it is associated with the dimming of the crystals." Aki slipped off Rhen's back and sucked up some of the stream water, crafting a new body.

"Do tell," Rhen said.

There was a deep, whining *snap* and the tree atop a hill near the stream tipped toward them. The fat trunk careened toward the party, but they were too spread out to run the same direction.

"Head's up!"

Rhen grabbed Bort and dragged him out of the way. The tree crashed into the water, branches snapping and sending wood shrapnel out in all directions. The party was split—Jakira and Olliat on one side, Aki, Rhen, and Bort on the other.

Wild arboreal combat continued all around them. The smaller, immature trees bent their boughs and bashed against the larger mammoth trees, but their bases were thick and unyielding. Vines whipped out at Aki, exploding his watery body with a snap. Aki soared through the air and landed in the downed tree.

"Aki!" Rhen ran toward his friend.

The Prelusk was stuck in the branches, eyes closed, no water bobble surrounding his head. His fins didn't flutter, and Rhen couldn't get him to rouse.

More sapling vines snapped out at the massive, felled tree. Jakira yipped in pain, and Bort hit the sand with an *oof!* But the vines couldn't reach Rhen, nestled among thick leaves and branches.

"Everyone under the tree!" Rhen called.

He gently pulled Aki from the branches and crawled toward the stream. The tree trunk crossed the stream, leaving an open space just below on the shallower banks. Rhen rushed Aki to the water and held him under.

"Come on, buddy, breathe—or whatever it is you do!"

Jakira splashed into the water beside him. "Aki! Is he okay?"

"He's not moving!"

She put her hands under Rhen's, cradling Aki's tentacles. "Wake up, Aki! We need you!"

The last vestiges of blood-red light from the crystals above winked out of existence, leaving the party in loud, terrifying darkness. Rhen wrapped his other arm around Jakira, the three of them hip deep in the stream.

For thirty seconds of eternity, it was chaos. Trunks whined and roots snapped as massive trees fell. Deep rumbles vibrated out through the forest as trees collided, their branches splitting and spitting shards into the black. Then it stopped.

Leaves fell all around them, making soft *splats* as they hit the cluttered forest floor until...

Silence.

"Aki, get up," Rhen urged, shaking him.

His skin glowed a very faint blue and his fins fluttered. "I seem to have involuntarily fallen unconscious."

Rhen smiled. "That tree spanked you right out of your body."

They crawled out from under the tree, Aki conjuring up another water body for himself. After a moment he seemed to shake off the blackout and return to normal.

"Just what the hell was that, Dungeon Owner?" Bort asked, accusation in his tone.

"I don't know. I've never seen a dungeon do that."

Sparkling anima drifted up from the hundreds of down trees, their bodies dissolving into the dungeon once more. It looked the same as when Rhen fell backwards through the sky on goddess fruit. The whole forest was alight with the massacre, and Rhen could see what the damage was.

All of the tallest trees—including the ones they had used to mark the dungeon exit—had been ripped from their roots and pummeled to death. But a glint of white caught his eyes and Rhen focused on it.

There, in the distance, was the glow of a node.

Finally.

Rhen whooped. "There it is! Come on!"

He took off across the annihilated forest, bouncing over fallen trees, feeling like he was on cloud nine.

"Rhen, wait!"

"It's just right here!"

He ran faster, the glow in his vision getting brighter. He was making such a racket, he didn't hear what Jakira yelled next, but he certainly felt whatever she was screaming about when it hooked a claw into his shoulder.

21

DOWNPOUR

Pain lanced through Rhen's shoulder, and he was hauled into the air. Rhen pulled his crescent blade from its holster and slashed at anything he could above his head. There was a monstrous hiss and the claw's grip slipped. Rhen's flesh ripped, and he dropped back to the forest floor.

Rhen rolled onto his back, both weapons poised to slash at the sky. Creatures as silent as the night sailed overhead, long black cloaks of mist trailing behind them. They had three sets of hooked claws dangling from the sides of their bodies, but unlike a sky predator, their claws were turned inward.

One of the monsters ghosted down and latched its claws on either side of a fat tree trunk. It lifted with all its might and two more creatures joined in. They hovered in midair, no flapping wings to be seen, and feasted on the wood. Mouths opened all along their bellies and they forced their bodies against the trunk. Thousands of razor-sharp teeth shifted back and forth, cutting into the wood and stripping the trunk down in seconds.

Sawdust fluttered to the ground all around Rhen as he watched, horrified to think that could've been him.

"Are you okay?" Jakira asked, dropping to Rhen's side.

"Mostly fine, just, holy hell. Look at that." He pointed to the tree feasting.

Aki sloshed up to Rhen's side, and healed his shoulder with cool, green mist. "We must get to the Resurrection node. It is too far to the exit. We must save anima profiles, now."

"Don't have a lot of hope for our survival, huh?" Rhen rotated his shoulder, feeling the stab reduce to a sting. When the wound was mostly healed over, Rhen came up to a crouch.

"I'll blast fire ahead, Aki, use Shadow Snare behind, and we'll all run like hell. Got it?"

Rhen could hear their nervous agreements. He climbed to his feet and put himself in front, then sucked down a deep breath.

Inferno.

He charged forward, blowing a searing gout of flames into the sky as he did. Rhen tripped on a log, but Jakira caught him. She wrapped her arm around his waist and guided him through the mess while he breathed fire.

The monsters—hexawraiths he'd dubbed them quickly—ghosted away from the flames, dropping their trees in the process. Heavy *thunks* sent wood shrapnel flying and tossed felled branches into the air on impact.

"That's not helping!" Jakira yelled and punched a falling branch out of their path.

"I noticed," Rhen wheezed, then sucked down a painful breath.

He activated his light breath instead, and instantly regretted it. The spell illuminated hundreds of the terrifying hexawraiths. They swarmed the free-floating anima and absorbed it into their blackened bodies.

A particularly bloated hexawraith charged Rhen and Jakira. Rhen did the only thing he could and gave it a powerful Tremor Blast. The creature exploded in a shower of warm water, knocking them to the ground. Its little crystal core rolled to a stop at Rhen's feet, and he jammed it into his pocket.

They were only a few paces from the Resurrection node now. Rhen gained his feet once more, dragging the others up with him. They climbed the muddy hill on hands and knees while hexawraiths ripped the dead branches from the ground, pulverizing them into dust.

Rhen reached the top and stretched out for the node, placing his hand on the slippery surface.

[Congratulations – Rhen Zephitz!]

You have claimed a Resurrection node! The D.O.G. has been informed of your progress.

You may restrict access to the node at any time—

=====

"Stop it! Give me Resurrection Control!"

[Resurrection Control Center]

Allow anima profile saves: Disabled
Allow all saves to immediately resurrect upon death: Disabled
Allow expedited gestation: Disabled
Allow—

=====

"Enable all!" Rhen screamed. He reached back and pulled Jakira up to the node with his other arm.

[Resurrection Control Center]

Enable all Resurrection node abilities. Cost: 2,050 per anima profile.
Current anima reserve: 41,837/102,050
{Confirm} {Decline}

=====

"Confirm!"

Jakira got her hand to the node, and so did Bort. Rhen pulled Olliat up next. Aki climbed the node pedestal and laid a tentacle on the crystal.

"Save all profiles!"

The node flashed brightly, sending hot anima down all their arms to their id syntials. Hexawraiths descended all around, hissing and clawing. The bright light and transfer of anima must've attracted them!

Claws raked over his back and Jakira screamed in pain beside him, but they all held tight to the Resurrection node. Fat raindrops fell from the sky, making the node pedestal slick. A claw caught under Rhen's arm and lifted it off the node right as the anima save completed.

Rhen turned and gave the monsters another thick blast of inferno breath, but the rain dampened his range and power. The hexawraiths sucked up the spell, their bodies glowing like rainbows.

"We have to get out of here!"

Jakira swung her club at the nearest monster, bursting its belly. Warm water splashed across the hillside and the other hexawraiths scooped up the defeated one's core, eating it greedily.

A flash of light burst overhead from one of the crystals, illuminating the chamber but for a second. An opening in the cavern wall blazed in the afterlight on Rhen's eyes.

"Cave!" Olliat yelled and pointed to the spot along the wall.

"There are terrocken in that cave." Aki said.

"Better than out here!" Rhen swiped at a hexawraith that got too close. It backed off a measure, then surged forward. Rhen hit it with Tremor Blast, exploding its water-bloated body. The explosion sent him tumbling backwards down the muddy hill. His head struck a tree, and his hearing went tinny.

Pink light filled up his vision, then beautiful blues and greens.

"Run!" Aki shook the world with his cry.

The hexawraiths swarmed the Prelusk, his aura of anima drawing in a feeding frenzy. Aki conjured the water about him into a massive sphere, then charged down the hill, pulling the monster swarm with him.

"Aki, no!" Jakira screamed, chasing after him.

Olliat ran down the hill to where Rhen lay, his head spinning. She jerked him up to stand and put his arm over her shoulder. Bort did the same, and they stumbled toward the cave entrance.

Rhen's ears popped, and his vertigo vision ended with a snap. He looked over his shoulder to see Aki deftly evading all the monsters, keeping to the center of his huge orb of water while rolling around the forest. Jakira was not far behind him, bashing her club into anything that got in her way.

"Wait." Rhen pulled himself out of their grasp.

"We need your protection, Dungeon Owner," Olliat said, fear in her wide eyes.

Rhen stood at the mouth of the cave, mind torn in two. Olliat and Bort were his responsibility as the delve leader. If he, Aki, and Jakira all died, the dungeon operation would be without a leader for at least a week... his dungeon would be vulnerable to Welsh.

Rhen turned back to the cave and urged them inside. He stopped at the mouth and dropped into stealth, watching Aki lose his glow little by little while the hexawraiths fed on him. Jakira cried out, but Rhen couldn't see her anywhere on the ground.

"No, damn you, fluffers!" She was hovering above Aki, claws gripping her sides.

She gave a gurgling scream and Rhen saw blood rain down into Aki's water, turning it black. Rhen closed his eyes, nauseated as her scream slowly faded. Then, the glow of Aki's magic faded, too. Rhen opened his eyes. The pounding rain was all he could hear or see.

"It'll be okay," Olliat said, laying a gentle hand on his shoulder. "They'll respawn soon."

Rhen wanted to throw her hand off his shoulder and scream at the gods.

He'd *let them die.*

He'd just sat here. And he hadn't even watched the consequences of his choices...

"Yeah," Rhen said, jaw clenched.

Olliat backed away. She took a seat next to Bort, leaning against the cavern wall and watching the rain.

"Ten minutes left on the Enon bag," Bort reported.

Rhen ground his teeth. Why in the realms would he care about something like that right now? He refrained from asking Bort, knowing that thought was driven by anger that wasn't Bort's fault.

Rhen took a deep breath and closed his eyes. He had to do what he could now.

He got up and then sat next to Bort. "Give me a bag. Let's unpack. We can't risk damaging them."

They got to work, organized at first, but hastily as the timer on the bag counted down. By the end of it, they were surrounded by piles of feathers, claws, meat, ores, gems, and monster cores. The only benefit was *maybe* the smell of the feathers and meat would keep the terrockens far away from them.

As the first half-hour elapsed in the darkness, Rhen found himself getting weary. Olliat took the first watch, letting them sleep for four hours before rousing Rhen from a weary, nightmare-filled sleep. Two hours into his shift, the rain began to slow and the flashes of light from the crystals above increased in frequency. It was as if they were trying to restart. By the third hour, it had become a gentle drizzle.

It hadn't escaped Rhen that Aki had saved an anima profile, something the Prelusk had said was against the laws of his people. He wondered, with his ample time waiting out the black storm, what sort of consequences Aki would face.

The crystal ceiling came to life with orange-pink light, waking the others. The crystals became brighter and brighter, illuminating the forest. Suddenly, hundreds of the trees and bushes glowed and pulsed with white light. They grew in size, their limbs healing and flowers blooming.

Rhen looked on the regenerated forest with awe. Aki had been right about the closed ecosystems needing balance. What a violent balance the rainforest chamber had achieved.

Rhen heard the distant voice of Joseph calling through the trees. "Olliat! Bort!"

"We're here!" Olliat yelled in return.

Rhen put a hand over her mouth, but it was too late. The deep *click-click-clack* reverberated off the walls behind them.

"Let's go!"

Bort stammered. "But the materials—"

"Leave it!"

Rhen hoisted Bort to his feet and they ran into the flooded forest.

"Where are ya!" Joseph yelled again.

The splashing of heavy footfalls were loud in Rhen's ears but he could still hear the thunder of fat, terrocken thighs behind him. He spun around and unleashed Tremor Blast at the ground, splashing water into the air.

Cold. He exhaled hard, freezing the water into a solid wall of ice.

The terrocken crashed through the wall, shards of ice stabbing into its gut. It dropped to the ground, tripping the next closest pursuer. Rhen whirled back around and chased after the others.

Joseph appeared between the trees, relief washing over his face. Olliat ran into his open arms and he lifted her off the ground in a huge hug. There were three other delvers with Joseph, smiles on their faces.

"No time for that! Keep running!" Rhen yelled.

Joseph's eyes bulged when he caught sight of their pursuers. He grabbed Olliat's hand and pulled her along. They stumbled their way through the forest, following the rope the delvers left to find their way back.

Somewhere along the way, the terrocken gave up the chase, but Rhen couldn't slow down. They ran all the way back to the cavern exit, then collapsed on the cool stone of the traversing tunnel.

"What happened?" Joseph demanded angrily, shaking Rhen's shoulders.

And why shouldn't he? His daughter's life was on the line.

Rhen couldn't breathe, his throat still raw from fire and ice.

"Tell me!"

Olliat pulled her father away. "We were heading back, the chamber changed. We fought and found a Resurrection node!

But Aki and Jakira died... Rhen protected us through the night."

The last part was a stretch since Rhen was certain it was the scent of the terrocken's own blood that spooked it off enough. Joseph relaxed, his shoulders falling away from his ears.

"I, uh... sorry." Joseph patted Rhen on the back.

"We need to get to that node, protection detail," Rhen croaked. "They'll be naked and vulnerable when they respawn."

"Sir." Joseph nodded.

Rhen trudged last in line up to the dungeon exit. Devastation dragged his mind back to the rainforest, Jakira's screams, Aki's fading light. He'd done *nothing*.

Not anymore. He'd rather die than hear her screaming again.

Rhen went to the coffers at the master chamber. They were nearly full of Lafite, gems, and other minerals. Good, they were going to need everything they had.

"Listen up." Rhen clapped his hands and pulled the attention of everyone in the room. "We located the Resurrection node."

The group cheered, save for Joseph, Bort, and Olliat. Everyone knew the Resurrection node had been a big item on Rhen's to-do list, but had no idea what had happened.

He quieted them with an upraised hand. "We don't have control of the node. It's surrounded by monsters, and two of our own are waiting on respawn. They *will* respawn as soon as they are ready, which could be hours, or days. If we're not there when they do, the monsters will tear them apart."

"What do we do?" Eli asked.

"We need a master craftsman, fast."

22

BURY THE HATCHET

All mining operations had stopped, and round-the-clock shifts had been posted at the Resurrection node. Everyone saved an anima profile, and Rhen adjusted the setting so that they could afford to resurrect everyone if they died. It affected the speed of Jakira and Aki's resurrection, which Rhen could track from the Control node.

Three more days... that's how long he would be without them. But that was almost a good thing. He didn't want them respawning into the middle of a terrocken battle. They needed a more sustainable solution than a constant five-man guard posted, and he knew just where to go to get it.

Wyland.

Rhen made it to town in record time, out of breath. He went to open the door to Wyland's shop, but it was locked. He knocked, waited, knocked, waited, then started banging on the door nonstop.

After the third full minute of Rhen pounding and calling for Wyland, he opened the door, a deep scowl wrinkling his brow. "What could be so urgent to interrupt my teatime?"

"I'm sorry, truly. My friends died after saving their anima

profile, and we barely have control of the node. We're being attacked by monsters every hour, and we know there's an event in that chamber that wreaks a lot of havoc, but don't know when it will hit again. I need a creative solution for safe resurrection that doesn't require a constant guard within three days."

"Three!" Wyland laughed.

"Can you do it?"

Wyland frowned. "Said I wouldn't poke my nose in any dungeons again..."

"Please, sir, it won't be like Welsh. I'll listen to you."

The old man scratched his chin with his mechanical arm. "You got Lafite?"

"Yes."

"Telzonite?"

"No, I don't think so."

"Lafite's good enough I 'spose. All right, let me get a few things." Wyland opened the door and beckoned Rhen inside.

Rhen followed him down to his shop and milled about while the old man got ready. He wheeled a cart around his workshop, grabbing this tool and that, nothing Rhen really recognized besides oversized pliers. He wasn't a crafter himself but did find all that fascinating. If he hadn't developed such a passion for delving, he'd likely have become a crafter after earning his freedom.

"Help me with this portable smelter, would ya?" Wyland fluffed out a wide-mouthed pack and stood beside a waist-high cylinder with many knobs covering its surface. It had a lid that seemed to lock in place, and a large inner bowl that had been blackened by use.

Rhen stood beside Wyland and helped him fit the mouth of the bag over the top of the smelter. As soon as the top of the smelter passed the cinch it shrank and distorted, almost as if it were being stretched.

"How?"

The rest of the bag fit over it easily and Wyland smiled. "Enon syntials are a wonder."

"But where is the syntial?" Rhen looked all over the sack, but saw nothing.

Wyland pulled on the string that would close the bag. It flared a brilliant red at his touch. Six mandala-like inkings revealed themselves around the top of the bag, and then disappeared after a moment.

"They're the least understood of the syntial types, but so essential. I'll teach you 'bout 'em sometime… for a fee." Wyland winked.

"I'd happily pay it."

He gathered the rest of his tools, opting to shove the entire cart into the sack instead of dropping each tool in individually. Wyland passed the bag to Rhen. "You carry this one."

He went to his bed and stuffed a few shirts and other items into another, smaller backpack. Wyland slung the pack over his shoulder and looked around at his space.

"Okey dokey, let's hit the road."

"Wait, you're going out to the dungeon?"

"Whatdja think we were packing for?"

"I…"

"If you need it fast, there's no time for me to go out, survey the space, craft a design, come back here, build it, go out there, test it, yadda yadda yadda. If I'm there, bing, bang, boom, we'll get it done."

"That makes sense, though, I'm not sure if that will require delving paperwork signed by the Guild."

Wyland waved his hand dismissively and headed for the stairs. "I have no intentions of mining or monster hunting, and those are the two big no-no's if you don't have papers. C'mon, daylight's wasting."

Wyland shuttered everything up tight on their way out, activating the same anima locks on the workshop door and the front door of the shop before they left. They were on the path toward Rhen's dungeon when it struck him. Money.

"I really appreciate you doing this, but we haven't discussed a rate," Rhen said, apprehensive. He knew Wyland was good, so it wasn't the quality of craftsmanship that was the issue... or maybe it was. His work was *too* good, and therefore too expensive.

"I'll be usin' all your materials, you'll be puttin' me up and feeding me, protectin' me, oh and I'll need a couple apprentices—gophers."

"Gophers?"

"Yeah, you know, go fer this, go fer that, someone to hold the cast steady, etcetera."

"Sure, we have several delvers that can help, but what about your rate?"

"Impatient. I could tell by the way ya nearly banged down my door! I'm gettin' there, sonny. With all those things accounted for, you're just payin' for my expertise and time, so let's say thirty marks."

Rhen was shocked. "Total?"

Wyland's laugh filled up the whole forest. "No, sonny, per hour. 'Course you only pay when I work. I'll need breaks for sleepin' and eatin'; I am just a man, after all."

Thirty an hour was steep, but Rhen knew it'd be worth it. "Okay, agreed."

"No fuss? Huh. I expected you to counter with twenty or somethin'. Thirty it is! Now, where's this dungeon?"

Rhen shook his head, smiling. Damn kook had gotten him good.

"We're still a few miles out. It's to the south past the waiting tree."

"Better pick up the pace," Wyland said, then took off at a jog. He was surprisingly fit for his age. Rhen wondered if Wyland hadn't faked some of his feebleness for his own ends. What a clever ploy.

Rhen caught up to him easily and kept pace beside him, always watching for trouble. They made it to the dungeon in an hour, the sun already on its way down to the horizon.

Joseph had built a good-sized fire outside the inn. He'd also positioned some sitting rocks around it and dropped down onto one. He was roasting his feet and shoveling back soup. Joseph's voracious eating stopped when he saw Rhen and Wyland.

Joseph pointed to Wyland with his spoon. "What's *he* doing here?"

"He's going to build us something to protect the Resurrection node."

Joseph jumped to his feet, a furious grimace pulling at his lips. He jammed the spoon at Wyland's chest. "I don't want you anywhere near us, you hear me?"

Wyland nodded. "I hear ya, sir."

Joseph returned to the fire to eat and stare daggers at Wyland. His scars stood out to Rhen for the first time. He'd thought Joseph had earned them after years of being a bruiser, but now he saw differently. There were scars all up his fingers, and some of his nails were missing. The scar running up his face ran from chin to cheek, but only on one side.

Then it hit him. Joseph must've been the man ferrying delvers in Welsh's dungeon. When he lost control, he must've hit the wall of the dungeon, dug his fingers into it to slow his descent... after he'd dropped his daughter.

Olliat emerged from the inn carrying a tray loaded with bowls full of stew and a fresh baked loaf. She smiled when she saw Rhen, but her expression melted to worry when she saw

Wyland. She looked to her father, then stopped and set the tray on one of the sitting rocks.

"You can't be this way forever."

"Like hell. He got you killed."

"No, he didn't. Stop spreading your guilt around onto other people and get over it."

Joseph grabbed the loaf of fresh bread and chewed off a hunk, his death glare never wavering from Wyland.

"Unbelievable." Olliat grabbed two bowls and brought them over.

Rhen accepted the bowl and took a sniff. Smelled like father's fennel and terrocken thigh. The broth was thick and reddish, and there were other chunks of what looked like potato floating around in it. Rhen took a taste. The sour broth made his jaw clamp down, but he forced himself not to pucker his lips. Olliat was watching.

"Thanks, s'good," Rhen managed to say through clenched teeth.

He missed Jakira...

She chuckled. "It's better with bread... if my dear father would share!"

Joseph ripped off another hunk. "Need my fill for the dive. I'm night shift."

Olliat rolled her eyes. "You two sit, there's another loaf that should be ready soon."

"Thank you, dear." Wyland put himself on the opposite side of the fire from Joseph, making it difficult for him to glare without staring straight into the flames.

Olliat turned back at the door to the inn. "It's good to see you well, Wyland."

He raised his bowl to her. "Good to see you well, too."

Rhen wasn't going to touch this one. There'd be no quarrel if they didn't cross one another's paths. But still, Rhen realized he would need to start making rules of conduct for the village and the delvers who frequented it. No brawling would have to be at the top of that list.

So much to do.

After a few minutes, Olliat came back out with another loaf. Rhen and Wyland chowed down on the sour soup with its confused flavor palate, stuffing bread in after to soak up the taste. It wasn't the worst meal Rhen had ever had, but that wasn't saying a lot. They needed to start farming more ingredients.

So.

Much.

To do.

Rhen breathed deeply and reminded himself, *one thing at a time*. Build a protection solution for the Resurrection node. First things first, let Wyland inspect the area and form a plan.

Rhen drained the last of the broth from his bowl. "We should get down there."

"Lead the way, sonny!"

Rhen and Wyland curved through the dungeon down to the rainforest chamber. The delvers had set up a simple rope wayfinder solution by staking branches into the ground and tying the rope off around it. They'd painted the sticks and rope red to help them stand out. It was smart, but one more night of chaos would undo all of it.

The terrocken were learning that the delvers were dangerous prey, unlike the smaller creatures of the forest, and so he didn't think they'd be ambushed. Just in case, Rhen stayed on high alert and in full view of whatever may have lurked in the forest surrounding the path. He was ready to make trouble for anything dumb enough to try and stop them.

Rhen pushed through the last bit of underbrush to see the guard team had cleared the ground level bushes and branches from around the Resurrection node. It was much easier to protect from ambush now that they could see more than five feet into the forest.

"Deo," Eli said, tipping his head.

It was short for Dungeon Owner, since Rhen was adamant about them *not* calling him that. This was Eli's workaround.

"Any attacks?"

"None. What are you doing here, Wyland?" Eli asked the old man, his voice laced with scorn.

Wyland tried to smile but it looked like a wince. "Just makin' sure y'all can resurrect safely."

"Deo, this man's faulty machinery got my sister killed."

"That's only partly true," Wyland cut in before Rhen could say anything. "Yes, your father was operating my glider when they fell, but the cause was your dungeon owner's negligence in heeding my warnings, not because there was any fault with the machine."

Eli looked like he wanted to say more, but he held it in. He was younger than Olliat by a few years, only fifteen to her nineteen. It must've been difficult knowing his sister was dead but would *maybe* be resurrected when he was just a child. Thoughts like that, where death could be cheated but only if someone else flipped your bill, were terrifying.

"Wyland's machines are not perfect. They are limited, just like our magic," Rhen explained. "Tremor Blast takes a lot out of me, and I can only do so many before I can't cast anymore. Likewise, the machines that feed off our anima have limited use before we're tapped out."

Eli's shoulders slumped and he nodded.

Wyland was already walking the circumference of the cleared circle. "Hmm, good." He snapped at Rhen, "Gimme the, uh, ligimeter."

"The... what?" Rhen pulled the bag off his back and opened it up. He looked inside, his gaze roving over the miniature tools.

Wyland reached into the bag and removed a stubby cylinder with a bit of string sticking out the end.

"Hold that." He gave the string to Rhen, then pointed for him to stand at the node. Wyland walked around it, staring down at the cylinder. He stopped abruptly. "Someone mark this spot."

One of the guards used their dagger to scratch in the dirt where he pointed. They did this a few more times until there were six marks in the dirt.

"What is this all for?" Rhen asked.

Wyland chuckled. "Sonny, you're about to find out."

23

RESURRECTION

Rhen stood at one of the six transference rods imbedded in the ground around the node. The other five candidates, Olliat, Barrek, Gil, Patti, and a very reluctant Joseph stood holding the other rods. Eli, his mother, Valine, Bort, Barrek's wife, Leslie, and Caleb stood guard around them to make sure no terrockens decided to take advantage at a vulnerable moment. The Faust family had stayed topside at the inn, not wanting to get in the way.

They were all nervous, except Wyland. He looked like he'd done this a hundred times. Wyland said the rods would only need their anima to get started, but once the field was generated, the Resurrection node would handle all the load. The essential part was *getting out of the way* as soon as the field instantiated.

"All right everyone, hold onto yer butts!" Wyland called from the Resurrection node.

"I thought we were supposed to hold onto the rod!" Joseph yelled.

Wyland laughed. "That too. Three, two, one, starting up!"

The Resurrection node flared with hot, white light, and made a noise like accelerating vibrations. The cascading plate on top of the node shot into the air with a burst of illumination, propelled by Wyland's machine that was drawing off the dungeon's energy. Round and round the plate spun, accumulating anima.

A bright *zap* of power jolted from the cascade plate and hit Rhen's transference rod. Pain lanced up his arm to his chest and he pulled away from the rod.

"Not yet! It needs to connect!" Wyland yelled.

The zaps came more frequently, hitting everyone in the circle. Olliat yipped when the lightning hit her rod. A sustained stream of blue energy emerged, bouncing and dancing in the wind.

Wyland pointed to Olliat. "Let go!"

She jumped back and the color of the lightning shifted to white. Joseph's rod connected next, and then everyone else in turn. They jumped into the circle and joined Wyland at the node. The lightning arcs to the cascade plate became stable, losing some of their lightning type energy. A connecting line moved from rod to rod, spiraling up to the top of the plate.

The vibration accelerated until it was almost deafening.

"If we die, I'm killing you, Wyland!" Joseph screamed.

Wyland guffawed. "And when we don't die, you owe me a brew!"

Anima flashed faster and faster all around them, and Rhen's eyes started to cross. There was a *crack!* and the vibrations disappeared along with the flashing lights.

Surrounding them now was a dome of opalescent energy, rippling like gentle waves against the shore. It was quiet, hardly a hum in the background.

"I'll take your strongest," Wyland said, grinning at Joseph.

"I'm sure this thing'll break down any second, blow us all to bits." Joseph crossed his arms.

"Okay, show me how it works again?" Rhen stepped up to

the machine wrapped around the base of the node. There were six flat pieces of metal pinned to the crystal that aligned with the placement of the transference rods in the ground. Those flat pieces projected the anima up into the cascade plate above, but at the base of the node was a control panel.

Wyland crouched beside it. "Put your finger right there on that glassy bit."

Rhen did as instructed, and all the buttons on the panel lit up. There was a directional pad on the left, two toggles on the right, and a big round button at the top.

"Up targets up gate, down targets down gate. Toggle 1 is open doorway. Toggle 2 is open window—if you want to shoot an arrow out it. Circle is execute command. Each command will have a small extra anima charge, but on the whole, this thing only takes 'bout ten, maybe fifteen anima an hour."

Rhen stammered. "That's unbelievable. How is it so efficient?"

"Well, it's not *consuming* the anima, like our spells do; it's recycling it. Some is just lost by bein' exposed. 'Course when it gets attacked, that'll be a different matter. Probably five to ten anima per average melee strike. Want to try it out?"

"Please."

Rhen selected the "Up" gate, flipped the door toggle, and pressed the button. A split in the anima waves ran down the cascade plate and hit the "north" rod, the one pointing directly away from the chamber exit. The waves pushed back, opening a seven-foot by four-foot doorway.

Rhen stepped through the opening. The hairs on his arms stood on end as he passed through, and his skin prickled with a feeling of raw power.

The door snapped shut behind him and Rhen whirled around.

"Throw a rock!" Wyland yelled.

Rhen found the closest stone of decent size. He didn't want to throw a pebble, the effect had to be visible. He wanted Joseph to be satisfied with its safety, too.

Finally, he found a good head-sized rock. He held it up and chucked it at the shield. The stone smacked into the opal barrier, sending ripples across it. The rock cracked, and when it hit the ground, it was split in six pieces.

"Wicked..." Rhen whispered.

"Okay, now come back in."

"How?"

"Just walk on through!"

"I don't want to split apart, thanks."

"You won't! If your anima profile is saved to the node, you can walk right through without making a door or a window, from either side."

Rhen sucked in a deep breath and reached out for the shield. His hair stood on end and his fingers vibrated the closer they got. Well, if he died, at least he'd respawn in safety.

He lurched forward, just to get it over with. His hand passed straight through and into the powerful dome. Where the shield touched his forearm, the skin tickled, like after using an anima drill for too long.

Rhen stepped all the way through and Olliat clapped. "You're a genius, Wyland!"

The old man beamed. "I know."

"And this won't interfere at all with respawning?" Rhen asked.

"Not a bit. I've installed this type of machine in Desedra dungeons, function great."

"None of the ones I've been in..."

"Ha, bet not. These are rare, restricted dungeons with epic syntials and rewards, not the money pits."

Rhen scowled, but it made sense. No need to set up such a

machine on a Resurrection node that was easily guarded and under control, which was the case for most of the so-called money pits.

"So, why'd you make the door at all if we can just walk through it?" Joseph asked, his hand halfway through the shield.

Wyland sighed. "How would'ya get new people in here to connect with the node?"

Joseph opened his mouth, then shut it with a grimace of defeat.

"Now, I gotta warn ya. You said during the dark chaos that the creatures who came out fed on anima, izzat right?"

"I think so. Aki activated his soothing aura ability, which is supposed to make him less desirable to enemies, but it projects a field of anima around him. Instantly, they were on him like a dog on vomit."

Wyland nodded. "So, yer gonna want to be ready to deactivate this shield when that happens. I dunno if those monsters'll eat up all the dungeon anima. It's raw, and that might not be what they feed on... but just be prepared, cause if they do consume it all, no more respawns for you."

"Understood. We'll need to learn more about these dark cycles, but I believe the color changing of the crystals is what kicks it off. If so, we'll have a few hours of warning. I can change the respawn controls so that no one will respawn without my explicit permission, so that'll at least prevent people from spawning in that time."

"Good'nuff." He crouched next to the control panel again. "To cycle it down, flip both toggles and press down on the execute button for five seconds. You'll need seven people to start it back up again, and you just do it exactly the same way."

"Got it."

Rhen stood and watched the others messing with the shield.

They jumped in and out of it, giggled like kids at their staticky hair, and stared in awe.

One more thing down.

A million to go.

Jakira and Aki would respawn in a little less than two hours, and since everyone else was in the dungeon already, Rhen thought it was high time they do a bit of grinding. He broke them into two groups, Joseph taking Eli, Barrek, Leslie, and Caleb while Rhen took Olliat, Valine, Gil, and Pattie. Wyland stayed behind, relaxing in the shield for the time being—getting paid, of course.

It wasn't hard to find the terrocken nests now that Rhen had recognized the tracks they made in the dirt, and how to see their passing in the leaves. Even stealthed, Rhen could find a pair of terrocken hidden fifty feet away.

The oversized chickens were becoming fewer and fewer in the region near the Resurrection node, which was good, but also troubling. If their hunting of those monsters altered the ecosystem in the chamber, the whole thing could collapse. They'd have to be careful, and make sure they were appropriately balancing the terrocken's absence by killing and eating their prey themselves.

But not too much...

Dungeon management was a whole nother level of overwhelming. Not only did he have to manage the nodes, the village above, the trade, signing papers for join requests, on and on, but now he had to make sure the dungeon chambers with ecosystems were properly balanced. Rhen was starting to doubt whether he could've managed the Desedra dungeons better than they had.

After two encounters, it was time to head back to the Resurrection node. He gathered two big buckets of water for Aki, and had a nice, thick blanket ready for Jakira—as well as all the gear she'd left behind when her body dissolved into the dungeon. The jerkin had been shredded to pieces, but everything else made it well enough.

The Resurrection node vibrated with a deep bass feel in Rhen's chest. A slice of white energy appeared hanging in midair that popped open to an abyssal portal. The circle of energy around the black doorway whipped erratically, spinning at high speed.

Jakira's dark feet dangled out of the opening and Rhen positioned himself under it to catch her. She slopped out, covered in primordial respawn goo, naked as the day she was born. Rhen caught her and dropped to his knees, wrapping her up swiftly.

Jakira turned and coughed up more of the pink slime that coated her skin. She gasped and opened her eyes, gaze falling on Rhen's face.

"Welcome back." He smiled.

"Ouch," she whimpered, closing her eyes again.

"Catch him!" Eli growled at Olliat, who was holding one of the buckets up to the other portal.

Aki plopped into the basin and Olliat brought it down to the ground. After a few seconds, Aki emerged, conjuring a watery body about himself from the other bucket. It wasn't quite as much water as he was used to, and so his body was only about four feet tall.

Jakira rubbed her eyes and sat up. "What's happened since... since, ugh, it's hard to remember. The teeth. Lots of teeth."

"Lots of teeth, indeed." Aki remarked. "Is that how we met our end?"

Rhen nodded. "You saved us. But nothing like that has happened again down here. It's been a little over three days. Wyland came out to help build this shield to protect the respawn area."

"Neato burrito." Jakira moaned with desire. "I want a burrito."

"Before food, let's go get some new abilities. Once someone is registered with the Resurrection node, I can see their anima capacity; we're all ready for upgrades."

"Burriiitoooo," she groaned with hunger.

Rhen laughed. "All right, food first."

Everyone turned away to let Jakira dress, and then they made their way to the exit. By the time they reached the megahound room, Rhen knew something was wrong. Everyone was with him, but there was smoke—lots of smoke—wafting into the dungeon. Wait, no... the Faust family had stayed behind.

Rhen broke into a jog, worried something had happened and the Fausts needed help. Aki was right beside him, keeping pace.

Hazy red light shone down on the dungeon opening and white smoke billowed into the tunnel. Rhen held his breath and climbed the ladder up to a raging inferno. The entire field was alight. Trees around the inn burned wildly, and Rhen couldn't see an inch of his plot that wasn't covered in flames.

"Aki!" Rhen cried out for his friend. *We need to get to the river.*

The Prelusk latched onto Rhen's neck and surrounded them both in a thin layer of water. Rhen took another breath before the liquid protected his face. He ran through the flames, his feet burning with every step. Fire licked at his limbs and heated the water that protected them both. Rhen hoped they wouldn't boil alive before he could get them to the river.

He climbed up the dirt embankment and cleared the wall of flames. They collapsed into the river and Rhen gasped for air. Aki was back up in an instant, using his full psionic powers to whip lances of water at the biggest flames. Aki doused fire after fire until only a few patches of smoldering embers remained.

The inn, their tents, their homes... Everything was gone.

24

BURNED AND BROKEN

Rhen walked through the soaking wreckage of his village. The inn's foundation was all that remained, just charred and cracked stone barely holding together. He crouched at the place where his tent once was and grabbed a handful of mushy ashes.

"What happened?" Jakira clutched the towel around her shoulders as if it would protect her from the hurt that came with losing everything. Rhen did the same thing, long ago, like wrapping himself in his mentor's cloak would've hidden him from the world.

"It could have been an ember from the fire pit," Aki offered. "The inn roof was highly flammable."

"Not a chance. I doused it cold with water before we left," Joseph said.

Rhen threw the ashes down and stood, his heart pumping fire through his veins. "It was Welsh."

"That's a hefty accusation to throw 'round," Wyland said. "Though *I* would believe it, yer gonna have a hard time comin' up with the evidence to do much about it in terms of the D.O.G."

Obviously, proving it would be impossible. Unless...

"Aki, if you could get in a room with Welsh and ask a few questions, you could get the truth out of him, out of his thoughts, right?"

Aki fluttered, turning blue. "Alas, the word of a Prelusk who is in your employ may not mean much to the Guild."

Rhen growled. Aki was right, of course. If there *was* any physical evidence in the wreckage, it would take days to find. And so what if he did? Welsh's dungeon was dry, so any reparations he'd be owed from a D.O.G. settlement would come too little and too late. Rhen needed to fix their living situation *now*. Just another thing cutting in front of the Nexus node, another thing needing his immediate attention.

Olliat pulled a metal frame from her tent and ashes crumbled away from inside.

"It's just stuff," Jakira said when Olliat started to cry.

She sniffled. "It was the last picture I had of my mom."

"I'm so sorry." Jakira put a comforting hand on her shoulder.

Rhen gritted his teeth. This was why he hadn't wanted to take anyone on in the dungeon. Now he was responsible for all this pain, all the things they'd lost. Rhen was their dungeon owner, he was supposed to take care of them…

Aki tried to comfort him, laying a tentacle on his shoulder like he'd seen Jakira do for Olliat. "You have been doing your best."

Angry heat filled Rhen's cheeks. "Not good enough."

"You are one man—"

"And I'd wanted to keep it that way!" He pushed away from Aki, a flurry of dark emotion culminating in his chest. "I didn't want a village. I wanted to delve my dungeon, alone. And now I have to go handle this…"

Rhen closed his eyes and took a deep breath, then another. The angry pressure that made his body feel like it would explode lessened, and he was able to think straight. The sun was directly overhead, and his stomach growled. Getting to Yu and back would put them returning right at dusk. Still, it was doable.

"Four people need to stay here, guard the dungeon entrance so they can't get to our coffers. The rest of us are going into town to buy new supplies. Who's staying?"

No one raised their hands.

"Someone needs to stay," Rhen said with more urgency.

Everyone looked at each other, shocked. No one wanted to stay in a burned-out broken village. But someone had to. Someone had to protect the dungeon.

Rhen sighed. "Fine. Jakira, Eli, Joseph, and Barrek, you stay. The rest of us will be back soon."

"Why am I staying?" Jakira whined.

"Because I said so!"

Jakira jumped, holding tighter to the cloth around her shoulders. Only the sound of crackling embers filled the space between them. Rhen saw fear in her eyes, and for the first time, he felt shame in the way he'd spoken.

He closed his eyes. "I'm sorry. You, Joseph, and Barrek are strong, and Eli is fast. If anyone or anything attacks, there's a good chance the four of you will win."

Jakira nodded, her eyes glossy. "Okay."

Rhen wanted to say more, but what? How could he make it better?

"We oughta get movin'," Wyland said.

He picked up his pack and headed to the trail back to town. Slowly, the others followed. Joseph, Eli, and Barrek sauntered back toward the dungeon, leaving Rhen and Jakira alone in the ashes. The anger turned to ice in his veins as he realized how much he'd hurt her.

"I'm sorry."

"I know."

"What... what do you want me to do?"

"Get new tents for everyone. Bring back something to eat."

"No, I mean. How can I erase what just happened?"

Her eyes narrowed. "You mean the part where you yelled at me, or when you told everyone you didn't want them here? Sorry Rhen, you can't just make those disappear."

Was that really what he'd said?

"I didn't mean it."

"You sounded like you did."

"That's just stupid. Without you, and everyone else, there's no way I'd ever stand a chance at getting to that Nexus node myself."

She scoffed. "That's what's most important. Great."

"No, but..." Rhen sighed. He might as well set himself on fire and join the ashes underfoot, that was about how highly she thought of him. There was nothing left to say that would do any good.

"I'll be back before nightfall."

Rhen turned and walked away. Jakira didn't follow or call after him. That was fine. He was angry, she was angry, it was probably best they didn't speak for a while.

They made good time back to Yu with their boat cart, and Rhen stopped at the inn first. He ordered everyone food, then got the barkeep to fill up one of his pots with enough to feed those left behind.

There weren't enough tents at the outfitters, but Leslie said she could sew something together if he got the raw materials. They picked up heavy canvas cloth and a few other supplies, then made their way to Fennica's bakery. Someone was already inside taking up all the counter space.

The sight of that familiar orange hair and beefslab arms were enough to make Rhen's heart race. The dungeon owner turned slowly at the sound of the door jingling.

"You look like you've been dragged through seven hells, boy. What ever did happen?" Welsh asked, a snarky smile on his face.

"My business is none of yours." He gritted his teeth and stepped into line behind Welsh.

"You like keeping to yourself, don't you? Not the best way to make friends..."

"I don't need friends like you."

Welsh laughed. "Seems like you do."

"What would you know about it?" Rhen could barely contain his rage. He wanted to pummel Welsh into the counter.

"Covered in ash, cart full of supplies; looks like you had a little fire incident. It's okay, happens to inexperienced dungeon owners all the time."

"Happens when a slimy welp is jealous of what he doesn't have."

Welsh feigned innocence. "You think *I* did this? Why ever would I risk my own position just to burn down a few tents and a pathetic little inn?"

He knew what they'd lost, then. Someone must've been reporting what was there. Rhen couldn't believe it was any of the families that had joined him—though the Faust family was decidedly absent...

"You didn't have the balls to come do it yourself, because you're a pathetic weasel."

Welsh frowned in distaste. "Name calling really is so childish. Despite your horrible manner, I'm willing to extend a helping hand to you and your poor delvers."

"Never on my life would I accept your help."

"And what about their lives," Welsh said, all joy leeched from his expression. "What happens when the fall freeze comes and your delvers are still living in tents? How long will they stay?"

"Stop saying *my* delvers. I don't think I own them, unlike

you. And I wouldn't worry about the fall freeze, we'll have another solution before then."

"Oh yes, the Nexus node," Welsh said with a smirk. "You think you have enough delvers for whatever threat is down there? Sleeping in tents in the cold. No kitchen to cook from. Nowhere to bathe. What kind of shape will they be in for that fight?"

"Here's your order sir," Fennica returned from the back, a tray stacked high with bags of father's fennel bread. She looked between Welsh and Rhen with sympathy.

Welsh took three of the bags off the top and thrust them at Rhen.

Rhen pushed the offering away. "I won't be owing you any favors."

Welsh tutted. "Charity for a charity case. Let me know when you've got enough *balls* to admit you need that help, before time runs out."

"What did you say?" Rhen grabbed Welsh's shirt collar, unable to hold back his rage any longer.

Welsh only smiled and pulled Rhen's hand away. "Tick-tock, or so I hear. Don't let your arrogant pride make this opportunity slip through all our fingers."

Welsh left, dropping the three charity bags on the counter.

Rhen's heart felt like it would explode if he didn't go beat the piss out of Welsh.

Don't let emotion control you. He repeated his mentor's words in his head, in his voice. It was comforting to hear him... but it was still so hard. That bastard burned down their village because he knew the Nexus node was down there. He wanted to manipulate Rhen into cutting him in for providing safety for the delvers.

If he let Welsh take advantage of them just to unlock the Nexus node, was he worthy of it? Would any of the delvers trust him if he partnered with the very man who'd burned down their homes? Rhen wouldn't.

"You okay, love?" Fennica asked.

"Fine."

But he wasn't fine. He wanted to rage. He wanted to pull down the system that had put Welsh in power and made him the way he was. He wanted revenge for Olliat's picture, and Barrek's tables, and Leslie's drapes. And he didn't want to share that Nexus node with anyone but the people who had *earned* it.

It wasn't about pride. It was about doing what was right.

Opening the Nexus was important to him but keeping Welsh's grubby hands off a new world was more important. He wouldn't let a Desedra have partial control of a whole realm, and Welsh was just like them. If the Nexus slipped through any fingers but his own, it would be for the best.

But he wasn't going to let it slip.

Rhen took a deep breath and let his anger fuel his determination. "I'll take ten rejuvenating loaves please."

25

ZEPHITZ INN

Rhen was quiet on the way back, thinking through his speech. He had a lot to apologize for, but apologies wouldn't win them over—a plan would. He had that, but how to present it... especially when it relied heavily on Wyland's machines?

Maybe he should let his actions do the talking, first? No, that would be weird. He had to tell them what he was thinking.

They arrived just before dark and Rhen called them all down into the Control node chamber. Jakira, Barrek, Joseph, and Eli, famished from waiting so long to eat, were digging into the food they'd brought while Rhen gathered his courage to speak.

"Rebuilding the inn won't work right now, we don't have time. I'm sure some of you have been hearing Jakira, Aki, and me talking about the raid, and that it's important... time dependent. It's not just a Nexus node. It's an unexplored realm."

Olliat gasped. "How do you know this?"

"I divined it while, eh, accidentally under the influence of goddess fruit."

Aki fluttered confidently. "I am very sorry about that, but also not sorry at all because of the discovery."

"The potential discovery," Rhen corrected.

He sighed. This wasn't really going the way he'd hoped. He had to stop avoiding the awkward emotion and just do it. He messed up, he yelled, he was rude to everyone, and what he'd said wasn't even true.

When he'd started out, he wanted to delve the dungeon alone, but Aki and Jakira changed everything. He loved having teammates who weren't fluffers, and sitting around the firepit after a long delve, exchanging stories and laughs was amazing.

"I'm sorry. I've been rushing everything, everyone. There's nothing more I've ever wanted in my life than to found a new realm... but seeing our homes destroyed reminded me of who I'm doing this for. What would I do alone in my own realm? I want a place like this... like the home we made. We share, and we help one another without thinking about getting paid back because we know we will. We laugh and enjoy one another's company"—Rhen looked between Joseph and Wyland—"mostly."

"Anyway, I've been pushing us to this node, but it hasn't been about the discovery, or the fame, maybe a little bit about the fame, but it's about making a safe place for us, all of us. For everyone who isn't a fluffer like Welsh, or Desedra.

"It's not safe up there," he said, pointing toward the dungeon exit. "But I can make it safe for us down here."

With that said, he placed his hand on the Control node and filled his mind with the idea of an inn made of dungeon stone. After a quick sensation of falling, Rhen opened his eyes to the control center of the dungeon. He floated weightlessly in that space and watched as the inn took shape.

It had twelve rooms, and a nice big kitchen with a stove and a chimney running to the dungeon entrance. There was a sitting area right outside the kitchen where they could eat and relax, with three big tables crafted from the dungeon floor.

But it was so dark. Without anything to light the area, they'd have to use a lot of torches. Unless...

Rhen envisioned windows overlooking the rainforest and the location of the inn shifted. The tunnel leading down to the rainforest chamber widened and three stories of rooms cut themselves into the rock on either side. The tunnel into the chamber had a passageway right above it that connected the left and right sides of the inn. On the left side of the first floor was the large kitchen and dining area. On the right he made two more rooms for crafting, both designed sort of like Wyland's workshop.

The windows were midway up the wall inside the rainforest chamber; too high for a terrocken to jump, he hoped. Maybe he could get Wyland to craft some barriers on the windows to keep bugs out. Oh yeah, and the insane hexawraiths.

As he thought it, sheets of thin, clear glass covered the windows. Well, he'd want them to be able to open in case people wanted to let a breeze through. Again, the windows adjusted to become double pane with a divide down the middle and a track the panels could slide on.

Fantastic.

He adjusted little details here and there, adding closets to all the rooms, a nice pantry for the kitchen, some kitchen layout adjustments for several workstations, and other quality of life changes.

Quality of life...

Aki...

While he didn't really need a place to sleep, Rhen wanted him to feel like he had his *own* space within the inn. Rhen imagined a recessed room near the bottom of the inn that pooled with water from the river above. More changes took shape and Rhen realized he could create those bathing rooms too! Maybe he was getting ahead of himself. Nah, he was going for it.

Beside Aki's space he carved out two more similar rooms with walking areas around wide circular tubs. He envisioned a heating element below them, and a way for the water to flow out of the bathing rooms and back out into the stream above. He got a negative buzzing in his ear for that adjustment and text appeared over the inn view.

[Alteration not possible without {Power Gem: Corraphine}]

"Is there Corraphine within the dungeon?"

[Corraphine likely within the {Aquatic} chamber.]

Hmm. Well, the baths would have to wait until they took out the gigafish, then. He removed the bathing rooms, then zoomed out and spun the view around. Not bad at all, and built in a fraction of the time of a real inn.

[Dungeon Editing]

Cost for current adjustments: 45,500 anima points
Current chamber allotment: 15,300
*Warning, to complete this change, you will need to siphon anima from other dungeon chambers. Select chamber to siphon from: Mastery node {32,450}, Resurrection node {240,042}.

=====

Rhen choked when he saw the cost. Good thing he hadn't put those baths in...

He didn't want to risk throwing off the balance of the rainforest, so he stole from the Mastery node chamber, setting them back in abilities. It was fine; they had the time to make it up if they worked hard.

[Dungeon Editing]

You are about to create {Zephitz Inn} chamber outside of {Rainforest} chamber using 30,200 anima from Mastery node and 15,300 from Control node. Are you ready to accept these changes?
{Yes} | {No}

=====

Rhen selected Yes and he was released from the control center. The room shifted underfoot, much of the open space being redirected down to the inn. Rock ground against itself and metal in the walls whined.

"What's happening?" Jakira crouched, holding tight to her bowl of stew.

"Layout adjustments!" Rhen yelled over the noise.

Finally, everything settled.

Rhen grinned, giddy. "Let's go see our new home."

He led the way down the tunnel to the rainforest chamber. After a few dozen feet, the tunnel widened to a brand-new chamber, the inn. There were windows on both sides of the inn, and light from the rainforest shone through.

"It's beautiful!" Olliat ran toward the building carved into the walls and Eli followed fast behind her.

Joseph slapped Rhen on the back. "Good work, Deo."

"Ah, I see there's a spot right here for my work," Wyland said, moving right toward the crafter's room. Rhen had tried to mimic the design of Wyland's workshop below his store, but he was sure he got some of the details wrong.

"I'll make some blankets and pillows for now," Leslie said, picking through the supplies in the boat-cart.

"I have some feathers we can use," Bort said, holding up his bag.

Barrek grinned. "We'll have this inn furnished in no time at all."

The three of them gravitated toward the other room, pushing the boat-cart along full of supplies as they chatted about what to work on first. Everyone smiled while they explored the inn. Rhen sat outside, watching them through the windows. Aki plopped down into a little watery bubble beside him, as if to sit.

"You have made everyone very happy."

Rhen tutted. "Like buying a kid candy after screaming at them..."

"No. You did not placate their sadness with gifts. You showed them your heart, and they love who you are."

Rhen chuckled. "You certainly have a way with the common language."

He wondered if it was true. Did they like him for who he was? Or did they just like that he had a profitable dungeon?

"You worry too much."

"Worrying is how I've survived."

"Or maybe worrying is preventing you from living."

Rhen scowled. How did that work?

"Come." Aki blooped himself back up into a man-shaped body. "Show me my room."

Rhen climbed to his feet, and they entered the inn. The walls of the living room were smooth, laced with bits of sparkling Celinom. Rhen could feel his boots pulling extra energy from the magical stones, chasing away his weariness.

Jakira was in the kitchen, checking out all the features he'd installed. A double oven for baking bread, a stovetop for sautéing or boiling, and a big spit for roasting large animals. Her face glowed when she saw him and she charged, arms open.

She gave him a huge hug and kissed his cheek. "This is the best thing ever!"

"I'm glad you like it."

"How much did it cost?"

Rhen grimaced. "A lot. Those new abilities we were gonna get are on hold until we can farm some of those crystals out of the aquatic chamber."

"I can help with that," Wyland yelled from his workshop.

Apparently, noise traveled in here... He'd have to fix that later.

"How so?" Rhen called back.

"You'll see. Give me three days!"

Rhen counted down in his mind. That would leave them with sixteen days to farm crystals for the Mastery node, level up, craft enough gear and weapons for every delver... all the while someone had to be making food for everyone, and Rhen really needed to get on with finding a good apothecary. They'd gone too long without in-combat potions that could really make a difference.

Not to mention, he *really* needed to find a way down into the aquatic chamber and spar with a few of the smaller fish to get a feel for their abilities. He didn't want the whole team going in there blind.

So much to do.

Aki slapped him on the back the way he'd seen Joseph do it. "We are here to help you, Rhen. Share the work."

"Yeah, how can I help?" Jakira asked.

Rhen thought about how he could divvy up the work. "Okay, here's what we need to do."

26

HERE FISHY, FISHY

There had been just enough anima left for Rhen to craft a passageway down to the shore of the aquatic chamber, and while it hurt to use it all up, he didn't want to waste any more time searching for a way in. With that done, he put a team together to go hunt some fish.

Aki was essential. It was going to be his responsibility to keep an air bubble around the team as they dove down to do battle with the fish. Then he asked for Eli and Olliat. Jakira and Joseph protested, saying the team needed a bruiser. Rhen wasn't so sure. They'd need to be agile and deal piercing damage, things a bruiser couldn't do. Plus, it was a scouting trip. Too many bruisers and every fish in the lake would come after them.

After a good night's rest and a roasted terrocken leg sandwich, the team was ready to go. The tunnel down to the aquatic chamber was steep and short. Rhen wasn't able to afford anything else. They took it carefully and emerged down on the sandy beach of the new chamber.

The sand underfoot was crushed crystals so fine it felt soft. The massive hanging crystals above glimmered with untapped power. He'd have to leave some of them behind for unlocking the Nexus node, but as far as he was concerned, they were going to farm the ceiling bare to fuel their abilities.

The walls sparkled with more crystal fragments, and the calm waters reflected them perfectly. The cavern went on for what looked like miles. It wasn't very wide, but it was long. This too was a closed ecosystem. Rhen wondered if it underwent a night of chaos like the rainforest, or if it balanced itself some other way. He'd be spending most of his time down here trying to find that out with the time they had left: nineteen days, he reminded himself, and they wouldn't even be farming the crystals for another three.

Through the clear water, Rhen could see a fish about half his size swim up into the shallows. It was picking at some stringy kelp-looking plant, perhaps eating other little fish out of it. After a moment of picking, the fish glowed hot white and increased to about Rhen's size.

"We saw the trees do this in the rainforest chamber. They destroyed the neighboring trees then glowed, and grew."

Aki hummed. "This may be a visible representation of their anima well growth. If these creatures do not have syntials, or the conditions under which they can get one is difficult, to grow their anima well they must literally grow their bodies."

Olliat scowled thoughtfully, then turned to Rhen. "You said the crystals on the ceiling are an immense source of anima. The trees must maintain balance by keeping the tallest ones down, away from the crystals."

"And it developed the hexawraiths to convert the dead material into water, to keep the forest thriving. I noticed none of them had body material outside of a core... they just exploded into warm water when they were hit."

"The hexa-what-now?" Eli asked.

"Hexawraiths."

"Six... ghosts..."

"Six-legged ghosts," Rhen corrected.

Olliat chuckled. "What do you call the big bird monsters?"

"Terrockens."

Eli sighed. "Terror chickens?"

"The Guild is gonna go wild for those names." Olliat rolled with laughter.

Rhen scowled. "Yeah, fine, how about you name this fish-thing then if you're so good at it."

Aki lifted the fish from the water and flopped it out onto the sand. The fish wiggled and beat its tail, the only sound coming from its mouth was the *mop-mop-mop* as it gasped for breath. Its scales were an opalescent purple-green, with hues of pink around the fins and gills. It was pretty, for a fish.

A pink syntial beside its gills glowed and a gush of icy water blasted Rhen's stomach. The sucker punch sent him reeling, the only noise coming from his mouth the *hup-hup-hup* of failing to fill his lungs.

Eli chopped down on its neck with his short sword, but the scales shimmered, deflecting his blade. Olliat dug her scythe into one eye and stabbed her dagger into the other when it tried to flop away. Its next wiggle was weak, and then it was still.

Rhen caught his breath and approached the dead monster. "Water jet and shielded skin abilities. We'll want to target the mouth and eyes, and get Wyland working on something to remove those scales."

Olliat pulled her hook out of its eye. "Prismageyser."

Rhen tutted. "*That's* what you're going to name it? And you're giving me grief over Terrocken?"

"Mine sounds better."

"Eli, please. Help me out."

Eli wrinkled his nose. "It's a little better."

"Traitor."

They got to work descaling the prismageyser—stupid name

—and then cut out a few filets. Aki brought the cuts of meat up to Jakira while Rhen, Eli, and Olliat pulled out interesting crafting bits; thin, flexible bones, magical scales, teeth, and finally the core. Aki may have been onto something about the anima well, because the creature's core was relatively small for its own size. It must've needed time to grow.

Aki returned with Bort a few minutes later to collect the goods. Rhen stared at the water. It got darker the farther out he looked, and he couldn't see the bottom after about thirty feet. He exhaled long and slow to calm his nerves. He was never a big fan of the ocean.

"Are you ready?" Aki asked.

Rhen nodded. "Yep. Yeah. Very much."

Olliat and Eli didn't look convinced.

Rhen gritted his teeth. It was time to stop pussyfooting around, and dive in.

He charged the water and ran into the shallows. The water was not as cold as he expected. Not that he wanted to bathe in it, but after a hot day in the rainforest chamber, it might be nice to take a swim here.

Tiny sparkles of bright blue and green rippled away from Rhen where he splashed, like the water was disturbed by his presence. He got to waist deep and took a deep breath to dive under. The water didn't surround his face and dampen sound like he expected.

He opened his eyes to stinging water and saw a thick air pocket clung from his shoulders up to his nose, but the rest of his body was fully submerged in water. Rhen breathed normally in the little air pocket. He blinked a few times until the water felt more normal on his eyes and looked around.

The light pierced the water easier when he was under it, revealing a grassy field of kelp off to the left with little finger-sized silver fish flitting through it. One of the more colorful prismageysers swam along the bottom, making close circles around the kelp. Finally, a silver fish broke away from the school, and the prismageyser struck like lightning. Great... they were fast, too.

Olliat and Eli dove in beside him, similar bubbles of air around their shoulders. Aki splashed into the water and zipped forward, making quick circles around the group. He pulsed bright yellow, his tentacles surging behind him as he cut through the water fast enough to make a bubble trail.

He was really in his element here, for the first time since Rhen had met him.

"This is much more agreeable, yes." Aki's words traveled through the water and hit Rhen a little slower than he experienced them on land. "I will be able to communicate simultaneously between you underwater. Rhen, give us direction and I will relay the message."

"Just think it?" Rhen used his monologue to speak.

"Exactly."

~And how do we communicate back to Rhen? Olliat's voice came through just as clearly as Aki's did.

~This is so cool! Eli was grinning inside his air bubble.

"Okay, get the novelty out of the way now. We have fish to hunt—

~Prismageysers.

"Right, prismageysers. Stay behind me, flank right and left. Aki, you're insanely fast, so please be our lookout. Use Shadow Snare at the first sign of an approaching enemy. Maybe we should run in a small school with soothing aura?"

"A fair plan. How far out should we go?"

"How long will the air last?"

"If you breath shallowly, perhaps twenty minutes?"

"Let's see where ten minutes gets us."

Rhen kicked forward and swam deeper into the shallows.

Around thirty feet out from the shore, just as Rhen had seen from above, there was a steep drop off into deep blue. The sight of it sent a shiver down Rhen's spine.

"Incoming." Aki floated up to Rhen, pointing his tentacle about three o'clock.

"Already?"

Rhen turned to see what he pointed at. A silver fish three times Rhen's size was floating just over the edge of the shallows. Its huge eye, like a fully grown pumpkin, was locked on the party. Its fins fluttered as it hovered like graceful death. It could swim into the deeper shallows to reach them, but it waited.

~Should we attack? Eli asked.

"Aki, can you hear what the fish is thinking?"

"Its thought pattern is very basic, but it is trying to decide if we are prey or predator."

"Well, let's show it what we are. We don't want any of the fish in here getting thoughts of eating us." Rhen swam closer to the edge, his heart beating faster as he saw just how deep it went. Twenty feet from the fish, he stopped. The fish sucked in a deep breath, "smelling" him and the others. Rhen put out his hand and triggered a narrow Tremor Blast.

The effect vibrated the bubble of air around his shoulders and sent waves out in all directions, but barely affected the fish. Rhen put a little more anima into the spell and fired it again. The disturbed water hit the fish and it backed away a measure.

"I do not know if that ability will be effective here."

"I'm sensing that."

Rhen thought of his other abilities... Primordial Breath was useless down here unless he wanted to fill up his air bubble with fire. Swift Twitch and Caress of Night were all he really had going for him.

"All right, silvish, try this on for size."

~Silver fish... silvish? Really? Olliat groaned.

Rhen pulled out one crescent blade and activated Swift Twitch. He kicked his feet and surged forward, catching the fish off-guard and scoring a good slice along its pectoral fin. The silvish darted off into the darkness of the depths below, leaving Rhen alone at the edge of the precipice.

He kicked again and backed away from the edge, his heart thundering.

~Way to scare it off, Deo.

"I believe that is the opposite of what we wanted to do."

"Right, sorry. Let's patrol the shallows and see what we can find. Maybe a few cores could unlock some aquatic abilities for us."

Rhen removed the other blade from its holster, swimming with his arms behind him to make his profile smaller. They reached the kelp field where Rhen discovered Tremor Blast was quite useful in getting enemies to reveal themselves. The kelp parted at his spell, showing that several more man-sized silvish were hiding inside and a few prismageysers.

Three of the fish charged all at once, their orange eyes following Aki. He must've looked like a tasty treat compared to Rhen. But Aki was quick, avoiding them easily and pulling the fish into striking range for the others.

Olliat's scythe worked wonders in hooking the fish. She let the fish drag her along through the water as she stabbed into various tender areas, bringing her fish down quickly. Eli struggled with his short sword, so he switched out for a dagger, which worked better. Rhen's crescent blades were designed for fast swipes, which were difficult underwater. He managed to hook his blade in an eye socket, then de-fin the silvish, rendering it dead in the water.

They dragged their kills up to the shore, where Bort waited to dissect them. Eli stayed to help, feeling a bit useless in the water. Rhen and Olliat returned to the shallows to find a clutch of eggs nestled deep in the kelp. Rhen felt a *little* bad about murdering the ones that had been protecting the eggs. They left those be, despite probably being delicious. They didn't want to upset the ecosystem too much.

They made their way to the west end of the cave through the shallows, which seemed to wrap all the way around the lake. On the opposite side they discovered interesting crab-like creatures, most of them the size of Rhen's chest, with spindly legs as long as his. There were clams of some sort too, no doubt guarding nice little pearly cores. Rhen pocketed a few of the clams, who seemed not to notice their change in fate.

Only two more silvish made an appearance in the shallows, and both were small enough that Rhen didn't want to kill them. The four cores they had would likely be enough to get some aquatic abilities for a few of them... though they were going to need a lot more.

One thing at a time, he reminded himself.

Aquatic abilities for his primary delve team first, then they could fight the bigger fish and help everyone else. They made it back to the exit side of the lake and Aki pulled the water from their clothes, drying them instantly.

Rhen sighed, looking at the flayed carcasses. "If this is all we're going to be able to hunt, we're going to need a lot more of them. There don't seem to be that many of this sized fish in the shallows."

Aki hummed. "I would like to explore the deeper water alone."

Rhen tensed, a thousand thoughts of worry washing through him.

"Do not fret. I am fast, and with soothing aura I can remain nearly invisible. In case of extreme danger, I am also a proficient magic user. We must map the depths so we can understand what is waiting for us."

"He's right," Olliat said. "He's made for this."

Defeated, Rhen nodded. "Okay. Bort and Eli, stay down here and work on these fish while Olliat and I go check what abilities we can get to make things easier. Aki, you will check in with them every fifteen minutes, yes?"

"You are like a concerned mother. Yes, I will check in." Aki dove into the water. His glowing body zipped toward the depths and out of sight in a second. Damn, he was *fast*. He must've been holding back so the others could keep up.

Rhen plucked the fishy cores out of Bort's pack. "Time to roll the dice."

27

FIN UP OR FLUFF OFF

Rhen held two of the fish cores in his hand and stared at the Mastery node, unsure what to ask for. He didn't think Aki would be able to maintain every air bubble for everyone in the raid party, so perhaps long-breath or water-breathing would be good choices. What other abilities that would work well underwater?

Ranged attacks would be good. Having to get up in a fish's business every time they wanted to kill one wasn't going to work for the gigaprisma... no that just didn't roll off the tongue well. Gigafish.

What kind of underwater ranged attacks might there be other than the water jet? Rhen was sure he wouldn't be able to get that due to his Primordial Breath, but it may be useful to the others. No, that was still too weak. He needed a game changer.

Think!

Tremor Blast was essentially useless. The vibrations went everywhere and dispersed into harmless slaps by the time they reached the target, so anything vibration related was out. Speed and water breathing would be necessary, but not yet, while the diving team was still small enough for Aki to manage. Ranged attacks...

Maybe he was overthinking it. Maybe he should just keep it simple.

Rhen sucked down a deep breath and placed his hand on the node. "We need to effectively fight underwater."

[Syntial Additions and Expansion]

Available Options: 16 {Expand? Y | N}
Recommended Options: 6
{Amphibian Lung}
Prima I | Active:Persistent | Kinse | Life | Cost: 10% Anima to transition

Water, air, as long as it has oxygen, it's all the same to you. You may transition your breathing style between aquatic and atmospheric for ten percent of your current anima capacity. You will retain your selected breathing style until changed.

*Warning, attempting to switch styles without a five-minute cooldown between may cause permanent respiratory damage.

{Hydromirage}
Prima I | Passive | Mana | Light | Cost: 1.5% Anima/Minute

You're here... No, you're over there! WHERE ARE YOU? While underwater, it will not be possible for friends and foes alike to visually determine your exact location. Creatures using sonar and other non-visual methods will not be fooled by your distortion projections.

{Sea-Shell}
Prima I | Active:Persistent | Mana | Death | Cost: 12% Anima

The ocean holds you tight and keeps you safe. While underwater, you surround your body in a protective shell once every ten minutes built from the sediment of the sea floor. This shell is flexible at the joints, and resistant to both magical and melee damage, but varying amounts based on the materials used. Shell can be double stacked to increase resistance but reduce flexibility.

*Shells constructed of magical materials will damage attackers on hit.

**Warning, shell layers reduce buoyancy.

{Toxink}

Prima I | Active | Mana | Death | Cost: 5% Anima

When you get spooked, they get splooged. While underwater, release a {2} cubic foot cloud of toxic black ink that causes varying levels of blindness, asphyxiation, and reduced anima efficiency. Cloud will persist for up to ten minutes in still water.

*Used on land, the effect will take a gaseous form.

**Warning, Toxink does not differentiate between friend and foe.

{Cephaloshifter}

Prima I | Active | Kinse | Chaos | Cost: 40% Anima

Ever wanted between five and two hundred tentacly limbs? Now's your chance! Transform your body into a giant cephalopod for up to {5} minutes. Retain all the abilities of your syntials and gain any innate abilities of the selected cephalopod. Transformation is made at random, pulling genome from any connected realm.

*Cooldown: This ability can only be used once per {2} hours.

{Compbomb}

Prima I | Active | Enon | Chaos | Cost: 5% Anima

What happens when you compress matter really fast? Who knows! The material compressed will cause varying outcomes—super heating, gaseous transformation, solid transformations, etc. But what happens when that compression is quickly released? Usually an explosion.

Select any target material in line of sight within {100} feet that is {5} cubic feet to compress. Compression can be held for up to {10} seconds. Holding compression may cause different results.

*Warning, this is an expert level syntial. Experimentation is required, and death is likely.

=====

That was a lot for just two little cores. Rhen was happy with all the dungeon had been able to find, but none of it really struck his fancy, except maybe transforming into a giant squid. Maybe then Rhen could read Aki's mind...

"What are you going to pick?" Olliat grinned, her eyes pinned on Celphaloshifter.

"Amphibian Lung for now. Swift Twitch already helps me move quickly through the water, but I'm sure Aki can only support so many air bubbles at once. You?"

"Cephaloshifter, for sure. What an incredible ability!"

"You think a lot of people are going to like it?"

"Oh, yes. I mean, just think about it. Five minutes of being the biggest, multi-armed monster in the lake."

An idea was taking shape in his mind. Rotating squid-tanks with Sea-Shell against the boss. They would only need four or five people to take up the mantle, and they would have the gigafish in the bag.

But Rhen couldn't *force* anyone to get syntials they didn't want. Still, he could ask for tank volunteers. He had no doubt Jakira would step up in a heartbeat.

And he couldn't discount Compbomb. While the outcome would be hard to perfect, if they could learn to create explosions around the gigafish, or *on* it... but five cubic feet of gigafish was like a fingernail to Rhen. No matter. All the abilities presented would make up a good raid team.

"Okay, I'd like Amphibian Lung, please," Rhen said to the node.

Anima flowed up his arm and traveled to his neck. On either side, Rhen could feel the pinpricks of the anima tattooing itself into his flesh. The blue light faded, and the pain vanished from his neck.

Olliat practically pushed Rhen aside to get to the node. "Cephaloshifter, please!"

Blue power surged up her arm to the top of her head, making her hair glow. She winced and gritted her teeth, but held out through the process until it finished.

She rubbed the top of her head. "That was the most painful yet."

They made their way back to the inn. Without the sun, it was difficult to know what time it was. Was it time to rest? Rhen didn't feel tired, but he also knew that his anima siphoning boots helped keep him energized for long raids.

"I'm going to check in with Wyland. I'll be back at the lake in a few."

"Okay." Olliat waved and headed toward the steep tunnel down to the aquatic chamber.

Wyland had gotten well set up in his workshop in just a few hours, and was already plugging away at... something. He was in the middle of welding two pieces of metal together, so Rhen waited.

"Oh, hello. Can I help you?" Wyland asked with a kind but absent smile.

Rhen scowled. "Wyland, it's me, Rhen?"

Understanding dawned on his face and he waved Rhen's concern way. "Yes, I knew that, of course I knew that! Whaddya need, sonny?"

"I just wanted to see if you want to come take a look at the aquatic zone to get more ideas?"

"More ideas…"

"For the crystal farming?"

"Oh yes, that'd be a good idea."

Rhen helped him down, since the tunnel was quite steep.

"Wow, wouldya look at all that anima." Wyland whistled. "Why, that's gotta be enough to fuel an army!"

"And we're going to need a small, but ruthless army to take down the gigafish."

"The gigawha?"

"Step back to the tunnel." Aki summoned his aurora spell and flitted the light over the deepest part of the lake. Everyone climbed the rocks up to the tunnel entrance and waited. After a moment, the gigafish breached, chomping at the glittering spell. It hit the water with an ear-splitting *crack*, sending a huge wave up to the sands and crashing into the wall. The lake water sprayed up into the tunnel, misting them.

The walls of the cavern trembled, and the glowing crystals twinkled. Some of the longer ones cracked at the base and plummeted toward the lake. Some were snatched out of the air by enterprising silvish, but the others hit the water with a smack.

"I see. That's one big fluffer!"

"It is, which is why we'll need all the firepower we can get to go up against it. I think I have a good plan forming, though; now we just need the anima for everyone's syntials."

"Well, I can definitely getcha something to get those things out. Gimme three days."

"Isn't that what he said yesterday?" Olliat asked.

"I didn't make no promises yesterday, girly. Mind yourself."

"No problem, Wyland, everything's fine. One more thing if you could work on it in your spare time: a clock."

"Ha, spare time for a clock. Sure, sonny, whatever you want." Wyland hobbled his way back up the tunnel to his workshop.

Another day down... What the heck had Wyland been working on?

Eli cringed. "Is something wrong with him?"

"He's just a bit kooky," Rhen said, but he felt worry growing in him. There was definitely something wrong with his memory. Rhen had heard of diseases eating the mind. What a tragedy for such a brilliant one.

Rhen patted Eli on the shoulder. "C'mon, let's get you some abilities to help hunt these fish."

They went up to the Mastery node for another round of upgrades. There wasn't a lot of anima left in the node, so Eli just grabbed Amphibious Lung, despite wanting Cephaloshifter *badly*. Rhen guessed he wouldn't have to ask for volunteers to tank. Everyone was going to want a shot at a kraken kaiju battle, and maybe that was the plan.

They returned to the shallows where Aki projected a luminescent map of the area just beyond the precipice. There were openings along the rock face all the way down for what looked like a mile. Rhen's jaw dropped as the light projection kept going, and going, zooming out and making the shallows area smaller and smaller until he hit the bottom.

"It does continue to get deeper farther into the lake, but this was as far as I felt comfortable going. There are very large fish, some nearly comparable to the gigafish. There is plant life hanging from the walls and along the floor, and a few of the crab-creatures we saw before, but much larger.

"The openings in the rock face are mostly shallow, but some are deep enough to hide in. I believe a strong tactic will be to lure enemies close to these pockets where several others lie in wait to ambush the monsters."

"No time like the present to test that tactic."

"I speak only to you now, Rhen. You seemed apprehensive about the depths. Are you afraid?"

"Nothing I can't get over for the sake of the Nexus."

Eli pulled out his dagger, grinning. *~Let's fluff some fins up.*

With that, they got to work hunting silvish and prismageyser—which proved effective at stamping out the team's "hide in holes" tactic. The fish would blow their water ability right into the dimples and push the hiding ambusher out. Olliat came within a few feet of getting chomped before she activated her Cephaloshifter ability.

The attacking prismageyser's jaw was ripped straight off when she morphed into a ten-tentacled monster. Her skin shimmered, but was translucent, revealing all kinds of guts inside, as well as the massive sharp beak nestled under her tentacles. She rammed the beak into the fish's eye and ripped it out, then wrapped her tentacles tight around its body, crushing it.

She brought the fish up to the surface and chucked it at the beach where Bort waited to harvest it.

~By far the coolest thing you've ever done in your life, Eli said, the snark thick in his nasally pubescent voice.

She wrapped a tentacle around him and pulled him close to her eye. *~Watch yourself, kiddo. I'm the boss monster, now.*

They hunted down several more fish in the next five minutes, each one larger as Olliat tested her strength. Rhen and Eli sat back and watched for the most part. She was a wonder for those five minutes, using her new body as if she'd had it her whole life.

And that was how the days went on. With each core, Rhen rotated the raid party up to the Mastery node for abilities. His plan unfolded without any prompting as nearly everyone selected Cephaloshifter. Now, they'd just have to get enough anima for the other abilities to make this whole crazy scheme work.

Gods, he hoped it would work.

28

A CRAFTY PLAN

A week later, everyone had gone through the aquatic chamber with their new aqua-syntials, practicing their abilities on the smaller fish. There were only twelve days left, but Rhen was feeling confident the small raid of thirteen could make it happen. Everyone had agreed to get Cephaloshifter—because who *wouldn't* want that—and Sea-Shell. This was the core foundation of the plan.

Rhen wandered into the kitchen, following the scents of roasted terrocken with some spicy spice that was *not* father's fennel for once. Okay, maybe it was in there, but there was something else even *stronger* in it.

Jakira was at the stovetop, stirring a huge pot of bright gold gravy with chunks of meat and tubers.

"What is that masterpiece?" Rhen asking, grabbing a spoon from the counter.

Jakira blocked his ladling attempt with a parry of her own spoon. She grinned, and Rhen tried again with no success.

He grinned back. "You're getting really good."

"All thanks to you and Joseph for training me." She dipped a smaller tasting spoon into the broth and held it out to Rhen.

He licked the modest taster. Smoky, spicy, earthy, and rich. He loved it. "What is this?"

"Terrocken leg of course, but the broth is a surprise... It's actually part of our plan, if you want."

"I'm listening," Rhen said, dipping the spoon back into the broth for a chunk of meat.

The small spoon got past Jakira's guard and she groaned. "Double-dipper, gross..."

"The heat'll kill my germs. Anyway, tell me."

"So, the herbs I used to make the broth are actually from the burned inn. It's just super heated hakir salt and father's fennel. Something about being trapped in those airtight metal jars kept everything inside, but like, changed it. I can't explain it because I don't know enough about roasting spices, but I want to find out more.

"Anyway, *how* it was changed is important. I made a small portion yesterday for myself with the spices, just to test if they were still okay to eat—don't want to waste, ya know? So about ten minutes after eating I started feeling... different. Not sick to my stomach, but like, I felt a fire in me. All my anima spells were stronger, and my Cephaloshifter transformation lasted almost nine minutes instead of five. That's a *huge* deal!"

Rhen punched her shoulder. "Genius! We'll all go into battle on full stomachs."

Jakira's grin faded. "Yeah well, uh, I have more testing to do, you know? More people need to try full portions to test the effects, and also... I'm going to need more roasted herbs to replicate this before the fight. I have no idea how long they roasted for, or at what temperature, so it's going to require some experimentation."

"That's okay, we have some time. How can I help you make this a priority?"

Jakira giggled. "Rhen the dungeon owner, you're so cute. I

guess what I really need other than time and materials is a gear upgrade. Chainmail is *not* going to work underwater."

"Lighter, underwater gear. I'm on it." Rhen snapped his fingers and pointed to the stew. "Let me know when a full serving of that is ready. I'm starving."

Rhen walked across the way to the crafters' shops. Leslie was working away with a foot-press sewing machine, making some light undershirts.

Leslie smiled and set the sewing aside when she saw him. "Ah, Dungeon Owner, how are you?"

"Hungry, but good. I was hoping I could ask a favor. I know you're working on some spare clothes since we all lost everything, but I was hoping I could convince you to prioritize a prototype armor."

"Cloth armor? I'm not a syntial worker, Dungeon Owner."

"Leslie, call me Rhen, please. And it's okay, I think I've got someone who can manage it. I just need the raw materials put together."

"All right, I can give it my best effort. What are you thinking?"

Rhen whipped one of the colorful terrocken feathers out of a materials bin. "Feather armor. I've seen these feathers deflect blades when activated, and I think we can figure out how to do the same. We'll need to dress the bruisers first since their armor is too heavy for underwater, and if that's all we can manage, I think that'll be a job well done. Let's start with something small and simple, a bracer maybe."

Leslie nodded. "I'll see what I can whip up. Thank you, Rhen."

"Why you thankin' me?" Rhen smiled incredulously.

"For this opportunity to challenge my skills."

He beamed. "You're good people. I think you should have all the opportunity in the world."

Well, that felt awkward.

Rhen cleared his throat and took a step backwards, then dropped the feather back in the bin. "Anyway, let me know when it's ready so I can take it to Yu. I think Ghwan is familiar with syntial work on many materials."

"Surely."

Rhen sped out to Wyland's workshop. "How's the next machine coming?"

Wyland cranked down on his ratchet, tightening a bolt on the weird spiderlike object. It had a flat back, eight legs, two claws coming out of the shoulders and a wide mouth with mandibles to guide material inside.

"Almost there." The bolt stopped and he let off. He set the ratchet aside and pointed to the underbelly of the spider-mech. "This baby's got a far superior anima capacity to the last one. It can be out for at least two hours on its own."

He pointed to the crab-like claw and sawblade up front. "I made some mathematical adjustments to the blade height—now it'll only cut off the tips of the longer crystals, sorta mowin' the lawn if you would. Then the crystals can regenerate over time, and we can come mow again.

"Next I increased the storage capacity." He pointed to the back and the wing-like storage compartment opened up, revealing two upside-down buckets inside. "When this thing is hangin' from the ceiling, the buckets'll be right side up, don't worry."

He pushed a button on the beetle-looking face and the legs moved of their own accord, flipping the spider-mech upside down. It opened the compartment again, and Wyland removed the whole machine, leaving just the buckets.

"Bort helped me with that enon syntial," he said, pointing to the glowing symbol around the edge of the thing's wide mouth. He put the machine back together and righted it.

"Let's see, what else... Spring-loaded foot wedgers," he said, compressing and releasing the spring that opened and closed the foot. "It'll find cracks in the ceiling and wedge itself in. Only three legs needed to keep it up on the wall, so if two or three go down, it's okay."

Rhen scratched his chin. "How does it know what to do?"

Wyland laughed, but he sounded offended. "You wanna see that? Most people just say thanks and take their tools."

"I meant no offense. I'm not questioning your work."

Wyland grunted. "Good. Nothin' worse than a know-it-all dungeon owner tellin' you how your own machines should function."

Rhen chuckled, relieved to see Wyland was back to his sharp-as-a-tack self. He hoped it was just loneliness that made him forget who Rhen was from time to time, but a gnawing sensation lurked at the back of his thoughts that whispered it was something worse than just a distracted mind.

"Anyway, I want to understand it better, that's all."

Wyland hummed, squinting at Rhen beneath bushy eyebrows. "Well, all right."

He moved to the beetle-like head and opened its mouth, then clicked a latch that kept the top of the head down. Inside were myriad little cogs, gears, and metal cards inset with yellow anima crystals. "One of my syntials allows me to transfer simple instructions to anima crystals.

"It'll go up, look for longer crystals and cut'em free, shove them in its mouth, and repeat for one and a half hours. After that, it's gotta come back to this base plate." He got up and moved over to another wide-based machine on the ground.

He tapped his foot on the glassy surface of the machine and it came to life with yellow light. "I infuse this platform with my anima every morning, enough for two machines to make five trips. Of course, as they start havin' to go farther and farther out to find crystals, they're gonna bring back less day over day."

"That's okay, we need a lot *now*, so we'll deal with later when later comes. Priority one for those crystals is a Respawn Reserve. I want to make sure we have enough to revive everyone in the dungeon. Next will be distributing them to the lowest syntial level raiders first until we're all on the same playing field, or aiding anyone who has useless underwater abilities. And of course, keep fifty percent of them for yourself as they come in."

"Fifty!" Wyland screamed, his bushy brows climbing all the way to his hairline.

"That's what I said. You made the machines that are making this possible."

"Rhen! Lunch," Jakira yelled from the kitchen.

Wyland mumbled under his breath. "I wouldn't even know what to do with that much raw anima..."

Rhen shrugged and backed away. "Sell it? Use it? Either way, it's yours to do what you want. Have a good one, Wyland, I've gotta chow down."

He found Olliat, Eli, and Joseph too, asking them to come do the food test. They all ate the same portion of savory, earthy, tangy, *nomnomnom*. Rhen salivated even as he was shoving spoon-loads into his mouth. It was so, *so* good. Maybe weeks of eating fish and bread had helped readjust his tastebuds to bitter, because he was liking that earthy richness.

They sat back and Jakira started a timer on her kitchen clock. It was nice knowing what time of day it was with their perpetual afternoon coming from the rainforest chamber. It only took Eli five minutes before he felt the fire, and Joseph took the longest at fifteen, but they were all feeling it.

Time to test the effects.

The well-fed crew headed into the aquatic chamber feeling

like champions. Their power and excitement were palpable, like hot static electricity.

Rhen rushed the water, activating Swift Twitch. He leaped high in the air and sailed out over the deepest part of the water. Fear gnawed at his bones but he told it to fluff right off, and triggered Cephaloshifter.

Just as he hit the water, his body contorted into an enormous black and red, chambered nautilus. His perspective shifted and everything looked small around him. The silvish that were at least three times his size looked like little toys in his fifty tentacles.

He used Swift Twitch to hyper accelerate and bash his strong shell into a megafish that had been giving them trouble the past few days. Two of the others appeared beside him as glowing octopi, one a bright red with long tentacles, and the other more rainbow with shorter, stronger-looking tentacles. Rhen wasn't sure who it was since they hadn't managed to find any species that shared Aki's unique mind-talking abilities.

The glowy-pi wrapped their legs around the megafish's back fin and constricted. A spear-headed squid with a razor-edge shell surged at the side of the megafish, ripping open its side and spilling blood all around them. Together, the four of them gutted the fish right there and removed the massive core.

Rhen pulled out a few crafting bones, finding it easy to work with fifty functional fingers. Wow, it wasn't even weird being a giant chambered nautilus. It was as if he'd *always* been one. They delivered the goods to the beach where Bort and Jakira waited, then returned to the fray.

For eight, glorious minutes, Rhen wreaked havoc on the monsters of the near-deep. He hadn't yet found the courage to venture closer to the gigafish, but now, in an experiment, certainly wasn't the time to try.

When the spell elapsed, Rhen triggered Amphibian Lung,

Caress of Night, and Swift Twitch, propelling himself quietly toward the shore. The others trailed behind, their transformations fading within minutes after Rhen's.

Aki appeared not far behind them and followed them to shore. "I caught the last moments of battle. Incredible strength."

~*So much fun! I'll never get sick of this,* Olliat said.

~*It's a lot easier to take the big'n's down in a group,* Joseph said.

They climbed out into the shallows and switched back to atmospheric breathing. Rhen felt electric. He whooped, high fiving the others. Eli pushed Olliat playfully and they splashed around. Rhen charged across the beach and pulled Jakira into a big, sopping wet hug.

That stupid gigafish wouldn't know what hit it.

29

CEPHALO-RAIDERS

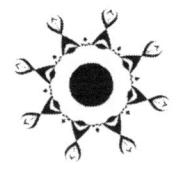

Leslie and Ghwan moved about the gathered bruisers, securing their colorful feathered armor into place and giving instructions.

Jakira looked *incredible*.

Multi-colored reds, blues, greens, oranges, and yellows cascaded across her dark body in a rainbow. Everything was form fitting, with no need for gaps at the waist or joints to allow movements. She sported dark leather pauldrons with megahound teeth jutting from the tops, protecting her from getting chomped. Around her waist and across her shoulders was a dark belt and holster for her club, as well as a pair of daggers. She had a few pouches around the belt that could store potions—which Rhen hadn't managed to get.

An alchemist would be a post-raid problem. They had done what they could with the time they had, and Rhen was feeling pretty good about their chances. With four days left, they could make two attempts at the raid, but Rhen knew they'd only need one.

Everyone was decked to the teeth. They'd all been able to level Cephaloshifter to Prima II, and Rhen unlocked a special

Ancilla I that allowed him to select a specific species he'd become before, or transform into something random. That, and the other two primas for Amphibian Lung and Compbomb, and they were ready to execute the master plan.

Rhen stood to address the crowd, half of them well-dressed in feathers. Everyone quieted, looking at him. He held each of their gazes for a fleeting moment, then spoke.

"These are the minutes before our greatest victory. There is no doubt in my mind that we will succeed, but that does not mean death isn't waiting for us out there. Stay sharp, stick to your pod, communicate, and improvise. That is how we'll win.

"Everyone made this possible, and we will all share in the wealth of its returns. A new realm... our lives will never be the same."

Rhen pulled the parchment out of his pack and held the stack out to Jakira to distribute them. "As a dungeon owner, I can make this promise that no matter what we find on the other side, everyone will get a share I feel is fair. Granted, we'll also be sharing with the D.O.G. and the Imperial Kingdoms, so that's why the number might, uh, seem a bit low."

Everyone read over their contracts.

"What if I don't want any of this?" Eli asked. As a fifteen-year-old boy, Rhen could understand him not wanting anything to do with owning his own land or dungeons. It was a lot as it was for Rhen just owning one dungeon.

"You can relinquish it to your father, sister, mother... you could sell it back to me. This contract states you own two-point-five percent of whatever we find there. It may be nothing, but it may be a new realm. It may be a new *sapient populate* realm, in which case we will get very little for many years as the D.O.G. representatives negotiate the terms of realm connection, broker infrastructure deals, and on and on."

They all stared.

Joseph cleared his throat. "Forgive my frankness, but fluff the politics. I just want to delve. You're a good dungeon owner, you treat us right. I know whatever we find over there, you'll do with it the things we need to keep on living our best lives."

"Here, here," Wyland said, lifting his mug of brew.

"These contracts are to protect you."

"But we trust you," Leslie said.

Rhen sighed. "That's great, but... you shouldn't. Not about this. Please, sign the contracts."

Wyland shook his head and whipped out a ballpoint pen. "Boy don't even know himself." He scribbled a signature and pushed the page away, then passed his pen around.

Everyone signed, their mood dour. He knew he should've done the contracts sooner, but he hadn't found the time to run an errand all the way back in Desedra. It wasn't until wind really caught of his raid that a D.O.G. representative was sent to stay at the Bustling Brood for documentation of the find, giving him the opportunity to write up these contracts—and get Wyland a work order.

"Oh, the stew!" Jakira dashed toward the kitchen, trailed by Eli and Olliat. They returned with a huge bubbling pot of the rich, golden-brown stew, another pot of some pearl-like grain, fresh bread, and some place settings.

Everyone gathered around with their bowls and Jakira ladled out measured servings of the anima power boosting food. Wyland took a spot at Rhen's table, digging in with vigor.

"Are you planning on coming with us?" Rhen asked.

"Me personally? Fluff no! Figure I could maybe send in some help. Got a coupla mechs I've been workin' I think you'll like, and I'll be needin' all the power I can get to operate 'em."

Rhen smiled. "Then we're grateful for the help."

"Yeah, well I was grateful for all that anima. Got me enough to start up a shop in a respectable dungeon."

"Oh... where at?" Rhen said, keenly interested.

"Here, stupid. I need a bigger workshop that's not attached to the inn. I've been savin' up these crystals for that modification. We can do it after the Nexus raid."

Rhen grinned. "Great. I can't wait to see your designs."

"We'll need to expand Leslie and Barrek's space too. They're too cramped in there tryin' to do woodworking and needlework in the same place." He shifted uncomfortably. "And it's nothin' heartfelt or some nonsense like that. If I can't get my wood and cloth materials in a timely manner, I can't do my own work in a timely manner."

"Okay, Wyland," Rhen chuckled.

It was obvious in the way Wyland buried his face back in his bowl that he was embarrassed about his act of generosity. He didn't use cloth or wood very often, and much of the multimedia crafting he did need, he could construct himself.

Pride swelled in Rhen.

They'd made a great place.

"Eat up everyone! We'll need to wait here for about fifteen minutes for the magic to take effect."

"And then we're gonna crush some fins!" Eli yelled, fist-pumping.

The group roared, everyone in battle-ready spirits.

When the bowls were emptied, the raid team left everything as it was, and headed down toward the beach. Wyland went to his workshop to get his mechs while Aki displayed his most accurate map to date in the shallows of the lake.

Rhen pulled out his dungeon owner's map, just making sure for the hundredth time that it was there. Without that, the whole journey and battle would be for naught. He needed the dungeon owner's map to register the Nexus node and secure his find. If done improperly, the D.O.G. could seize his find, boot him from his own dungeon, and take over. Just like his id syntial documented everything Rhen was—almost everything—the dungeon map documented his dungeon.

They podded-up: Rhen with Aki, Jakira, Olliat, and Eli; Joseph leading Bort, Barrek, and Leslie; and lastly Valine shepherded Gil, Pattie, and Caleb. Olliat and her lanky brother, Eli, waded into the shallows, and everyone followed. They dove under, triggering Cephaloshifter. Their bodies exploded out in all directions, tentacles flying. Eli become a spiky-bodied octopus with pale skin and Olliat morphed into a spidery creature, each leg armored on the top with vicious stingers hidden inside her suckers.

Rhen and the rest of the raid triggered Amphibian Lung and dove under. Moving the cold water in and out of his modified lungs was laborious, but not painful. The raid grabbed onto anything they could of the massive cephalokids. Rhen latched his fingers between the armor plating on one of Olliat's legs and laid himself flat against her. Jakira wrapped her arms and legs around a thinner tentacle, giving it a huge bear hug.

"Everyone is secured," Aki reported.

Behind them in the shallows, four snake-like mech dove in. They were four feet long each with tiny retractable legs for walking. They slithered like eels, cutting a wake through the water.

"These will shine bright lights ahead, and upon our enemy as we fight," Aki said. "They may also deploy grappling hooks we can anchor into the walls. Wyland says he will be watching us from the comfort and safety of the inn."

The group chuckled, a strange, dampened sound underwater.

"Let's go kill a boss monster." Rhen thought

Eli zipped off over the edge of the precipice, losing Joseph in the process. Olliat accelerated slowly at first, then picked up speed, grabbing her father as she passed. They moved into the depths and the pressure on their bodies increased, but it wasn't uncomfortable. Yet the fear ebbing at the edge of Rhen's consciousness remained. The deep water was dangerous.

But he was more dangerous.

The mecheels, Wyland's creations, kept pace with the cephalokids easily. Their eyes glowed, projecting beams of light ahead sixty feet, illuminating their first combatant. It was a lone dreadshrimp, one of the spiny backed, many-antennae-having evil creepers. It curled in on itself, preparing its strong forelimbs to attack.

Olliat dodged left and the incoming shrimp's punch missed by twenty feet. The speed of its punch made a vacuum, sending a shockwave of force rippling out against them. It shook Rhen's eyeballs and made him a little sick, but he was much happier he hadn't been directly on the receiving end of that strike.

Eli rammed his spiked head into the monster's underbelly, then wrapped his unoccupied tentacles around its back and squeezed, pinning it in place. Olliat captured the dreadshrimp's punching arm and ripped it free. She wrapped her tentacles over the monster's face and stabbed with her needles.

The dreadshrimp flailed as black toxin leaked from Olliat's needles. After a few seconds, it went still. Eli jerked his head around until the monster's belly opened. Olliat tore into it and ripped free its core, a massive thing the diameter of a wagon wheel. Bort opened his canvas sack wide enough to get the core past the threshold where the Enon syntial took over, shrinking it down for travel.

They moved forward with ruthless efficiency, killing anything that got in their path. Aki assumed when the battle with the gigafish began, it would attract a lot of attention. While they had a plan for that, taking out any extra combatants beforehand could be a saving grace.

The black around them was crushing, the mecheels barely able to pierce it. Rhen looked up to see the crystals above sparkling like distant stars. A silhouette moved overhead, blotting out the crystals.

"Up!"

Rhen watched, horror-struck as the silhouette turned, revealing its four, talon-tipped mandibles. The mecheels turned, opening the panels behind their heads in a huge dish shape. They projected light upward, illuminating the horror that was the gigafish.

Its armored flesh was bright red, blue, and yellow, while the thick-looking plates were a matte black—reflecting no light at all. It had ten eyes in a semicircle around the crown of its head, and two fat antenna that glowed yellow at the tip. It was a lure.

Olliat tried to dodge but the gigafish was moving so fast, propelled by a pair of alternating tails. It snatched up two of her tentacles in its serrated mouth, shredding them. Olliat ripped free, carrying the delvers to safety while she bled out.

Oh gods, if she lost her tentacles, what happened when she transformed back? Would Olliat have to kill herself to avoid being an amputee her whole life?

"Not now!" Aki barked and Rhen snapped out of it.

"Joseph, deploy transformation early!"

From the darkness, Rhen saw a huge beast explode into view. Twice the size of Olliat with a powerful blue glow emanating off him, Joseph lurched for the gigafish's tails. He snapped two tentacles around each and squeezed. There was a crackling sound and then one loud *pop!*

The gigafish roared and curled in on itself, snapping at Joseph's tentacles. He unfurled a tentacle at high-speed, smacking the gigafish's mouth away. The cephalokids dropped their delvers in a semicircle around the action. Olliat moved in to help Joseph while Eli made his Toxink pass behind the monster, preventing intruders and escape.

The mecheels fired grappling pins into the wall at their back, then took aim at the squirming boss monster. They fired the attaching rounds, two striking true between the plates of armor while two bounced off. They reeled in their lines for another shot.

The gigafish twisted and curled, making Olliat's body flop dangerously close to the monster's mouth. Joseph constricted the tails harder, pulling them together.

"*Compbomb the head!*"

Rhen tried to target the gigafish's eye, but it flailed so wildly his spell got water instead. He held it for a count of three until the creature's head moved close to the spot. He released and the water bubbled, rippling out and smacking the beast in the eye. It didn't seem to have an effect.

The mecheels fired their shots again, one of them hooking right into the boss's neck, but it didn't hold. The gigafish wriggled and ripped the anchor from the wall. Olliat lost her grip on the last flail and her body drifted too close. The gigafish got its clawed mandibles under her, then forced her head into its wide mouth.

It ground Olliat's flesh back and forth, keeping its head still for just a few seconds. Rhen used Compbomb again, getting one of its many forward-facing eyes. He held it for a second and released. The glossy black globe popped, spilling even more blood into the cloudy water.

The gigafish sucked in Olliat's remains and swallowed. Twenty-feet down, Rhen saw a bright purple pulse of light wash over the cavern. The pulse hit the gigafish and lit it up like a lightbulb.

Then, the gigafish grew.

30

FEAST FOR THE BEAST

Joseph's tentacles slipped off the monster's tail as it grew too large to be held. Eli zipped out from the darkness and smashed into the monster's underbelly, his thorny head piercing through the armor and cracking it.

A purple syntial glowed on the gigafish's neck and the monster roared. The shockwave smashed the raid party up against the wall, hitting them over and over with multiple waves. Rhen felt like he was going to lose his mind, not just his stew.

~*Transforming!* Jakira called out.

Jakira's nautilus body burst off the wall, blocking the team from the waves. A syntial flared on her side and she channeled the gasses in her shell through a vocalizing chamber. A low horn-blast reverberated out of her body, counteracting the gigafish's opposing spell.

Rhen swallowed his guts and took a breath.

The gigafish lunged at Jakira and she retracted into her shell. It clamped down on her and pusher her toward the wall. Rhen grabbed the nearest delver and used Swift Twitch, pulling them out of the way. Jakira slammed into the rock, sending a shudder through the dungeon. Crystals fell from the ceiling, making splashes above that filled the water with noise.

Rhen looked up to see the crack in the gigafish's armor made from Eli's attack. He swam up and placed his hand on the shell, triggering Tremor Blast at full strength. The spell vibrated through the plate and it split farther, revealing its orange belly.

The gigafish pulled back and rammed Jakira into the wall again, snapping her shell open. Blood leaked out from the cracks, and her legs drooped. The boss shoved its face into the opening in her shell and used its teeth to pry it open, exposing her organs.

"Eli, underbelly plate shattered!"

~I'll make him pay!

Joseph wrapped his tentacles around the monster's tail again, doing his best to keep it still. The boss dug into Jakira, pulling out her guts and feasting. Eli rocketed in from below and slammed into the monster's belly, but he missed the armor opening. The force of his attack pushed Rhen back and sent him floating away from the action.

Another cephalo-raider appeared in the darkness, this one a pale octopus with black diamond designs covering their legs. They climbed on top of the gigafish and pried up the shell plating. The boss finished off Jakira, letting the empty shell drop to the ground.

Eli lined up for another attack run, but mid-swim, reverted to his human form. The gigafish turned and in a single lunge, swallowed the kid whole. Joseph beat at the monster's back with his tentacles, as if trying to get him to regurgitate his son. Compbombs went off all around its face, but it didn't even flinch.

The gigafish turned, smacking its tail into the wall and jostling Joseph free. Rocks from the shore above tumbled into the water, turning the area into a dangerous debris field. The monster charged at Bort, who was passionately casting Compbombs.

Another raider transformed into a billowy squid with fat, fluffy tentacles. They descended on the boss monster's face, wrapping around the four deadly claws and clamping them shut before it could swallow up Bort.

The gigafish flailed, twisting and turning all the way over to try and shake off its attackers. Bort transformed, becoming a purple cuttlefish that looked almost like a giant Aki. He brought two of his tentacles out like wings, and speared the rest. Then, his skin shifted from purple, to blue, to green, in undulating waves.

The boss's rolling stopped, and it floated to the bottom, immobilized.

"Nice work, Bort!"

"I taught him that." Aki said, pridefully.

The raiders descended on the hypnotized gigafish, stabbing, bombing, and pummeling with tentacles. Bort lowered himself to keep in line of sight with the boss, ensuring that the tranquilizing effect of his spell didn't lose its hold.

Joseph's transformation ended and he took up position with the others bombing any exposed space they could find. Leslie transformed into a razor-sharp squid and covered her skin in a layer of the sea floor crystal debris. She grabbed the fallen rocks from above and used them like hammers against the gigafish's back.

Purple glowed from under the boss, and it too donned a layer of Sea-Shell.

"Don't!" Rhen thought in a panic, but it was too late.

Leslie slammed the stone down against the creature's shell, causing a massive blast of energy that ripped her in half. The concussive force sent Bort spinning, unable to maintain his hypnosis spell. The gigafish thrashed free, head-banging the fluffy octopus on the ground until their grip failed. In three big chomps, it shredded their fat tentacles clean off, leaving them stranded. Two more chomps and their body was turned to pale debris.

Icy dread filled Rhen's lungs. Five raiders dead, and seven of the thirteen transformations were already used up, but the gigafish didn't show any signs of slowing down. They just weren't strong enough to take it the traditional way. He needed to get creative... or use the forbidden ability. With so many witnesses it would surely be the end of Rhen's ruse, and if they failed, his freedom, too.

The gigafish turned its gaze on the floundering Bort who was getting back in position for hypnosis. Valine morphed next, becoming an enormous, long-tentacled octopus. The gigafish surged forward and she snatched it by the tail. She slapped three of her tentacles against the wall, finding suction enough to hold the monster back.

The boss twisted, mouth open wide, ready to chomp off Valine's tentacles. That's when Rhen saw it: the perfect opportunity. Its wide-open throat was big enough for Rhen to swim right inside.

"That idea is madness!" Aki declared loudly, making Rhen cringe.

Valine released two of her tentacles and the boss missed. She latched on at a new spot, dodging his every assault.

"I'm going for it. Tell Valine to use her mage powers to slow him down." Rhen activated Swift Twitch and kicked his legs with all his might.

Aki appeared beside him, swimming for the same opening. "I am smaller and faster, let me."

"But if it doesn't work—"

"Then you can still use Piercing Detonator. We will lose the core but win the fight." A surge of water pushed Rhen back from the mouth of the monster and Aki passed him. "I can do this."

"*Gods' speed, buddy.*"

The gigafish twisted for another attack and a bright orange syntial came to life between Valine's eyes. Coral-colored magic glowed around the boss and it slowed to half its speed. Valine closed her eyes, channeling all her remaining power into the spell to hold it still.

The last two raiders used their transformation, grappling the boss. Aki swam through its open mouth and down into its throat, disappearing in darkness. A moment later, the monster bulged around the middle. Its rubbery flesh pushed out against the protective plates like a cat trying to fight its way out of a knapsack.

Valine's spell faded, and the gigafish snapped his mouth around her legs. Despite the war inside his guts, he bit into her ferociously, not stopping to swallow. Aki continued to beat on the monster from the inside, but he was slowing down.

"The acid is strong." Aki's transmission was quiet.

The gigafish curled in on itself and regurgitated Aki, then bit down before he could escape.

Two of the mecheels surged forward, their heads transformed into deadly harpoons. They jammed themselves between the gaps in the armor made from Aki's banging. They used their legs to burrow deeper into the beast. The gigafish reeled against the other two raiders' holds, but it couldn't reach the smaller mecheels burrowing inside it. They disappeared into the beast and then detonated with electric zaps.

It still wasn't enough.

The gigafish turned on one of the octopi and bit down on their head. Their tentacles went limp, and the boss started swimming for escape. No, not when they were so close.

Rhen was torn between Cephaloshifter and Piercing Detonator. Who knew if he could summon enough anima and hit the core with enough force to kill the beast? But could his squid form be strong enough to finish him off with the help of just one other raider?

The gigafish was wiggling to escape. He had to choose now.

Rhen activated Swift Twitch and charged forward. He found the hole made by the mecheel and held his breath, then climbed inside. His head was getting woozy, and the acid from the beast's stomach burned his skin, but he crawled deeper.

He summoned every last ounce of anima left in his body and forced it into his palm. The pressure mounted, threating to blast his arm apart. He pointed his hand toward the creature's chest, hoping his aim was true enough. Would this kill him, too?

The power in his hand became unbearable, and he released Piercing Detonator. White light ripped through the space and Rhen clenched his eyes shut. His body trembled at a monstrous roar, then he was ejected. His head hit something solid. Darkness swallowed him.

Rhen jolted awake in the black, his heart racing. Chunks of gigafish littered the sea floor, slowly dissolving into the dungeon as red sparkles. Rhen was barely strong enough to pull in breath, so for a while, he just laid there, hoping nothing swam by and decided to make a meal of him.

"Time is short," the dungeon voice whispered, and a purple glow beckoned him from beyond the monster chunks.

You can wait ten minutes, Rhen thought. He placed the soles of his boots on the dungeon floor, soaking up the spare anima radiating off it. After a few minutes of this, he had enough energy to sit up.

A lone mecheel scanned the sea floor with its light. What it was looking for, Rhen didn't know. Its long legs picked up and discarded pieces from one pile, then moved on. Its light cast over Rhen, and the mech moved with purpose toward him.

Rhen waved, though he wasn't sure if Wyland could see him, or if the machine was just going off the programming it had been given. The mecheel did a turn around Rhen, then pointed toward the Nexus node.

"I know," Rhen mouthed the word, since his vocal cords could make no sound when full of water.

The mech circled him again, then squeezed its fat head under his armpit. Rhen grabbed onto the plating of its side, and it took off across the sea floor toward the node. Rhen's vision faded in and out. His head was so heavy.

He dropped to the ground at the foot of the Nexus node pedestal. The purple light flared and pulsed, excited by Rhen's presence. Rhen grabbed onto it and hoisted himself up, then patted his interior pocket. Map was still in there.

He stared into the clear depths of the multifaceted node. Little zaps of anima fired within at random intervals, making it look alive.

"Time is short," the node glowed with the syllables.

Rhen lifted his hand to the glassy crystal, feeling warmth radiating off it. His fingers touched the surface and a shockwave rippled out across the dungeon. Light beamed straight up through his fingers, past the ceiling and into the sky. Rhen could see it open, felt his body pulled along too.

He entered the stream and knowing dawned on him. His existence was so small, but so essential. Grow the great Tree of Being. Return the realms to their natural states. Connect, learn, evolve, live.

He was one with the universe.

And then he was gone.

31

PARADISE

Rhen gave a gurgling gasp and spit up water. Right, Amphibian Lung. He activated the spell to swap back to atmospheric breathing, sputtering all the while.

Water rushed behind him and lapped over his feet. The sand beneath him was warm and soft. There was a gentle breeze that licked the warmth from his skin. Chirping birds called somewhere nearby, and leaves rustled in the wind. When he was ready, Rhen pushed himself up, and opened his eyes.

He was on the beach of a lake half surrounded by waterfalls. Above the waterfalls were towering peaks of lush, green forest. The water was clear blue, and there at the center, Rhen spotted the pulsing Nexus node, awaiting his return. Fish flitted about around the node, poking it curiously. Rhen chuckled. They did *not* want to go where that would take them.

He turned and looked behind him. The beachhead ran all the way up to a retaining rock wall about ten feet tall, and above that was a line of palm trees. Fat brown fruits were nestled among the broad green leaves, and colorful birds with comically long, orange beaks pecked at them.

Rhen lay back on the sand for a moment, his head woozy. He

let a big breath of air fill up his belly and he looked up to the wispy clouds. The sun was warm, but didn't burn his skin like Cadria. The breeze was cool, but not harsh like Ptahl. The scents on the wind were floral and fruity. The rushing falls were a perfect ambiance to complement the lapping waves.

Ah. Paradise.

For a second, Rhen wondered if maybe he'd died and landed in the afterlife instead of a new realm. He pinched his arm and winced. Still hurt, so it wasn't a dream, and probably not afterlife paradise. How had he gotten so lucky?

At first, he grinned, but soon that smile turned to a laugh. Energy returned to his body, and he jumped to his feet. "I founded a new realm!"

The birds chirped curiously in reply, and a few of the long-beaked fellows even came down to the retaining wall to inspect him. Rhen wondered how intelligent they were, and how much more life was here. He couldn't wait to explore it all, and the world's many dungeons.

He looked back to the Nexus at the bottom of the lake. He really didn't want to return to the crushing black of his dungeon and fight his way to the surface, where only Wyland and maybe Gil or Pattie waited for him.

Poor Aki, and Jakira... and all the others.

As soon as they respawned, he was bringing them all here for a celebration beach party. Tiki drinks, huge bonfires, roasted terrocken legs, and relaxation. They'd earned it. Speaking of earning.

Rhen pulled the map—which somehow repelled water—from his soaked pocket and pulled it open.

[Congratulations – Rhen Zephitz!]

You have discovered a new realm! What an accomplishment

for all the Imperial Kingdoms. The Dungeon Owner's Guild is grateful for your discovery, and anxiously awaits your arrival at the nearest tower for paperwork and proceedings. Please, make haste so we may get underway with exploring this new territory!

=====

Rhen groaned, the joy leeched from his body.

Paperwork. The bane of his existence.

Well, he'd better get used to it now. Realm founding came with a *lot* of rules, and it would be a long time before they'd explore all that the new realm had to offer. There was sure to be more along the way.

He folded the map up and stuffed it back in his wet pocket. He took one more look around at the wonderful place he'd found. Incredible.

Rhen waded into the warm water, then dove in. He triggered Amphibian Lung and took his time exploring the lake. There was a tunnel behind the waterfalls that might lead to the very first dungeon. He wanted to explore it but knew the D.O.G. would have his ass if he did much more than visit the beach beside the Nexus.

He paddled down, cataloging all the interesting and colorful fish—which were not ginormous sized. The sandy lake floor was alive with little snakes, crabs, and coral, all of it so perfect looking. It was the absolute best he could have hoped for.

The Nexus node was before him now, but he loathed to go back. He took one last breath of the fresh warm water of the new realm, then laid his hand on the Nexus.

[Nexus Travel]

Would you like to teleport to {Zephitz} Dungeon in realm {Resplendare}?
Cost: 50 Anima
{Yes} | {No}

=====

Reluctantly, he selected Yes. He would be back soon with all his friends for a killer party. Until then, Paradise would be okay without him.

THE END
Deathless Dungeoneers Book 1

J. D. Astra

Deathless Dungeoneers

Book Two

THE ADVENTURE CONTINUES...

... in *Deathless Dungeoneers Book 2*.

Even in a new realm, Rhen can't hide from his inescapable past.

Gigafish slain, nexus node activated, and a new realm discovered. Rhen is on cloud nine... until the paperwork comes in.

Now he's charged with preparing his dungeon to become a transport hub to the new realm, but the regulations are maddening. To help manage the insanity, Rhen hires a specialist to handle his contracts while he slays the boss monsters.

But soon enough his hired help is creating new issues, uncovering secrets that Rhen thought were buried for good. Will his past ruin his future, or can Rhen keep his skeletons in the dungeon long enough to make a killing?

From J.D. Astra, author of Monster Haven, Bastion Academy, and Viridian Gate Online: Firebrand, comes a brand new LitRPG adventure that delves the deepest dungeons in order to turn the steepest profit.

BOOKS AND REVIEWS

If you loved *Deathless Dungeoneers Book 1* and would like stay in the loop about the latest book releases, deals, and giveaways, be sure to subscribe to the Shadow Alley Press Mailing List.

www.ShadowAlleyPress.com

Sign up now and get a free copy of our bestselling anthology, Viridian Gate Online: Side Quests! Your email address will never be shared and you can unsubscribe at any time.

Word-of-mouth and book reviews are beyond helpful for the success of any writer, so please consider leaving a rating or a short, honest review on Amazon—just a couple of lines about your overall reading experience. Thank you in advance!

You can also connect with us on our Facebook Page where we do even more giveaways: facebook.com/shadowalleypress

BOOKS BY SHADOW ALLEY PRESS

Shadow Alley Press

ENTER THE SHADOW ALLEY LIBRARY to take a peek at all of our amazing Gamelit, Fantasy, and Science Fiction books! Viridian Gate Online, Rogue Dungeon, Snake's Life, Dungeon Heart, Path of the Thunderbird, School of Swords and Serpents, the FiveFold Universe, and so many more... Your next favorite book is waiting for you inside!

A WORD FROM (JESS) J.D. ASTRA!

Henlo there my dudes! I hope you enjoyed the read, and really look forward to seeing your thoughts online! Come hang out in my discord server:

https://discord.gg/ZRSSvgRh6k

Not a fan of Discord? Follow me on Facebook for memes and updates here:

https://www.facebook.com/theastralscribe

If Facebook isn't your thing, you can sign up for my mailing list for a free novella set in the Bastion Academy series, and get monthly updates here:

http://subscribe.astralscribe.com/bastionsubs

If you're looking to support me (<3 thank you!) and get super exclusive access to early chapters, arts, special updates, and more, you can find me on Patreon here:

https://www.patreon.com/jdastra

Here's some of those awesome Patrons, my Friendly Townsfolk+:

Tyler O. | eden H. | Janet S. | Joseph O. | Ken R. | Laura L. | Remy J. | Ray Allen | Daniel M.

STILL not seeing your jam? These things receive less love, but…

I have a website: www.astralscribe.com

You can email me directly: contact@astralscribe.com

TikTok: @jd_astra

ABOUT THE AUTHOR

About me... I'm a baller. Keyboard crawler. 20 inch display, on my ink scrawler. Holler. Getting flayed tonight, all my characters getting splayed tonight!

In my spare time I love to cook, hike, play video games, and spend quality time with my people.

Three questions people never ask me are; how do I look at myself in the mirror, what's in the box, and what does it take to build a story with likable characters in an interesting setting with important goals?

The answer to the last is determination, dedication, and sacrifice. I've been working at being a writer since before I could string more than two sentences together, and it never gets easier, but it does get better.

I'm surrounded by people who love and support me, which is the most amazing gift the universe could ever give. I will never give up, never surrender, and hopefully, keep on entertaining for the rest of my life.